The Russian Enigma

Clive Egleton

THE RUSSIAN ENIGMA

HODDER & STOUGHTON
LONDON SYDNEY AUCKLAND TORONTO

British Library Cataloguing in Publication Data

Egleton, Clive
  The Russian Enigma.
  I. Title
  823'.914[F]   PR6055.G55

  ISBN 0-340-28508-7

This book is for Harry and Marie Gommersall

The Russian Enigma

1.

The fifteen-year-old boy and the large Saint Bernard dog went on down the slipway and, turning right, passed under the catwalk leading to the lifeboat station at the end of the pier. A thick sea mist cut visibility down to a few yards and somewhere in the direction of Nab Tower, a ship was slowly feeling her way up the Solent toward Southampton, her foghorn blowing a mournful warning at two-minute intervals. The ebb tide was a glassy millpond and the muggy atmosphere, the boy thought, was a further sign that once the haze lifted they would have another warm, humid day with the temperature hovering in the mid-seventies. Early September was the best time of the year in his opinion; the weather was invariably good, and with the season almost over, the number of tourists dwindled to a mere trickle. That meant there were fewer chores for him to do around the hotel his parents owned and he had more leisure time to himself.

An impatient jerk on the lead interrupted his train of thought and bending down, he unclipped the chain from the dog collar. Free now to roam wherever he wanted, the Saint Bernard put his nose down, picked up a fascinating scent, and took off, making a noise that sounded like a vacuum cleaner on the blink as he disappeared into the mist. Ambling after the dog, the boy kicked an empty beer can along the beach, mentally planning how he would spend the rest of the day. If there was enough wind later, he would take the dinghy out, except that his girl friend, Caroline, had gone back to boarding school and it wasn't much fun sailing *Nimrod* single-handed. Maybe he'd do a spot of fishing instead? Or regrind the valves on the engine of his motor scooter? That was something he'd intended doing all summer. He gave the beer can another hefty kick, then veered over to the rocky outcrop, where he was pretty sure he would find his dog, Disraeli, licking the seaweed as usual.

The Saint Bernard met him halfway, trotting toward him out of the mist, a canvas shoe clamped between his jaws. At first, the boy thought it was just a piece of flotsam washed ashore by the tide, but after he'd pried it free, he saw that the sneaker was fairly new and bone-dry, apart from a few traces of saliva. Curious to know where Disraeli had found it, he crossed the narrow reef and followed the paw marks in the wet sand to a bank of shingle in front of the sea wall. The other canvas shoe was on top of the bank, along with a pair of brown corduroy slacks and a roll-neck sweater that looked decidedly the worse for wear. Somehow he didn't think the moths could be blamed for the large ragged hole in the right sleeve and, somewhat guiltily, he rearranged the clothing, placing the sweater under the corduroy trousers and weighting them down with the pair of canvas sneakers.

Disraeli was a hundred and seventy pounds of pure mischief, a scatterbrained dog for whom Dizzy was an apt nickname. He was easily the most undisciplined hound in Bembridge; the boy's father had said so repeatedly, and it was one of the few things on which they agreed. You couldn't let Dizzy out of your sight for more than five minutes before he was up to no good. The boy could hear him now barking furiously down by the shore, and it was a fair bet he was having a whale of a time intimidating the man who'd left his clothes on the shingle be-

4

fore taking an early-morning dip in the sea. Dizzy's bark was far worse than his bite, but not many people believed that, and the boy ran back down the beach, his feet skidding wildly on the smooth rocks.

He found the Saint Bernard performing his ritual war dance, darting forward and back, then crouching, his forelegs bent, his rump stuck up in the air, before making another sally. Disraeli had learned from experience that this gambit had an unnerving effect on all other dogs and most humans. Not the most intelligent canine in the world, he seemed genuinely puzzled as to why the piece of driftwood wallowing in the shallows did not turn tail and run. As the boy stretched out a hand and grabbed hold of his collar, Disraeli charged forward again and went into the sea, dragging the boy with him.

The man was lying flat on his back under the clear water, the lower half of his body obscured by a tangled mass of floating weed. He was old, the boy could tell that from the graying hairs on his chest and the scrawny throat. His face reminded the boy of a bird of prey, the nose curved like an eagle's beak, the eyes black as coal and staring up at him in a lusterless but oddly calculating way that made his flesh crawl. A small wave broke over the body and the head rolled over to the right and the bloodless lips suddenly parted in a ghastly caricature of a smile. Then the foghorn blared again and the boy almost jumped out of his skin. His hands shaking, he clipped the lead on to Disraeli's collar, dragged the Saint Bernard away from the corpse, and started off toward the lifeboat station. A few strides later, he broke into a run and kept on running until he reached the hotel at the top of Lane End.

Winter left his empty champagne glass on the nearest table and strolled out of the marquee that had been erected on the lawn behind their large Edwardian house on Spaniards Road. Hampstead's wedding of the year was steadily drawing to a close: the Dom Perignon had flowed like water, the father of the bride, the bridegroom, and the best man had made their speeches, and now his daughter, Amanda, was upstairs changing into her going-away outfit. Except for a few hardened drinkers determined to get their money's worth, the other wedding guests had already assembled in front of the house, armed with the usual bags of confetti and rice. He assumed Geraldine was there too, busy giving last-minute instructions to the harassed photographer, something she had been doing from the moment the little man had arrived at the house at eleven o'clock, before Amanda had left for Saint Margaret's Church. Four hours of Geraldine in one of her organizing moods went a very long way, and the poor bastard was probably wishing he'd never heard of the Honorable Mrs. Charles Pelham Winter, let alone met her.

It occurred to Winter that Geraldine would undoubtedly dream up a few errands for him and, changing direction abruptly, he headed toward the French windows leading to the drawing room. Knowing his daughter, it would take Amanda at least half an hour to get herself ready, and that would give him plenty of time to have a quiet drink in the privacy of his study. Champagne wasn't his favorite tipple by a long chalk; it always made him thirsty, and what he needed now was a good stiff whiskey and soda. As he was in no mood to make small talk, Harry and Eunice Lang were the last people he wanted to bump into, but as he crossed the patio, they emerged from the drawing room and it was impossible to avoid them.

"Well, if it isn't the father of the bride." Lang greeted him with a swift, effusive smile. "Eunice and I were just saying what a splendid wedding this has been. We've enjoyed every moment."

"Good. I'm glad you were able to come, Harry. It wouldn't have been the same without you."

"Winchester's not the far side of the moon, Charles, and I am Amanda's godfather."

"Yes." Winter clasped both hands behind his back and made a determined effort to conceal his impatience. "Of course you've always had a soft spot for Amanda and you've been very

6

generous too, almost embarrassingly so. You really shouldn't have given her such an expensive wedding present, Harry. You spoil her."

"Nonsense, I can afford it." The smile came on again and flickered briefly like an intermittent neon sign. "Besides, it was a joint present. I mean, had it been left to me, I'd probably have given my goddaughter a check, which wouldn't have been all that original."

Lang had his arm around Eunice, as if to suggest the Minton dinner service and the Waterford crystal had been her idea, but Winter knew different. In his customary oblique fashion, Harry had been referring to his first wife, Katherine, who had died of cancer at the age of forty, over five long years ago, the vivacious brunette who'd also been the love of Winter's life. Lang hadn't discovered that until after her death and then only through Geraldine, but he never ceased to put the knife in whenever the opportunity presented itself. In the circumstances, Winter thought it was just as well Harry had sold the Regency terraced house in Clifton Avenue and moved down to Winchester, otherwise they would have been continually at each other's throats.

"It's been a wonderful day, hasn't it, Charles?" Eunice squeezed his arm and looked up at him, saccharine-sweet. "Geraldine's obviously enjoyed it too. I don't think I've ever seen her so radiant."

"I expect that's because everything has gone exactly the way she planned it," Winter told her.

"You mean Geraldine arranged all this?" Eunice released his arm and waved a gloved hand toward the marquee on the lawn.

Winter nodded. Amanda had wanted a quiet wedding, just family and intimate friends, but her wishes had been ignored. A guest list of under fifty had expanded to more than three hundred by the time Geraldine had been through inviting everybody who was anybody in Whitehall, the arts, and the theater, no matter how casual the acquaintance. She had also taken steps to ensure the wedding would be featured in all the society magazines, especially *Queen* and *The Tatler*. That was

7

something she would come to regret when Amanda's condition became more apparent, but of course his wife wasn't aware that their daughter was already two months pregnant. No doubt when the time came, Geraldine would claim that premature births ran in the family and remind everybody that their son, Lance, had arrived eight months to the day after they were married, while conveniently ignoring the fact that it had come about because she'd had too much to drink at one of their innumerable dinner parties and had fallen down the staircase.

"I'm full of admiration," Eunice gushed.

"So am I. You're a very lucky man, Charles." Lang clapped him on the shoulder. "If I know Geraldine, I bet she's already planning the next big occasion."

Winter clenched both hands under the tails of his morning suit, digging the nails into his palms. First Eunice squeezed his arm, then Harry felt obliged to pummel him, both of them presuming on close bonds of friendship that no longer existed. "Lance isn't even engaged yet," he said tersely, "and anyway, it's the bride's parents who are responsible for the wedding arrangements." He turned to Eunice, an acid smile etched on his lips. "Still, I daresay Geraldine will be only too happy to lend you a hand when your stepdaughters take the plunge."

"Actually, I was referring to your silver wedding anniversary next year," Lang said hastily. He frowned, giving the impression the date had momentarily slipped his memory. "When exactly is it now?" he asked.

"September the third. War was declared on our first anniversary," Winter said dryly, adding, "Against Hitler, of course."

"God, how time flies. We're getting to be a couple of old fogies, you and I."

You speak for yourself Winter thought. They were the same age, fifty-two, but with his pot belly, florid complexion, and gray hair, Harry looked a good ten years older.

"Rubbish, darling. You're just reaching your prime."

"There's a loyal wife for you, Charles," Lang said, and winked.

Winter unclasped his hands, pushed his cuff back, and stared

8

at his wristwatch. "You're right about one thing, Harry," he said. "Time certainly does fly. If Amanda doesn't get a move on, she and Rupert will miss their plane to Rome."

"You'd better hurry her along then."

"That's just what I was thinking."

Winter gave Eunice a brief kiss on the cheek, told Harry they would find Geraldine around the front, and walked into the house. The drawing room, dining room, main lounge, and entrance hall were a mass of pink carnations and roses arranged in cut-glass and silver vases. The study, however, was outside Geraldine's jurisdiction, the one room on the ground floor apart from the kitchen she'd been unable to transform into a miniature Chelsea Flower Show. Taking the key out of his pocket, he unlocked the door and went inside.

The whiskey bottle and soda syphon were kept in the cabinet under the bookcase. Finding a clean glass among the half-dozen tumblers on the top shelf, Winter fixed himself a generous double and then sat down behind the desk to drink a silent toast to Amanda. The vicar in his address had warned Rupert and Amanda that their life together would not always be one long primrose path, but he didn't know the half of it. All he knew was that Amanda was the great-granddaughter of a prosperous Lancashire mill owner who had been knighted for political services to the Liberal Party before the turn of the century, and that one day, her husband, Rupert Swarburg, would inherit the Merchant Bank of Swarburg and Mays from his father. The vicar merely saw an exceedingly attractive young girl of twenty-one whom he had just joined in wedlock to a good-looking young man from an equally well-placed family. His words of advice and the friendly warning were therefore simply a ritual, something to be said to every young couple standing before the altar. But that was not his fault. How could it be when he was not aware of the poisonous atmosphere that had existed between the bride's parents from the time Katherine Lang had been admitted to the hospital with cancer on Friday, October 26, 1956, and the effect that atmosphere had had on a fifteen-year-old adolescent?

Winter thought he and Geraldine had a lot to answer for. Their constant bickering had turned a bright, intelligent school-girl into a promiscuous rebel. Although at his insistence Amanda had stayed on at Roedean until she was eighteen, she had deliberately failed all her A-levels. Instead of Oxford or Cambridge, she had gone to a secretarial college in North London and had left home to share a pokey flat in Bayswater with three other girls. A competent enough shorthand typist, Amanda had subsequently changed jobs and boyfriends with equal abandon until, largely as a result of his influence, she had been offered a secretarial post with Swarburg and Mays. In a rare moment of confidence, his daughter had told him that Rupert certainly wasn't the first man she had slept with, but he was easily the nicest, and for his part, Swarburg seemed genuinely fond of Amanda. Winter just hoped that his daughter had finally found the happiness she had seen so little of at home.

The telephone at his elbow rang loud and insistently, and for a moment he was tempted to ignore it. People had been ringing the house all morning to wish the happy couple well, but this particular number was unlisted and Winter knew it must be somebody from the office. Reluctantly lifting the receiver off the cradle, he found he had Frank Edmunds, the head of Administration, on the line.

Edmunds said, "I'm sorry to intrude at a time like this, Charles, but I thought you should know that George Deakin is dead."

"How and when did this happen?" The question was auto-matic. Deakin had been the best double agent the SIS had had since the war, and there had been nothing wrong with his health when he'd started his annual summer holiday a week ago.

"Sometime between seven and eight this morning." Edmunds cleared his throat. "A boy who was exercising his dog on the beach found him lying on his back in two feet of water. From what Ross can gather, it seems George must have slipped on a piece of seaweed and cracked his skull on a rock. The exact cause of death won't be known until after the post mortem, but the local police figure that the blow knocked him unconscious and he fell into the sea."

"And then drowned," said Winter.

"That's the theory, Charles."

"What the hell was George doing on the beach at that hour?"

"Well, he was wearing a pair of swimming trunks, so I assume he must have been going for an early-morning dip."

Winter frowned. That wasn't the Deakin he knew. George was fifty-six and round-shouldered, a dried-up husk of a man with a strong aversion to any kind of physical exercise. "How did his wife take the news, Frank?" he asked.

"That's just it," said Edmunds. "Marjorie doesn't know yet that he's dead. She returned to London yesterday afternoon. Apparently her daughter had called them on Friday morning, pretty hysterical, to say that she had broken off her engagement, and Marjorie went back to sort things out; at least, that's what George told Ross when he met him for a drink in the Hare and Hounds pub last night."

A watchdog was assigned to keep an eye on Deakin whenever he went away on holiday. There was nothing secretive about it; Deakin knew he was being kept under surveillance and it was also standard practice to introduce him to the security officer who'd been detailed to look after him. He was like a dog on a long leash, free to roam within certain well-defined limits. In an emergency, he was expected to contact his watchdog, but as far as Winter was concerned, George had no business approaching Ross just because his stepdaughter was having problems with her love life.

"What have you done about contacting Mrs. Deakin?" he asked. "I assume you've called their house in Hendon?"

"Several times," said Edmunds. "I've also tried her daughter's flat in Notting Hill Gate, but it appears she isn't home either."

"I don't like it. This whole business is beginning to smell like bad fish."

"Yes, I've got to admit it doesn't look too good, Charles."

"The local coroner is bound to hold an inquest, but we can't afford to wait for that," Winter said, voicing his train of thought aloud. "We'll have to hold an internal investigation and I don't believe we can leave that to our own Security branch, not after the way Ross has goofed. I'd like an outsider to conduct it, somebody from the Training School at Gerrards Cross who doesn't have an axe to grind."

"How about Richard Burman?" Edmunds suggested.

Until last April, Burman had been the resident officer in West Berlin. He was an experienced field agent, had a quick, incisive brain, and as a national serviceman had won an MC in Korea at the age of nineteen. Released from the army in July 1952, Burman had then read philosophy, politics, and economics at Magdalen College, Oxford, where Winter had also been an undergraduate from 1931 to 1934.

"I think Burman will do us very well, Frank."

"Right. When do you want to brief him?"

"This evening," said Winter. "My office at five-thirty."

There was some other point he wanted to raise with Frank which had occurred to him earlier on in their conversation, but for the life of him, he couldn't remember now what it was. Suddenly aware of a low murmur of voices in the hall, Winter heard his daughter laugh nervously and decided it couldn't have been very important anyway. Hanging up on Edmunds, he left the study to join them.

One look at the happy expression on Amanda's face was enough to reassure him that everything was going to be all right. He hugged her close, gave her a warm kiss, and shook hands with a somewhat bewildered Rupert. Then, ushering them forward, Winter followed his daughter and son-in-law out of the house into the bright sunlight and a hailstorm of confetti and rice.

2.

Over the years, the dividing wall between the two buildings had been systematically demolished, certain rooms had either been partitioned or enlarged, and additional windows had appeared in the fabric, so that it was now impossible to tell where the elegant Georgian town house at 21 Queen Anne's Gate ended and 54 Broadway began. Winter's office in the SIS headquarters was on the top floor of the complex. A high-ceilinged, double-size room with an oblique view of St. James's underground station, it was furnished in accordance with the scale deemed appropriate for a deputy undersecretary in the Civil Service. That meant he was entitled to three leather armchairs, a hatstand, a round swivel chair with padded armrests, and a large kneehole desk. There was also a fitted wall-to-wall Wilton carpet and two oil paintings, a Monet and a Cézanne, both on permanent loan from the National Gallery. Among the personal memorabilia on Winter's desk were a somewhat dated photograph of Geraldine and the children in a silver frame, a cut-glass ashtray, an old-fashioned pen and ink stand that had once belonged to his father, and an engraved paper knife which Katherine and Harry Lang had given him one Christmas long ago.

Burman and Edmunds occupied two of the leather armchairs and sat facing Winter across the desk. Even allowing for the disparity in their ages, Winter thought that no two men could have been less alike. Edmunds was five foot seven but with his straight back and upright posture gave the impression of being much taller. Always well-groomed, he tended to wear conservative suits, and with his pepper-and-salt short hair and his clipped speech, it was easy to see why strangers frequently mistook him for a retired army general. Burman, on the other hand, had the broad shoulders, deep chest, and angular frame of an athlete. He towered a good eight inches over Edmunds, but with his long legs, his true height was not readily apparent when sitting down. He had reddish-brown hair, gray eyes, and an elongated face that ended in a round chin. He was likeable, quiet, unassuming, and very tolerant, so much so that some people wrongly assumed this latter characteristic was a sign of weakness. Three Glaswegians who'd picked on him one Saturday night seven years ago in a pub off the King's Road certainly knew different. They had come down to London for the England-Scotland football match at Wembley and had been celebrating before and after the game. By the time they'd arrived at the Coach and Horses, the Glaswegians were in a truculent mood and looking for trouble. It just so happened that Burman was there having a quiet drink with his current girl friend, an attractive blonde who had immediately caught their eye. They had swaggered over to the table and made a number of obscene suggestions to the girl. Burman had politely asked them to go away, a request they'd found vastly amusing. One of them had then poured a whiskey over his head and asked him what he proposed to do about it, and so Burman had stood up and showed him. The Glaswegian who'd anointed him had woken up in hospital with a broken jaw to find his two companions occupying adjoining beds in the same ward. They too were a little vague as to exactly what had happened. All they were able to remember was that the tall Englishman had shot out two enormous hands, grabbed a fistful of their hair, and cracked their skulls together.

"This profile on George Deakin." Burnam looked up from the file he'd been reading and frowned at Winter. "It's not exactly informative, is it?"

"It gives you an insight into his background."

"And raises more questions than it answers. All I know about him is that Deakin spent eight years working for an oil company in the Persian Gulf before joining the Special Operations Executive in Cairo late in 1940. After the war, he stayed on with the British Middle East Office until 1950, when he was summoned home to head the Arabian department at 54 Broadway. He was then given the Russian desk in June 1956, an appointment which was abruptly terminated eighteen months later when he was shunted off to something called the JIAP Committee."

"Joint Intelligence and Planning," said Winter. "And George wasn't shunted off; he was selected to be a member of that committee because we and the Foreign Office decided his services would be invaluable."

"I see." Burman clucked his tongue, then said, "When did he first come to the notice of our security people?"

"A few days after the Suez affair."

"But that was almost six years ago."

"Yes." Winter smiled. "As a matter of fact, George only got the job because we knew he'd been recruited by the KGB. Mind you, his defection wasn't permanent, and at the time, Deakin sincerely believed that he was acting in the long-term interests of our country. Like a great many other people who disagreed with Eden's Middle East policy, he was violently opposed to the idea of using force to resolve the Suez Canal dispute with Nasser."

"And he did something about it?"

"Not immediately. George reckoned the Americans would dissuade us from invading Egypt."

"They certainly did their best," said Burman. "The Maritime Nations Conference, the Suez Canal Users Association—Dulles used every device he could to circumvent Eden."

"Well, it was election year in the States," Winter said

acidly, "and Eisenhower wanted another term in the White House. Since he was campaigning as a man of peace, it wouldn't have gone down too well with the voters if he hadn't tried to restrain us. With Eden and most of his Cabinet determined to invade Egypt, we had to persuade Ike it was in his own interest to take a back seat."

"How did you go about that?"

"We thought we could apply a certain amount of diplomatic pressure," Winter said vaguely.

There had been nothing diplomatic about the sort of pressure the SIS had tried to apply. Under Winter's direction, they had forged a bundle of love letters and a hotel bill to prove that Eisenhower's wartime romance with his driver, Kay Summersby, was still going strong when he was Supreme Commander of NATO forces from 1950 to 1952. In a subtle variation of the usual blackmail routine, Winter had then made damn sure that Tom McNulty, the resident CIA officer at Grosvenor Square, knew exactly what his people were up to. The message was simple enough; either the CIA persuaded Ike to take a softer line over Suez or the forged letters would end up in the hands of the biggest muckraking columnist in the States.

"Diplomatic pressure," Burman repeated, breaking a lengthy silence. "That hackneyed expression can mean almost anything."

"We didn't send a gunboat," Winter said affably, "we'd run out of them. It just so happened that we were in possession of certain facts which could have made life very embarrassing for the Eisenhower administration had they been made public. Unfortunately for us, George Deakin got wind of it and decided it was his duty to pass the information on to the Egyptian Embassy in South Audley Street. Their intelligence officer contacted the KGB and when he and George met face to face, the Egyptian was wired for sound. You can guess the rest."

Burman nodded. "Who finally recruited Deakin?"

"Vasili Korznikov. He was supposed to be a trade counselor

at the Soviet Embassy, but our friends in MI5 knew different. They had him under surveillance and were there when he met Deakin for the first time in Waterlow Park in Highgate. That was on Guy Fawkes Night, 1956, the day before we agreed to a cease-fire and our troops halted their advance on Ismailia. Deakin was the one plus factor to emerge from that debacle. Once we knew the KGB had got their hooks into George, we turned him around and for the last six years we've been leading those people in Dzerzhinsky Square around by the nose, feeding them false disclosures."

There had been other spin-offs. On a number of occasions, the KGB had asked Deakin for specific information and their questions had been very revealing. The CIA and the State Department had been allowed to join the game, after they had paid their dues. The entrance fee hadn't been cheap either; Winter had seen to that. Polaris missiles at knock-down prices were only one of the items on the bill he'd presented to Tom McNulty.

"Is it possible the KGB discovered that Deakin was a double agent?" Burman asked.

"That's what we want you to find out." Winter unbuttoned his jacket and leaned back in the chair. The atmosphere was becoming more and more oppressive and he could hear the distant rumble of thunder in the still air. "You'd better start with his wife and stepdaughter. I'd like to know why they aren't answering the telephone. Frank here will give you their addresses."

Edmunds suddenly came to life. "I already have," he said in his usual clipped fashion. "Before you arrived at the office. There wasn't much I could tell Richard about the family background. I thought I'd leave that to you. After all, you know the Deakins better than I do."

"Quite." Winter turned to Burman. "George didn't get on with his stepdaughter. Coral was sixteen when he met her mother at Zermatt back in January '51 and it seems she took an instant dislike to him. Her attitude didn't change when he and

Marjorie were married; if anything, she became even more hostile. I hold no brief for George, but I had some sympathy for him in that area: Coral Hughes is a very unpleasant and vindictive young woman. She's a dedicated left-wing socialist and a member of just about every protest movement you can name. A couple of years ago last Easter, she met a Mr. Dennis Keefer while taking part in a march organized by the CND, the antinuclear group. Keefer is a lecturer in social sciences and they set up house together a few weeks later. Coral then gave up her job as a schoolteacher to work full time for the CND and they moved into a basement flat in Notting Hill Gate."

"Are they both tainted?"

"Keefer professes to be a Marxist, but he's pretty harmless, according to Special Branch."

"The mere fact that he came to their notice worries me."

"I've never lost any sleep over it," Winter said. "To my way of thinking, his activities strengthened Deakin's credentials with the KGB. All the same, I'd rather you steered clear of Mr. Keefer. He has a very suspicious nature."

"That could be a mite difficult," Burman said. "I don't see how I can avoid him if he's living with Coral Hughes."

"He's not any more—she's broken off the engagement. At least, that's what she's supposed to have told her mother yesterday morning."

"If you can believe the story Deakin told Ross when they met last night."

"Isn't that what I've just said?" Winter glanced at his wristwatch. It was already past six-fifteen and he'd promised Geraldine he would be home by seven-thirty without fail. Harry and Eunice Lang had apparently invited them out to dinner and there would be hell to pay if he was late. "You'd better try Deakin's place in Hendon first before you call on the daughter," he continued.

"Right."

"Let Frank know how you make out. He'll give you a key to the house."

"You want me to look the place over?"

"That's the general idea." Winter nodded briskly. "Now— do you have any other questions?"

"I can't think of any."

"Good."

It was some moments before Edmunds and Burman realized the briefing was over. When the penny finally dropped, Edmunds muttered something about Burman needing a copy of *Nicholson's London Street Finder* and then ushered the younger man out of the office.

Winter lifted his clipboard from the pending tray and uncapped his fountain pen. He would have to inform Tom McNulty that their business arrangement with Deakin had come to an abrupt end, but that could wait until Monday. Right now, there were a few loose ends that needed tying off. Vasili Korznikov had been moved on from 13 Kensington Palace Gardens to a similar appointment with the Soviet Embassy in Washington and it was important to know if he was still in circulation. The same applied to Anatole Gorsky, the KGB agent masquerading as a lowly clerk, who'd become Deakin's control after Korznikov had departed, but that was a job for Malcolm Cleaver and his people at MI5. Committing his thoughts to paper, Winter drafted a lengthy telex to the head of station in Washington and then delivered the flimsy to the duty communications officer to have it enciphered. Ten minutes later, he left the building, collected his Jaguar from the parking space in Queen Anne's Gate, and drove out to Acton.

Malcolm Cleaver had a flat in Sliema Avenue, a quiet side street off Acton Road. A former detective superintendent with the Metropolitan Police, Cleaver had joined MI5 in 1940, shortly after the disaster at Wormwood Scrubs when much of the untidy filing system that had been the hallmark of the counterintelligence organization in those days had been destroyed in an air raid. A short, stocky man with pugnacious features, Cleaver was noted for his shrewd intelligence and dogged perseverance, two qualities Winter greatly admired.

Leaving his car in the forecourt, Winter strolled into the

building and rang the bell to Cleaver's apartment on the ground floor. A plump middle-aged woman wearing a plastic apron over a green dress opened the door and gaped at him, her face rapidly turning crimson.

"Hello, Jean." Winter smiled. "Is Malcolm in?"

Jean nodded and opened the door wider. "Do come in, Mr. Winter," she murmured breathlessly. "You'll find him in the living room."

"It's Charles," he said, gently correcting her.

"Yes, of course." Jean cleared her throat. "We've only just got back from spending the day with our daughter and son-in-law at Woking."

"You made it just in time then."

"What?"

Winter pointed a finger toward the ceiling. "The thunderstorm," he said. "It's getting closer."

"So it is." Jean opened a door off the hall. "It's Charles to see you, dear," she called out, then backed off toward the kitchen, her face still pink.

As Winter entered the living room, Cleaver laid a copy of the *Evening Standard* on the arm of his chair and came forward to meet him. "Hello, Charles," he said warmly. "You're the last person I expected to see. How did the wedding go?"

"Amanda looked marvelous and everyone seemed to enjoy themselves. It's a shame you and Jean couldn't be there."

"Yes. Well, we hated to let you down at the last minute, Charles, but our grandson's been poorly since Thursday and Jean couldn't rest until she'd seen him. You know how it is with women of her age, they get broody."

"So I'm beginning to discover."

It was a lame excuse and they both knew it. The Cleavers had failed to show up at the wedding because the one and only time they'd dined with the Winters had been an unmitigated disaster. Some time between the entree and the main course, Malcolm had told Geraldine that he'd left elementary school at the age of fourteen to start work in a cotton mill and, exaggerating his Lancashire accent, had remarked that he must have been following in her grandfather's footsteps. Geraldine had no sense of humor and she didn't like to be reminded that her family had its roots in Oldham. Thereafter she had gone out of her way to make the Cleavers feel small, and although Malcolm had been unperturbed by it all, she had certainly made Jean squirm.

"What will you have?" Cleaver asked him, crouching in front of the sideboard. "Whiskey, brandy, or gin?"

"I could do with a large brandy."

"With soda or ginger ale?"

"Neat, please," Winter said.

"You sound down in the mouth." Cleaver glanced over his shoulder. "Nothing wrong, is there?"

"George Deakin is dead."

"What?"

"It happened between seven and eight this morning. George and Marjorie were on holiday at Bembridge on the Isle of Wight, and apparently he decided to go for an early-morning swim. The local police think he must have slipped on a piece of seaweed and struck his head on a rock. Anyway, it's pretty definite George was unconscious when he fell into the sea and drowned."

"Good God." Cleaver placed a bottle of Henessy on top of the sideboard and took out two brandy glasses. "How's Marjorie bearing up?"

"She returned to London yesterday, and up to now we haven't been able to trace her." Winter shrugged his shoulders. "I daresay there's a perfectly innocent explanation for her absence, but I can't help feeling a little uneasy. That's why I'd like you to run a check on Anatole Gorsky."

"Do you think George was murdered?"

"I don't know. If the KGB were on to him and suspected he'd been hoodwinking them for years, they would certainly recall his control to Moscow for a full-scale inquiry. That's standard procedure, but killing George simply doesn't make sense. In their shoes, I'd use him to spread misinformation to both the SIS and the CIA."

"You would, Charles, but then that's your style." Forked lightning lanced the dark sky outside the window and the thunderclap which instantly followed rivaled an artillery barrage. Cleaver never flinched; hand rock-steady, he continued to pour the brandy, then handed a glass to Winter. "Maybe the KGB didn't have a motive to kill George, but I can think of at least one man in your organization who did."

Winter froze, the glass of brandy halfway to his lips. "Bill Turnock," he said in a flat voice, suddenly recalling the matter he'd wanted to raise with Edmunds before the sound of Amanda's voice in the hall had disturbed his train of thought.

"Why not?" said Cleaver. "He had every reason to hate Deakin."

"Assuming it finally dawned on him that he'd taken the rap for George's little escapade."

"Yes, six years is a long time, Charles, but Turnock never was exactly quick on the uptake, was he?"

"You could say the same for me," Winter said in a subdued voice. "I thought he was pro-Arab at the time of Suez and was convinced he was the man who was passing information to the Egyptian Embassy. I should have looked at his personal file and read between the lines; then I'd have realized that Bill simply hated the Israelis."

Turnock was a former colonial policeman who'd spent the greater part of his service in Palestine before joining the SIS in 1947. One of the best officers in Special Branch, he'd been forced to leave the country in a hurry after Esther Rabinowitz, the twenty-two-year-old high school teacher he'd been living with, had betrayed him to the Irgun Zvai Leumi.

"It's ironic, isn't it?"

"What is?" Cleaver asked.

"Well, in the beginning, George was able to keep his hands clean because he used Turnock as a front-runner. Then, when the truth finally came out, I had to sack Bill because we needed a scapegoat to make the KGB believe that Deakin was in the clear. If I hadn't done that, we could never have set George up as a double agent."

"Maybe Turnock is after you as well." Cleaver swallowed the rest of his brandy. "Have you considered that possibility?"

"The thought had occurred to me. Of course it may be that Turnock can account for his movements today."

"I'll look into it."

"Thanks." Winter emptied his glass and set it down on the sideboard. "Say goodbye to Jean for me," he said.

"You're going?"

"Got to. I promised Geraldine I'd be home by seven-thirty and I'm already ten minutes adrift."

"You're mad. It's pissing cats and dogs outside."

"What's a little rain?" Winter said dryly. "There'll be a worse storm waiting for me in Hampstead if I don't get a move on."

3.

Burman replaced the receiver and backed out of the phone booth in the booking hall at Hendon Central. Edmunds had been trying to contact Marjorie Deakin all day and now this was the second time he'd called the house in Queen's Road himself with the same negative result. A small crowd of people were sheltering in the entrance to the station and, joining them, Burman edged his way to the front and looked up at the dark night sky. Although there was still some thunder about, the rain had slackened off and was no longer the torrential downpour it had been twenty minutes ago. Even so, the light showerproof raincoat he was wearing wouldn't afford him much protection, and he regretted having left his Ford Zephyr in a parking lot at Golders Green, two stops up the line.

A double-decker bus pulled up outside and most of the crowd surged toward it. Waiting until the sudden exodus was over, Burman walked out of the station, crossed the road, and then turned left to follow the route he'd memorized from *Nicholson's Street Finder*.

Queen's Road was much as he'd imagined it would be, a typical urban development of the early thirties, consisting in the main of identical-looking semidetached, three-bedroom houses. The architect responsible for the project had not anticipated the day when almost every family would own a car, and only one semi in eight had a garage built on the side.

The Deakins lived at Number 113, a bay-window type with mock Tudor beams under the eaves, a small bedroom over the porch, and no adjoining garage for their Morris Minor. Behind the chest-high privet hedge that enclosed the property on three sides was a small front garden, a circular rose bed in the center of the lawn and a narrow border of chrysanthemums on either side of a concrete path. Although the nearest lamppost was only a few yards away on the opposite side of the street, its orange glare, directed downward on to the road, left the near curbside in shadow. There were no lights showing in the neighboring houses, and as far as Burman could tell, nobody was watching him from across the street. Quietly opening and closing the front gate, he walked up the path and let himself into the house with the key Edmunds had given him.

He shut the door behind him and kicked off his shoes. Then, taking a small, pencil-thin flashlight out of his raincoat pocket, Burman trained it downward and switched it on. The Deakins had started their holiday a week ago, but there were no letters on the mat, which he thought rather unusual. Although their close friends might not bother to write if they knew they'd gone away, the unsolicited mail would still come through the letter box: the advertising circulars and special offers from local tradesmen. Moving slowly forward, he located the hall table and found two buff-colored envelopes on the brass tray. One was from the Inland Revenue, the other from the gas board; both were addressed to Mr. George Deakin and had been posted on Thursday.

There were two possible explanations. Either Marjorie Deakin had picked them up off the mat when she'd returned home yesterday, or else she had left a key with a neighbor who'd been asked to keep an eye on the place. Even allowing for the vagaries of the English climate, there was no danger of the pipes freezing up in September, but it could be that the Deakins were worried the house might be burglarized in their absence, which was both prophetic and somewhat ironic in the circumstances. Burman checked out the two rooms off the hall and the kitchen, but could find no evidence that the Deakins had a cat or any other kind of domestic pet which they'd left behind to be fed by somebody else. The fact that the indoor plants lining the shelf of the kitchen window had not been watered recently also cast further doubt on the theory that one of the neighbors had been given a spare key.

Burman glanced at the electric stove and saw that it had been switched off at the mains and the plug removed from the power socket. The larder appeared to be well stocked with nonperishable items, but the refrigerator was empty and it too had been disconnected. If Marjorie Deakin had returned to the house on Friday, it was now beginning to look as though she had departed again soon afterward. Leaving the kitchen, he went upstairs and checked out the bathroom.

Coral Hughes was supposed to have phoned her mother on Friday morning to announce that she had broken off her engagement. According to Deakin, she had been pretty hysterical and a worried Marjorie had gone back to London that afternoon to sort things out. Since it would have taken her at least three hours to reach her daughter's flat in Notting Hill Gate from Bembridge, it was reasonable to assume she'd had no intention of returning to the Isle of Wight that same night. The way Burman saw it, Marjorie Deakin would have brought a vanity case with her, if nothing else, yet there was no toothbrush in the mug on the glass shelf above the washbasin and no sign of a facecloth either.

There were three bedrooms off the landing, but the single over the porch was little bigger than a shoebox and unlikely to be in use. Not quite certain what he was looking for, Burman tried the double room immediately to his left which overlooked the back garden.

The large divan bed was made up and on the bedside table

nearest the door, he noticed a paperback novel by Georgette Heyer. A three-piece walnut bedroom suite was arranged in the shape of an inverted letter L, the dressing table in the window recess, the wardrobe and chest of drawers side by side against the dividing wall and facing the divan. The chest of drawers was full of Marjorie's carelessly folded sweaters, cardigans, silk blouses, and underwear, while the entire wardrobe, except for a few vacant hangers, was taken up with her clothes. George, it seemed, wasn't allowed a look-in and there was only one inference to be drawn from that. Going next door, Burman opened the built-in cupboard in the front bedroom and stood there gazing thoughtfully at the suits and sports jackets hanging from the rail and the shirts, socks, vests, and underpants neatly laid out on the adjoining shelves.

He wondered how long the Deakins had been living apart under the same roof, wondered too if their differences had reached the point where Marjorie had suddenly decided she'd had enough of George and had simply walked out on him. One thing was certain: Winter would feel a good deal less uneasy if he could prove that had been the case. Whether he could find any hard evidence to support that particular theory was an entirely different matter, however, but it was just possible the writing desk-cum-bookcase he'd seen in the sitting room might yield something. Nodding to himself, Burman went downstairs to give it the once-over.

The desk was tucked away in an alcove to one side of the fireplace. Its appearance suggested it was the oldest piece of furniture in the house, and the books on the two shelves underneath the drop leaf were yellowed and musty from lack of use. The key which opened the desk was missing, and at first he thought either George or Marjorie had locked the drop leaf and taken the key with them when they went away. Then he noticed the woodwork was scratched around the keyhole, as though a pair of pliers had been used to force the lock. Immediately, a montage of images flashed through his mind and he saw Marjorie's dressing table upstairs and the toe of a nylon stocking trapped in one of the drawers; and the contrast between the neat way her husband's socks, shirts, and underwear had been arranged on their respective shelves while her sweaters and underclothes looked as though she hadn't bothered to fold each one properly before putting them away. A feeling that somebody had been there before him was confirmed when he lowered the drop leaf and saw the mess inside the desk. Household bills, insurance policies, used checkbooks, personal letters, and four Kodak envelopes containing prints and negatives had been taken from the pigeonholes and then shoved back again any old way. Curious to know what the intruder had been looking for, he removed the Kodak envelopes and examined each batch of photos in turn.

The black-and-white snapshots were a record of past holidays. The panoramic views didn't convey a great deal to him, but one taken of George leaning against a stone wall with a walking stick in his right hand suggested that he and Marjorie had visited the Peak District of Derbyshire one summer. Unlike his wife, George wasn't exactly an expert with a camera, and there was not one photograph of the slender, dark-haired woman, whom he assumed was Marjorie, that wasn't out of focus. Despite the general fuzziness, it was, however, very apparent that she had a good figure, one that somebody half her age might well envy. Even the sensible clothes she was wearing couldn't disguise that.

Burman opened the next envelope, found that it contained only nine prints instead of the usual twelve, and immediately checked the negatives. Three were missing, and while the roll of film could have been spoiled, he knew Kodak would have returned the blank exposures to satisfy the Deakins that none of their snapshots had been mislaid by the processing laboratory. Marjorie could have given the missing prints to her daughter or to somebody else, but was it likely that she would have parted with the negatives as well? Burman stifled a groan; there was a flaw in his deduction. If the intruder had been after the snapshots, why had he then gone upstairs and sifted through her things? Unable to think of a satisfactory answer to that puzzling question, Burman tucked the Kodak envelopes into the inside pocket of his jacket, closed the desk, and walked over to the French windows.

The Deakins were obviously great ones for privacy. Like the small plot at the front, the back garden was enclosed by a privet hedge all of twelve feet high, which effectively screened them from the neighbors on either side. The hedge would also shield any would-be intruder from ground-level observation from either flank or from the house in the parallel street, the garden of which backed onto their property. True, he could be seen from the upstairs windows, but once it was dark, the curtains would be drawn in the neighboring houses. Burman frowned. If somebody had broken into the house, they certainly hadn't come through the French windows. The draw bar was still firmly embedded in the recesses, top and bottom, and even if the lock had been picked from the outside, there was no way the intruder could have opened the door without breaking a pane of glass. The same applied to the catches on both side windows, and that meant there was only one other place where the burglar could have effected an entry. Although time was running on, he decided to check out the kitchen again.

The large picture window above the sink and drainboard was intact and there were no obvious signs that the back door had been forced. For a few brief moments, Burman was inclined to believe he'd drawn the wrong conclusion, that there was a perfectly innocuous explanation for the missing prints and the scratch marks on the writing desk. Then he looked at the catch on the door to the larder and knew different. The hasp seemed okay at a casual glance, but two hairline cracks in the wooden frame told him that somebody had put a shoulder to the door and sprung the catch. He opened the larder door and examined the fly screen attached to the small window frame in the outside wall. No two ways about it, the screen had been cut out, then put back and held in place with black masking tape. The cunning bastard had applied the same technique to the windowpane, except that he'd used putty to secure the glass. Secure? One light tap and the whole thing would come adrift.

Burman glanced at his wristwatch, saw that it was twenty minutes to nine, and decided to give the storage room above the porch a miss. More than an hour had elapsed since he'd opened the front door, and there was no point in pushing his luck on the off chance that he might find whatever it was the intruder had been searching for. He went into the dining room, which faced on to the street and, satisfied nobody was about, collected his shoes from the doormat, slipped them on, and let himself out of the house.

Ten minutes later, he rang Edmunds from Hendon Central and told him he had found some interesting snapshots that would keep the photo interpreters busy all weekend.

Matthew Frayne placed his empty glass where the barman couldn't fail to see it, murmured an "Excuse me" to the blond German girl sitting next to him, and, leaning across, helped himself to a handful of salted peanuts from the dish in front of her. The girl didn't say anything, but her eyebrows rose in lofty disdain and, just before she turned her back on him, Frayne saw her long aristocratic nose twitch as though she had suddenly become aware of a very unpleasant smell. He didn't altogether blame her: the phone booth in the foyer of the Badischer Hof had been hot and airless and he was still perspiring. He didn't look exactly presentable either, but that too was hardly surprising. Paris to Baden Baden was a long haul, all of three hundred and sixty miles. Apart from just over an hour they'd lingered at lunch in Nancy, he'd spent the entire day behind the wheel of the hired Peugeot and, as a result, his suit was creased in all the wrong places. He'd meant to change, but a puncture outside Strasbourg had thrown his timetable out of gear and the phone call to Munich had had overriding priority.

"Yes, sir?"

Frayne looked up and saw the barman had finally condescended to serve him. "About time," he grunted.

"*Bitte?*"

"Forget it." Frayne pointed to his empty glass. "Just get me another Scotch on the rocks."

The bartender inspected the glass, shook his head at the sweaty fingermarks on it, and replaced the tumbler with a clean one. A lean man with a hard-boned face and graying fair hair, he was, in Frayne's opinion, the kind of German who'd idolized Hitler. He could just picture him twenty-odd years ago, sweeping through Belorussia with the SS Das Reich Panzer Grenadier Division, killing or maiming everyone who got in his way. The war had changed nothing, he thought bitterly, these Aryans were the same high-handed and arrogant people who'd turned Europe into one huge bloodbath. And the new generation were no different if Axmann, his contact in Munich, was a typical example. He was too young to have fought in the war, but he was tarred with the same brush and had spoken to him as though he were one of the *Untermenschen* of this world. Axmann, the efficiency expert, upbraiding him because he'd waited twenty-four hours before reporting that Deakin's wife had the missing photograph in her handbag. Shit, what did the stupid cretin expect him to do? Leap out of bed in the middle of the night to phone the office? He'd have had a hard time explaining that one away to Marjorie.

"Your drink, sir."

Frayne glanced at the tab that had been placed beside the glass and slipped a ten-mark note out of his wallet. The bartender hesitated just long enough to give him a chance to say "Keep the change." When Frayne didn't, he went through his purse and produced two marks fifty in ten-pfennig coins.

"Thank you." Frayne smiled. "Tell me," he said, "what time does the restaurant close?"

"The grillroom is open until ten-thirty."

"Great." Pocketing the loose change, Frayne raised his glass in a mock salute and then, as a final taunt, downed the Scotch in one go. Feeling inordinately pleased with himself, he slid off the stool, walked into the lobby, and took the lift up to the second floor.

Marjorie Deakin was staring at her reflection in the full-length mirror on the inside door of the wardrobe. As he entered the room, she turned to face him, still holding the black dress in front of her.

"Do you think it's my style, Matthew?" she asked.

"You'll look very fetching in it." Frayne removed his crumpled jacket and tossed it on to the bed. "Very fetching," he repeated.

"I don't know." Marjorie frowned. "I have a feeling it's too young for me."

"Nonsense." The obligatory denial, but it contained more than an element of truth. Marjorie was forty-eight, ten years older than he was, but Frayne thought no one would ever guess it. Her face was unlined and youthful-looking, and even if she did tint her hair, the glossy dark sheen looked natural. And she had a very attractive figure, one which the oyster satin slip she was wearing made even more desirable. "Tell you what," he said hoarsely, "why don't you go as you are?"

"You've got a one-track mind, Matthew Frayne." Marjorie turned about to face him again. "That's your trouble."

"Is George afflicted the same way?"

Of course he wasn't. Deakin hadn't made love to his wife in over two years and Frayne knew the reason why, which was more than Marjorie did.

"What do you really think, Matthew?"

Her eyes were on the dress, but in refusing to answer his question, he guessed it wasn't only the little black number that was bothering her. Marjorie was feeling guilty about the shabby way she had treated George and needed to be reassured that she had no reason to reproach herself. There was, Frayne thought, only one sure-fire cure for that and, slipping his arms around Marjorie's waist, he kissed her, forcing his tongue into her mouth as she entwined his neck with both arms. He stroked her flanks, feeling the softness of her body under the satin, and slowly moved on up, his touch feather-light. Then he hooked both thumbs under the straps of her slip and began to ease them off her shoulders.

"Now, you just stop that, Matthew Frayne." Marjorie arched her back and placed a restraining hand on his chest. "I'm not in the mood for any hanky-panky."

But she was. The way her eyes had narrowed told him so and he pressed his body closer.

"I'm hungry, Matthew."

"Oh, yes?"

"I mean it. If we don't get a move on, we'll be too late for dinner."

"The grillroom doesn't close until ten-thirty."

"Oh. Well, I suppose that does make a difference," she murmured and slipped her arms out of the shoulder straps.

Frayne unhooked and raised the bra, freeing her breasts so he could caress them gently, her head on his left shoulder, her limbs trembling the way they always did when she was aroused.

"Do you love me?" Marjorie whispered.

"You know I do," he said.

The stock question and the stock answer, he thought, the ritual that preceded a frenzied coupling. A hand undid his zipper and reached for him eagerly as he guided her toward the bed. He raised her slip, discovered she was naked underneath, and wondered, not for the first time, just who was seducing whom. Then Marjorie sank down and spread her legs to receive him and the question became irrelevant.

Vasili Korznikov closed the door of the phone booth, lifted the receiver off the hook, and fed a dime into the slot. Then he dialed a number and waited, his mouth becoming dry, his stomach knotting with nervous tension as he listened to the prolonged and intermittent burring noise at the other end of

33

the line. Finally the number stopped ringing and a bored, nasal voice said, "Yeah?"

"Is that Mr. Jessop?" Korznikov asked politely.

"You've got the wrong number, Mac," the voice told him.

"I don't think so. This is the standby number of the Zenith Technical Corporation on the fourth floor of the Potter Building on Nassau Street."

"So what? You happen to be talking to the janitor. If you want the Zenith people you'd better call back on Monday. They've all gone home for the weekend."

"I find that hard to believe," Korznikov said. "Especially as the Zenith Technical Corporation is a front organization for the CIA."

"What are you, some kind of nut?"

"My name is Vasili Korznikov and I'm a trade counselor with the Soviet Embassy in Washington."

"Yeah?" said the voice. "Well, I'm Jack Kennedy and right now I'm playing hooky from the White House."

Korznikov closed his eyes and struggled to control his anger. At a time when every second counted, he was dealing with an imbecile. "You don't understand," he said patiently. "Mr. Jessop and I are in the same line of business, but on opposite sides of the fence. In other words, I am a KGB officer."

"Now I know you're a nut."

Although the nasal voice sounded irritated, Korznikov sensed that the anonymous person at Zenith was merely putting on an act. "You're quite wrong," he said in a flat voice. "I'm as sane as you are, Mr. Duty Officer."

"Yeah?" There was a long pause, then the duty officer said, "What did you say your name was?"

"Korznikov, Vasili Korznikov."

"Well, look, Mr. Korznikov, you're still talking to the janitor and I'm way out of my depth. Why don't you do like I said and call back on Monday?"

"I can't do that. My train to Washington leaves in an hour from now." Korznikov licked his lips. "I've been in New York since Tuesday looking after the Soviet trade delegation from Moscow, and this is the first opportunity I've had to get in touch with Mr. Jessop." He took a deep breath and went on. "I want to come across."

"You what?"

"I want to defect." Korznikov clenched the phone, the palm of his hand wet with perspiration. Dear God, did he have to spell it out in words of one syllable to this idiot dunderhead? "They are going to kill me," he said tersely. "That's why I'm asking for political asylum."

"I think I've just about had enough of your bullshit, Mr. Korznikov."

"It isn't bullshit."

"Oh yeah? Suppose you give me one good reason why I shouldn't hang up on you?"

"George Deakin," said Korznikov. "He's a mole in the British Secret Intelligence Service, has been ever since I re-cruited him back in 1956. Believe me, Mr. Duty Officer, I have a lot to offer."

"I guess maybe you have at that," the American said slowly. "Where are you calling from, Mr. Korznikov?"

"Saks Fifth Avenue. The delegation wanted to do some last-minute shopping before they embark on the *Mordovskaya Prospekt*."

"Okay. Now the best thing you can do is leave right this minute and get yourself over to Radio City Music Hall on Sixth Avenue. Go up to one of the ticket takers and keep talk-ing to him until we arrive to collect you. Got it?"

"I'm afraid you're too late," Korznikov said in a dull voice. "I've just been spotted by one of my colleagues."

He put the phone down and backed out of the booth. Samarin, one of the security goons from the Soviet Consulate on East Sixty-seventh Street, was talking to a sales assistant at the leather goods counter in the next aisle, killing time while he waited for him to make the next move. Ignoring him, Korz-nikov eased his way through the crowd of shoppers toward the exit. As he neared the doors, he felt a sharp stab of pain in his right leg and knew that Samarin had gotten close enough to operate the dart gun concealed in his briefcase. One minute, he thought, one minute from now and he'd be in a coma. Somehow he made it to the street and into the arms of a surprised black patrolman. Then his legs gave out and he sank down on to the sidewalk.

4.

It was said of Tom McNulty that a man had to be either foolish, conceited, or an incredibly lucky gambler to think that he could take McNulty to the cleaners in a game of poker. Observing the tall, lean, dark-haired American as he read the brief on the late George Deakin, Winter could see just how and why he had earned that reputation. As the top CIA officer in London, McNulty should have been relieved in June 1958, on the completion of his five-year tour of duty, but instead of returning home, he had stayed on at Grosvenor Square to ensure that American interests in the Deakin affair were properly represented, and in doing so had prejudiced any prospect of further advancement. Now, every sentence, every line, of the report in front of him mocked the sacrifices he had made; but if McNulty was consumed with bitterness, no one would have guessed it from the calm, almost placid expression on his face.

"I never did like Monday mornings." McNulty looked up and smiled wryly. "And digesting this report of yours is one hell of a way to start the week," he said, tapping the folder on his desk.

"I'm sorry, Tom," Winter said quietly. "I know just how much this whole business has cost you."

"It's not your fault. Accidents do happen." McNulty retrieved the cigar he'd left burning in the ashtray. "I suppose it was an accident, Charles?" he said, blowing a smoke ring towards the ceiling.

"All the evidence points that way. Mind you, I can't help feeling that if George had to die, it would have been less inconvenient all round had he succumbed to a heart attack."

"Even heart attacks can be faked," McNulty observed mildly. "All it takes is a hydrocyanide crystal discharged in the victim's face."

"Quite."

"And we know the KGB have developed a gas pistol. One of their hit men used such a weapon to eliminate the Ukrainian nationalist, Stefan Bandera, in Munich last year."

"George was drowned after striking his head on a rock," Winter said tartly.

"Right—the day after his wife left him." McNulty opened the folder again. "And she's still missing, so it says here."

"I don't think you should attach too much significance to what is probably a minor domestic upheaval. I'm sure Burman will be able to trace her before the day is out."

"Burman?" McNulty frowned. "I don't recall hearing his name before."

"There's no reason why you should have. Richard Burman is an instructor at our training school in Gerrards Cross."

"Is he ace?"

"He's pretty reliable," Winter said.

"That's what I like about you, Charles. You're so free with your praise." McNulty glanced at the photographs on the inside cover of the folder. Arranged in haphazard order, they showed part of the coastline at Bembridge from several different angles and a small row of assorted bungalows, cottages, and dormer-type houses fronting Fisherman's Walk some fifty yards from the cliff top. "Who took the pictures, Charles?"

"Ross. He went down to the island last Easter to vet the place before we allowed George to go ahead and rent a bungalow for the first fortnight in September." Winter smiled. "That's been our standard practice from the day Korznikov recruited him."

"Then Ross went down there again ten days ago to keep an eye on Deakin. Kind of risky, wasn't it?"

"Not a bit. It wouldn't matter if someone did remember his face; lots of people spend both Easter and summer in Bembridge."

McNulty looked at the photographs again. A cross marked the bungalow Deakin had rented, but there was nothing to indicate where his watchdog was based. "Where was Ross staying?" he asked.

"The Grange Hotel in Lane End, the only road leading to the houses on Fisherman's Walk. George couldn't make a move without him knowing it."

"Yeah? Well, you could fool me. Deakin runs his wife over to Ryde last Friday afternoon in their car, puts her on a boat to the mainland, and it doesn't occur to Ross that perhaps he ought to do something about it. One lousy three-minute phone call to your security people and they could have had a surveillance team waiting to follow her the moment she stepped off the train at Waterloo Station. Then maybe she wouldn't have disappeared into thin air."

Winter said, "You're being a little hard on Ross, aren't you, Tom? Deakin was his primary concern and he could have lost him while he was calling the office. Besides, Ross had no way of knowing that Marjorie was returning to London. Even now, we've only got Deakin's word for it."

"So you don't believe that cock-and-bull story about his stepdaughter either?" McNulty jabbed his cigar into the ashtray and mashed the last two inches into shreds.

"He could have been lying," Winter conceded. "But it doesn't necessarily follow that George had a sinister motive for doing so. It could be that Marjorie had upped and left him after a fight and he was merely trying to save face, hoping she would eventually come back to him."

"That's one for the agony column," McNulty said dryly. "I can't go along with that theory, it's just a little too cosy for me. I have a nasty feeling that Deakin was murdered."

"By the KGB?" Winter shook his head. "Oh, come on, Tom, what could they hope to gain by killing George?"

"I had another candidate in mind." McNulty paused. "The guy who took the rap for Deakin after Suez."

"Bill Turnock? You can forget him. I asked Malcolm Cleaver to make a few discreet inquiries and Bill's in the clear. Apart from walking his dog on the common and the usual Saturday morning shopping expedition, he never left his house in West Byfleet."

"I guess we can forget that angle then." McNulty leaned back in the chair and clasped both hands behind his neck. "How about Anatole Gorsky?" he asked casually. "Is Deakin's Soviet friend still in London?"

"He was spotted in Kensington Palace Gardens earlier this morning by one of Cleaver's people. I've cabled the head of station in Washington requesting the latest information on Vasili Korznikov, but I haven't heard anything yet."

"Vasili has defected to us."

Winter stared at the American. He could understand now why McNulty had taken the news about Deakin so calmly. Korznikov was a definite plus entry in the profit-and-loss account and was almost as big an asset as the one they'd just lost. "When did this happen?" he asked in a voice that was barely audible above the distant rumble of traffic passing through Grosvenor Square.

"Saturday afternoon around four o'clock Eastern Standard Time. Korznikov was in New York chaperoning a Soviet trade delegation around town. He called the Zenith Technical Corporation on Nassau Street from Saks Fifth Avenue and told the duty officer he wanted political asylum. He said the KGB were about to eliminate him."

"And?"

"Well, right now, Korznikov is recuperating in Roosevelt

Hospital. I don't know what kind of poison they pumped into him, but he's still a very sick man and it's going to be several days yet before we can interrogate him." McNulty unclasped his hands and leaned forward, elbows on the desk. "Deakin and Korznikov," he mused. "You take the time-zone difference into account and there has to be a connection."

"You could be right," Winter agreed reluctantly.

"I figure they both knew something we didn't and the KGB decided they had to go." McNulty grinned. "Just thinking aloud," he said.

"I'm listening."

"Information concerning some crisis point," McNulty continued. "Could be Berlin. Khrushchev is still making noises about a separate peace treaty with East Germany."

"That's all he is doing," said Winter, "making noises. There has been no significant buildup of Soviet forces in recent weeks."

"How about Iran? We're pretty vulnerable there."

"Why not Cuba?" Winter suggested. "It was announced in Moscow yesterday that the Soviet Union has agreed to supply Castro with arms and strategic materials. That could cover a multitude of sins."

"Yeah. Maybe we should ask Pandora to do a little digging on our behalf?"

Pandora was the code name assigned to Oleg Vladimirovitch Penkovsky, deputy chief of the Scientific Research Committee, Foreign Section. A lieutenant colonel in the GRU, the Intelligence Branch of the Soviet Army, he had become acquainted with Greville Wynne, an engineer from Shropshire specializing in import and export trade with the Soviet Union, when the Englishman had gone to Moscow in December 1960 to organize the visit of a British trade delegation. They had met again the following April when Greville Wynne had returned to Moscow to ascertain why a reciprocal delegation from the USSR had failed to put in an appearance on the agreed date. Penkovsky had assured the English businessman that the Soviet delegation would arrive in London around the middle of the month and, at the same time, had indicated that he wished to get in touch with the SIS. The first meeting had taken place in the Mount Royal Hotel on April 20, 1961, at eleven P.M. Thereafter, for the next fifteen months, Penkovsky had provided a steady flow of ultrahigh-grade information to both the CIA and the SIS via a number of prearranged drops in Moscow.

"You're crazy, Tom," Winter said angrily. "You know damned well the KGB have been watching his every move since the beginning of July."

"So what? Let's make use of him while he's still in circulation. Penkovsky is the man on the inside and he's in a position to tell us what the hell is going on, provided we ask him the right questions."

"I don't like it. Christ, we'd be inviting him to put his head on the chopping block."

"I don't expect you to make a decision here and now," McNulty said affably. "Think about it, then get back to me and we'll talk about the Korznikov setup."

The implication was clear enough to Winter. If he insisted on protecting Oleg Penkovsky, the SIS would be denied a seat at the table when the CIA got around to interrogating Korznikov. "All right, Tom," he said quietly. "I'll be in touch."

"Good," said McNulty. "Meantime, have a nice day."

There was a fat chance of that, Winter thought. Leaving McNulty's office, he went downstairs, nodded to the marine guard on duty in the entrance to the United States Embassy, and walked out into Grosvenor Square.

Burman drove slowly past the tube station at Notting Hill Gate, flicked the traffic indicator down to show that he was turning left, and swung into Farman Street. Coral Hughes and her boyfriend lived at Number 29, halfway down the road on the left-hand side. Finding a vacant space some twenty yards beyond the terraced house, Burman parked the Zephyr at the curbside, then turned to Lorrimer, the police constable sitting next to him.

"How about it, Ted?" he asked. "Do you want to run through the script again before we go into our double act?"

"I think I know my lines." Lorrimer smiled. "Don't let the uniform fool you, I'm not exactly your conventional policeman on the beat."

Burman already knew that. An experienced police officer in his early forties, Lorrimer belonged to A Division, the Diplomatic Protection Group, and was assigned to the Iraqi Embassy at 2 Palace Gardens in Kensington. He was absent from his normal place of duty this morning because Winter had pulled a few strings and borrowed him for a couple of hours to add a touch of authenticity to the charade.

"All the same, we could have our hands full with this one." Lorrimer wrinkled his nose. "I hear the man she's living with is a bit of a sticky customer."

"You don't have to worry about Dennis Keefer," Burman told him. "He's lecturing today."

"Sounds as though you people have been watching the house."

"Let's say Special Branch did us a small favor." Burman got out of the car, waited for Lorrimer to join him, and then walked back to Number 29.

The terraced house dated back to the horse and carriage era, a time of gracious living when the original occupants employed a small army of servants to look after them. Now, sixty years later, the once elegant Edwardian residence was fast becoming a run-down tenement. Opening the iron gate in the railings, Burman went on down a short flight of steps to the basement and rang the bell. A few moments later, a painfully thin young woman, wearing a pair of faded jeans and a sweater liberally daubed with paint, answered the door.

"Miss Coral Hughes?" Lorrimer inquired politely.

"Yes." Her eyes narrowed and emphasized a mean, spiteful-looking face. "What is it this time?" she snapped. "Another complaint about the noise from those people above?"

"No, it's rather more serious than that. I'm afraid we've some very distressing news about your stepfather." Lorrimer removed his peaked cap and tucked it under one arm. "Perhaps it would be best if we came inside," he suggested in a suitably grave voice.

Coral hesitated, then, shrugging her shoulders, opened the door wider and showed them into the living room off the hall. "You'll have to excuse the mess," she said. "We gave a party on Friday night before we went away for the weekend, and I haven't had a chance to tidy things up yet."

Burman could see at a glance what she meant. Wherever he looked there were empty or partially filled wineglasses, on the window ledge, the floor, the mantelpiece over the gas fire, and in the hearth. Every ashtray in the room was brim-full of cigarette stubs, and a considerable quantity of salted peanuts had ended up trodden into the carpet. But somehow the chaos didn't seem at odds with the lurid orange decor and the colored, framed magazine picture of Che Guevara glaring at him from the far wall.

"Serious and distressing news?" Coral pursed her lips. "Is my stepfather dead?"

Lorrimer nodded. "His body was found on Saturday morning. Apparently, Mr. Deakin was going for a swim and it seems he must have slipped and struck his head on a rock as he was wading out to sea."

"Poor old George," Coral said without a flicker of emotion. "Mind you, I always thought he would die of a coronary with his high blood pressure."

"That's interesting," Lorrimer said.

"What is?"

"The fact that your stepfather had a heart condition, Miss Hughes. It may have been a contributory cause."

"You mean he could have had a mild heart attack and blacked out?"

"We won't know the answer to that until the pathologist has completed a post mortem." Lorrimer paused, then said, "Naturally there has to be an inquest to establish the cause of death."

"I see."

"And of course somebody has to formally identify the deceased. Unfortunately, we've been unable to contact your mother. We were hoping you might be able to help us."

"Are you saying you want me to identify the body?"

Burman couldn't make up his mind whether Coral Hughes was being deliberately obtuse or had simply misunderstood the question. Either way, they weren't getting anywhere. "No, I could do that," he said, chipping in. "I'm with the Civil Service Commission now, but I knew your stepfather quite well when I was at the Ministry of Land and Natural Resources. I don't know whether George ever talked about his colleagues at the office, but my name's Burman, Richard Burman."

"I can't say your name rings a bell, but then George was the strong silent type." Coral folded both arms across her chest. "Still, if the police have no objections, I'm quite happy for you to identify him."

Lorrimer said, "You may be happy, Miss Hughes, but from our point of view, it's a very unsatisfactory arrangement. Mrs. Deakin is the immediate next of kin, and she ought to be informed of her husband's death as soon as possible. There's also the matter of the inquest on Thursday. It's going to look very odd if she isn't there."

"Odd?" Coral frowned, her dark eyebrows drawing together in a straight line above the narrow bridge of her nose. "What exactly do you mean by that?" she snapped.

"Let's put it this way," Lorrimer said calmly. "What is the coroner going to think if we tell him we've been unable to trace your mother? Right now, all the evidence points toward death by misadventure, but the jury could bring in a very different verdict if they thought she was missing."

There was a long pause before Coral finally said, "George was a singularly difficult and unpleasant man to live with. My mother should have left him years ago."

"And at last she did?" Burman suggested quietly.

"Yes. Dennis and I met her train at Waterloo on Friday

afternoon and then drove her out to the West London Air Terminal on Cromwell Road. She was going to catch the five-thirty BEA flight to Paris."

"Do you know where she's staying?" Lorrimer asked.

"The Hotel Saints-Pères, but they were only planning to spend one night in Paris."

"They?"

"The other man," Coral said acidly. "His name is Matthew Frayne. There's not much more I can tell you; they didn't discuss their plans with me. All I know is they're touring the Continent, driving from one place to another as the mood takes them."

The rest of the story didn't amount to much, but it gave Burman a fresh slant on the Deakins. In a few terse sentences, he learned that her mother had met Matthew Frayne last summer when she and George had spent a fortnight in Scarborough. Frayne had been staying at the same hotel and had gotten into conversation with Deakin one evening before dinner, while George had been downstairs in the bar waiting for Marjorie to join him. He had played a round of golf with George the following day, and thereafter they had gone around in a threesome. It had rapidly become a twosome one month after the Deakins had returned to Hendon, when Frayne had rung Marjorie one day to invite her to lunch.

"Matthew's asked her to marry him," Coral said abruptly, "and I hope she will."

Unlike George, it seemed, Matthew was kind, considerate, good-humored, and fun to be with. He was also a successful businessman and much better looking.

"You've met him then?" Burman said.

"No, but I've heard a lot about him and I've seen a color photograph of them together." Coral ushered them out into the hall and opened the front door. "That's why I know Matthew is right for her." Then slowly and very deliberately she closed the door in their faces.

"You know something?" Lorrimer said as he followed Burman up the steps. "I'm not sorry that's over. A little of Coral Hughes goes a very long way."

"You can say that again," Burman grunted.

"Do you think it was worth the hassle?"

"We've got a few pointers: Matthew Frayne, the name of the hotel where they stayed in Paris, and the date and time of the BEA flight." Burman closed the gate in the railings. "If they're touring the Continent, Frayne must have hired a car from Hertz or some other rental agency."

"Even so, I doubt if the French police will be able to trace her before the inquest starts on Thursday." Lorrimer sniffed. "We should have asked Coral Hughes if she had a photograph of her mother we could borrow."

"There was no need," Burman said. "I've already got a snapshot of Marjorie Deakin."

Suddenly the penny dropped and he made the connection. Marjorie Deakin had shown Coral a color photograph of herself and Matthew Frayne, but the prints he'd lifted from the house in Queen's Road were black-and-white. The fact that three negatives had been removed from one of the Kodak envelopes only strengthened a growing feeling that the intruder had subsequently searched the house from top to bottom looking for that particular color transparency. If that were the case, then Deakin's widow could well be in serious trouble.

47

5.

Winter picked up the plate, emptied the bread-crumbs into the wastepaper basket, and then wiped his mouth on a handkerchief. A ham roll and a glass of milk in the office was not his idea of lunch, but it had been one of those mornings when he'd rushed from pillar to post, losing all track of time in the process.

Berlin, Iran, or Cuba? McNulty had certainly given him plenty to think about, and he had stopped off at the Foreign Office on the way back from Grosvenor Square to have a word with Bracecourt, a diversion that had proved a waste of time and effort. Bracecourt had been in one of his expansive moods, taking the best part of an hour to deliver a homily on Khrushchev's problems that could have been given in ten minutes, if he had been less enamored with the sound of his own voice.

According to Bracecourt, the Soviet grain harvest had fallen well below the Kremlin's expectations, there was increasing public resentment over the lack of civilian commodities, particularly housing, and Russia's uneasy friendship with China was crumbling. Khrushchev was under attack and badly needed to pull off a major coup in order to restore his prestige, but Winter figured he wasn't the only world leader in trouble.

Midterm elections were coming up in the States and the voters weren't all that impressed with Kennedy's administration. His popularity rating had slipped after the Bay of Pigs fiasco in April 1961, when the CIA had attempted to overthrow Castro with the aid of two thousand Cuban exiles. The summit meeting with Khrushchev in Vienna three months later had done very little for him, and it was no secret that Kennedy was anxious to rebuild his image as a strongman. The two leaders were therefore heading for a confrontation, and the way Winter saw it, Cuba was the most likely place for a trial of strength.

That Bracecourt didn't agree with him was no surprise. The Foreign Office was preoccupied elsewhere; all their energies were directed toward supporting Macmillan's bid to get the U.K. into the Common Market, and Cuba was way down on their list of priorities. It rated a lot higher with the SIS, but even so, the head of the Caribbean desk wasn't exactly sure what was going on down there.

There was no shortage of information; if anything, there was too much of it and it was difficult to see the wood for the trees. There were reports that a battalion of Soviet engineers had moved into Pinar del Rio thirty miles west of Havana and were busy turning the small fishing port into a major harbor. Army barracks were said to be going up all over the island, roadworks were in progress at San Cristóbal and Guanajay, and a large tract of forest had been cleared at Bahia Honda. Cranes, locomotives, freight cars, drainage pipes, steam rollers, and power shovels were piling up on the dockside at Havana, and brand-new military trucks were parked three abreast in the side streets. Finally, the number of dry cargo ships arriving in Cuba from the Soviet Union had jumped from a steady average of fifteen a month to thirty in July, and had then increased to thirty-seven in August.

Inevitably, there were several theories about this hive of activity. One group of analysts believed that Khrushchev intended to establish a Soviet military presence on the island to deter any future attempt by the United States to overthrow Castro. Another faction in the Caribbean department was convinced that the Russians were simply training and equipping the Cubans on a lavish scale to enable Castro to export his revolution to other Latin American countries. And a third school of thought maintained that, faced with Russia's internal difficulties, the Kremlin had something more spectacular in mind, and that Khrushchev was about to position some of his surface-to-surface missiles outside the borders of the Soviet Union.

Faced with these differing opinions, two things were very clear to Winter. First, it would be the CIA and not the SIS who would eventually solve the riddle. If they hadn't already done so, it could only be a question of time before the CIA ordered their U-2 planes based in Florida to photograph the suspect areas of the island. And secondly, the whole of Latin America had been accepted as an American sphere of influence from the time of the Monroe Doctrine in 1817 and, knowing this, no KGB agent in his right mind would raise the subject of Cuba with Deakin. No, if George had been eliminated because he knew too much, they would have to look elsewhere for the reason.

Winter glanced at his wristwatch, saw that it was past two o'clock, and was about to buzz Diana Franklin when she tapped on the door and walked into the office. With a somewhat jaundiced eye, he watched his assistant deposit an armful of files in the in tray and remove the empty glass and plate from his desk.

"It's mostly routine stuff," she said, smiling. "Course reports from Gerrards Cross, a few supplementary estimates which require your signature, and the audit proceedings for the previous quarter."

"I can see it's going to be an exciting afternoon," Winter said dryly.

"Perhaps you'd like to see Mr. Burman first?"

"Where is he?"

"In my office. He arrived about ten minutes ago."

Ten minutes? It didn't take much imagination to guess how Burman had passed the time. Diana Franklin was a very attractive young widow, whose personality matched her looks, the kind of woman, in fact, who would immediately appeal to Burman.

"Right," said Winter. "Let's have him in here."

The files could wait; they weren't that important, and the SIS was unlikely to come to a grinding halt for want of his signature on a piece of paper. Winter got up and moved round the desk to greet Burman as he entered the room, then waved the younger man to one of the leather armchairs grouped around the pedestal table.

"How did you get on with Coral Hughes?" he asked abruptly.

"Well, she wasn't the most communicative person I've ever met." Burman lowered his lanky frame into an armchair. "It took some doing, but after Lorrimer had leaned on her a bit, she eventually told us that her mother had gone to Paris on Friday evening with a Mr. Matthew Frayne. I checked with the BEA desk at Heathrow and they confirmed both parties were on the seventeen-thirty flight."

"Do you have an address?"

Burman nodded. "The Hotel Saints-Pères, but aparently they only planned to stay there the one night. Coral Hughes wasn't able to tell us very much, but I gather they're doing the grand tour of Europe. That being the case, I thought the best way to trace Marjorie Deakin was through Interpol, so I rang Edmunds from the airport and asked him to start the ball rolling with Scotland Yard. Between us, we cooked up a story that will guarantee a green tab."

"I'm glad you didn't go overboard," said Winter. "It could have been very embarrassing if we'd had to make out a case for extradition."

Interpol notices were graded according to a color code. A green tab was a request for information concerning the whereabouts of a wanted person while, at the top end of the scale, a red was the equivalent of an international arrest warrant.

"How wide have you cast the net, Richard?"

"France, Holland, Belgium, Denmark, West Germany, Luxembourg, Switzerland, Spain, Portugal, and Italy. I had to play the field."

"You didn't have any other option."

"Trouble is, the average Interpol Bureau receives around thirty thousand messages a year and most of them are red tabs. Our request for information could end up buried under the priority telexes, and even if it doesn't, there's no guarantee we'll get a feedback."

"You never know," said Winter, "we may get lucky."

"Let's hope the same goes for Marjorie Deakin."

"Why do you say that?"

"Because she could be in trouble," Burman said, giving as his reasons the missing photographs and the possible link with the color snapshot of Marjorie Deakin and Matthew Frayne which Coral Hughes had seen.

"I don't like mysteries." Winter drummed his fingers on the table. "If Marjorie intended to leave George, why the hell did she spend a week with him in Bembridge?"

"Who knows? Maybe she wanted to break the news to him gently."

"I suppose that is possible. What do you have on this Matthew Frayne?"

"Not a lot. Frayne met the Deakins last summer when he was staying at the same hotel in Scarborough. It seems he took a shine to Marjorie and I guess the attraction must have been mutual. Anyway, she evidently gave him her phone number, because he called the house and invited her to lunch a month after she and George returned to Hendon. Coral told me he's a successful businessman, and handsome, too."

"And?"

"That's it."

"You're right," said Winter, "it's not a lot."

52

"I do have one lead we could follow." Burman reached in-side his jacket and placed an airline ticket on the table. "I got this coupon from the BEA ticket office in Cheapside. Frayne purchased it through an outfit called Wayfarers three weeks ago. I looked them up in *Kelly's Trade Directory* and they're a small travel agency in Harrow."

"The travel agency would have asked him for a deposit," Winter said, thinking aloud, "and that means he would have given them his home address and phone number."

"Right."

"What are you waiting for then? You should be in Harrow making discreet inquiries."

"I'm slow off the mark, that's my trouble." Burman stood up and moved toward the door. "By the way," he said, "what exactly do you mean by discreet?"

"You've got a free hand," said Winter. "If necessary, you can break into Frayne's house, but don't get caught."

"Don't worry, I won't," Burman said and closed the door behind him.

Winter returned to his desk and sat down. Dumping the audit proceedings and the course reports into the pending tray, he signed the supplementary estimates. Then, picking up the phone, he rang Ainsworth, the head of the Russian desk, and told him to meet him in the reading room.

"I'm rather busy just now, Charles," Ainsworth said plain-tively.

"You always are, Henry," Winter told him.

"And it's not my turn for escort duty today."

"It is now," Winter said, and put the phone down.

The reading room was one of the innovations Winter had introduced during his first year in office as deputy control. Located in the basement of 54 Broadway, it resembled a lion's cage and was derisively known as the Cat House among those whose names were not on the select list of department heads authorized to use the facility. Apart from a large, bricked-in combination safe and an internal telephone, the only other items of furniture were two tubular steel chairs and a table with a formica top which had been removed from the staff canteen on the ground floor.

Although the reading room was not the only restricted area in the building, security procedures were far more rigid than elsewhere. The gate to the cage was fitted with a double lock to which authorized personnel were issued one key, while the chief archivist held the other. Unable to get in or out without his assistance, the user was also subjected to a body search by one of the War Department constables on duty in the basement before the gate could be unlocked and opened. As a final precaution, the user was not allowed inside the cage unless he was escorted by one of the department heads on the approved list.

The security check completed, Winter told the chief archivist he would call him when they were through. Then he opened the combination safe, removed a medium-sized loose-leaf file from the top shelf, and placed it on the table in front of Ainsworth.

"I want you to go through the case history on George Deakin," he said. "You're to look for any subtle change in his manner—any period when he seemed distracted, morose, worried, introspective, or particularly unhappy—that sort of thing. If you find any instances, make a note of the dates and check them against the diary to see if any of his moods occurred before or after George had collected his instructions from a drop. As a double check, look up the dates when Deakin actually met Gorsky or Korznikov and then go to the case history to see if any of us observed any kind of reaction by George."

Ainsworth looked up, eyes blinking behind pebble-lensed glasses. He had receding light-brown hair and tufty eyebrows that needed trimming. A large, untidy man, he could have made a Savile Row suit look like a purchase from a jumble sale within minutes of putting it on.

"I didn't know this was going to be a working session for me, Charles," he said.

"I wouldn't drag you away from your Baltic States, Henry, unless it was important."

"Actually, I was reading a paper on Soviet strategic missiles. It was extremely interesting."

His enthusiasm was genuine. Ainsworth enjoyed reading a complicated scientific paper the same way other people became immersed in a good novel. An intellectual, his sole form of recreation seemed to be *The Times* crossword puzzle, which he invariably completed within a self-imposed time limit.

"Morose, distracted, introspective, worried, or unhappy." Ainsworth pursed his lips. "You do realize that was George most days of the week? My memory may be at fault, but I can't ever remember seeing him with what you could call a smile on his face."

"I don't suppose you would feel on top of the world either if you were lumbered with a stepdaughter like Coral Hughes."

"Quite. That's the reason why finding something unusual about his behavior will be like looking for a needle in a haystack."

"I didn't say it would be easy," Winter cautioned.

"That's right, you didn't. So where do I start?"

"At the beginning, from the day Korznikov recruited him."

"But that was almost six years ago," Ainsworth protested. "We could be here all night."

"I doubt it," said Winter. "With your specialized knowledge, you should come up with a lead long before then, Henry."

A member of the Joint Intelligence and Planning Committee, Ainsworth had collated the bogus information Deakin had passed to the KGB and had sat in on all the debriefing sessions. As head of the Russian desk, he had also handled the bulk of the material supplied by Lieutenant Colonel Oleg Penkovsky and had met the GRU officer on three occasions, twice in London in April and July of 1961 and finally in Paris some two months later, toward the end of September. Winter believed that if a choice had to be made between Korznikov and Penkovsky, Ainsworth was the only man capable of helping him reach an objective decision.

"I didn't realize there was a connection between Deakin and friend Oleg," Ainsworth said, eying the second file Winter had just removed from the safe.

"There could be."

"I don't see how. Penkovsky is GRU and George was playing footsie with the KGB. And we both know the GRU is the intelligence branch of the Soviet army, while the KGB is controlled by the Council of Ministers."

"There's no demarcation line between the two organizations, Henry. They both engage in espionage. As a matter of fact, they spy on each other half the time."

"That's a very tenuous explanation." Ainsworth cocked his head to one side and squinted at him calculatingly. "You know, Charles, I have a curious feeling that you're holding something back from me. I wonder—could it be some snippet of information you learned from McNulty this morning?"

Winter hesitated. He would have preferred to keep the news about Korznikov to himself until Ainsworth had completed the task he'd set him, but there was no stopping Henry once he'd scented blood. "There's been a rather surprising development in New York," he said casually. "Vasili Korznikov was admitted to Roosevelt Hospital on Saturday afternoon. He was rushed there shortly after he phoned the duty CIA officer at Zenith and asked for political asylum. It appears the KGB tried to poison him."

Ainsworth gave a low whistle, then was silent for several moments, deep in thought. "And this happened the same day that Deakin's body was found?" he said eventually. His tufty eyebrows shot upward, lending emphasis to the note of incredulity. "I think that's too much of a coincidence."

"So does Tom McNulty."

"What has Korznikov to say for himself?"

"Nothing yet," said Winter. "I'm told he's a very sick man. It'll be several days before he's fit enough to answer any questions. Meantime, we're going to do some researching."

"On whose behalf? Ours or McNulty's?"

"We have a common interest in Korznikov. We'd both like to know what made him jump through the hoop, Henry."

"And you think that maybe Penkovsky can supply the answer?"

Winter sat down at the table and opened the dossier on the GRU officer. Ainsworth was getting close, too close for comfort. Once started on that track, it wouldn't be long before Henry put two and two together and guessed that McNulty wanted to use Penkovsky to do the spadework.

"Well?" Ainsworth prodded. "Am I right?"

"How the hell should I know?" Winter said angrily. "I haven't even started to read the bloody file yet."

Samarin left the IRT subway at Columbus Circle and headed west on Fifty-ninth. Tracing Korznikov to the Roosevelt Hospital had been easy: the rest of the security section from the Soviet Consulate had been deployed to watch every hospital in the area bounded by Ninth Avenue, Forty-ninth Street, Lexington Avenue, and Forty-second Street, and he had known where to find Korznikov minutes after the ambulance had arrived at the casualty department. From then on, a surveillance team had kept the Roosevelt under discreet observation, noting the routine. Much of the groundwork had already been done in a preliminary reconnaissance of the likely hospitals within a two-mile radius of Saks a week ago, when the Soviet trade delegation had arrived in New York, and the follow-up was something of a formality. Even so, Samarin would have preferred to wait another day before making the next move, but the director of operations had insisted they keep the pot boiling and he'd been overruled.

As he approached the service entrance to the hospital, one of the street watchers on the other side of the road gave him the all-clear and, wheeling right, he went on down the ramp to the basement. His mouth dry with apprehension, it came as something of a relief to find that the layout was much as he'd imagined it would be from studying the architect's plan of the building. The briefing he'd received had been equally thorough in other respects; he knew to the exact minute when the laundry truck was scheduled to collect the dirty linen and, more important, he'd been given a plausible cover story. Had anyone asked him what he was doing in the basement, Samarin would have said that he'd heard the Roosevelt was short of ancillary staff and was hoping to see the supervisor about a job. But the necessity didn't arise; luck, the random and unpredictable element nobody could anticipate, was on his side, and at that particular moment, the basement happened to be deserted. It wouldn't be for much longer, though; a low-pitched humming noise warned Samarin that one of the two service elevators was on the way down and, reacting swiftly, he ducked behind a concrete pillar.

The elevator jerked to a stop and he heard the gate open, then close again. A few moments later, a thin, dark-haired young man appeared in his line of sight, wheeling a laundry basket. Sizing him up, Samarin figured the hospital attendant was about an inch or so shorter and several pounds lighter than himself, but that was close enough. Silent as a cat stalking a sitting bird, he came up behind the younger man and chopped him down with a blow to the nape of the neck. In that same instant, somebody on one of the floors above pressed the call button to summon the elevator from the basement.

He swung around to check the position of the second elevator, but there was no indicator above the entrance. Mouthing obscenities, Samarin grabbed the unconscious attendant under both arms, dragged him behind the pile of dirty laundry stacked near the loading bay, and stripped off his hospital fatigues. That done, he tipped the contents of the laundry basket on top of him. Only too aware that every second counted, he changed into the hospital garb, dumped his street clothes into the empty basket, and wheeled it over to the service elevators.

There was no need to push the call button. The right-hand elevator was already on the way down and he stood there listening to the cables whirring in the shaft, his heart thumping. The noise grew louder and he looked up as the cage neared the bottom and saw that it was occupied. The car shuddered to a halt and, moving the laundry basket out of the way, Samarin opened the cage and then stepped to one side.

"Need a helping hand?" he asked cheerfully.

"Who do you think you are?" said the hospital attendant. "A boy scout or something?"

"Nope." Samarin grinned. "I'm just new here, started today." He trundled his laundry basket into the cage and closed the gate. "The name's Macklin, Eddie Macklin," he called as he thumbed the button.

Although he knew just how many rooms there were in the Roosevelt Hospital, Samarin had no idea which one Korznikov was occupying. Alighting at the tenth floor, he pushed the laundry basket down the corridor and circled the block until he was back at his original starting point. He went through the same routine on the ninth, eighth, and seventh floors, greeting every nurse or intern who happened to glance in his direction with a cheery smile and a "Hi there." As he emerged from the elevator on the sixth floor, two patrolmen, one standing at the far end of the corridor, the other seated outside Room 639, told him that he had located Korznikov. Hastily backing into the cage again, he rode the elevator down to the fourth and got out.

The two patrolmen had definitely seen him, and from the way they'd exchanged glances, Samarin got the impression that somebody had already collected the dirty linen from the sixth floor. If that was the case, his hurried exit could well have aroused their suspicions. One thing was certain, he had to leave the hospital and fast. He wheeled the laundry basket into the south corridor, found one of the examination rooms was unlocked and empty, and went inside. Stripping off the fatigues, he quickly changed back into his street clothes; then, checking first to make sure nobody was about, he left the room and walked around the corner to the public elevators. Less

than two minutes later, he strolled through Reception and out
into the street.

It had been a close thing, but he was satisfied the operation
had been successful. Sooner or later, the CIA would learn
that an intruder had tried to get at Korznikov, and that had
been the whole purpose of the exercise.

6.

Burman parked the Zephyr in the station yard at Harrow-on-the-Hill and walked around the corner into Lowlands Road. The Wayfarers travel agency was sandwiched between two shops in a small arcade that looked as if it had been erected around the turn of the century. There were the usual eye-catching posters in the front window: a bronzed girl in a scanty bikini sunbathing on a deserted stretch of beach against a background of palm trees, the Acropolis, the Colosseum in Rome, and the Champs Elysées looking toward the Arc de Triomphe. There was also a stand-up card which read, "Book now for the winter holiday of a lifetime."

This blandishment didn't seem to have attracted many takers; the only clients inside the agency were a retired couple and, eavesdropping on their conversation with the travel representative, it was apparent they were more interested in a coach trip to Bournemouth than a fortnight in a fashionable ski resort. The travel representative glanced in Burman's direction, smiled fleetingly, and pressed a buzzer on the counter to summon a blond woman with a bouffant hairstyle from the small office at the back.

The plastic tag pinned on her dress told Burman that her

61

name was Ann, and he noticed a half hoop of diamonds and a platinum wedding ring on the third finger of her left hand.

"Can I help you, sir?" she asked in a carefully enunciated voice.

"I hope so." Turning his back on the retired couple, Burman leaned against the counter, reached inside his jacket, and showed her the warrant card he'd obtained from Edmunds. "Detective Sergeant Burman, CID Department C1," he said quietly. "I'd like to have a word with you in private about one of your clients. Perhaps we could step inside the office for a minute or so, Mrs.—?"

"Crawford, Mrs. Ann Crawford." She raised the counter flap, opened the gate beneath it, and stepped to one side. "If you would like to come through to the back," she murmured, her face expressionless.

The office was long and narrow and looked as if it might have been a storeroom before Wayfarers took over the premises. A large desk from a furniture-rental firm and three filing cabinets took up most of the available space. With only a small skylight in the roof, the room would have been extremely gloomy without the fluorescent strip.

"What's the name of this client?" Ann Crawford asked him, closing the door behind her.

"Matthew Frayne." Burman dug the airline ticket out of his pocket and placed it on her desk, then sat down in the only spare chair. "You sold him two tickets on the seventeen-thirty BEA flight to Paris on Friday, the seventh of September. He purchased them from you three weeks beforehand."

"I can see that."

"You also booked him a double room at the Hotel Saints-Pères in Paris for one night."

"You seem to be very well informed." She raised her eyes and stared at him, lips pursed. "What exactly is it you want from us, sergeant?"

Burman said, "We've reason to believe Mr. Frayne rented a car. We'd like to know if he hired it from Avis or Hertz, assuming he asked you to make the necessary arrangements."

"If we did, it will have been itemized on his account." Ann Crawford moved around the desk, opened the top drawer of the left-hand filing cabinet, and pulled out a slim manila folder. "It appears your information is correct," she said presently. "Mr. Frayne hired a Peugeot from Avis for one month and was intending to travel through France, West Germany, Switzerland, Austria, and Italy. He also stipulated that the car was to be delivered to the Hotel Saints-Pères at nine A.M. on Saturday, the eighth of September."

"Do you mind if I have a look?" Burman reached out and plucked the file from her grasp before she had time to object. "19 Cumberland House," he said, noting Frayne's address on the invoice. "Is that as classy as it sounds?"

"It's a luxury building at the bottom end of Station Road, opposite Sopers' Department Store. Do you know where that is, sergeant?"

"Not exactly," he said.

She assured him that Cumberland House was easy to find. Provided he turned right outside the travel agency and kept on past the recreation ground, he would find himself in Station Road and from then on he couldn't possibly miss it.

Burman said how helpful she had been, apologized for taking up so much of her time, and backed out of the office. The retired couple were still there quizzing the travel representative, who was beginning to look decidedly harassed. It seemed they'd changed their minds about Bournemouth and were now inclined to think Worthing would suit them better.

Cumberland House stood well back from Station Road, had an underground garage, and was surrounded by a well-tended lawn. A large notice stuck in the grass warned that trespassers would be prosecuted, and there was a porter on duty in the entrance hall to ensure the residents were not pestered by door-to-door salesmen.

The hall porter wore a gray uniform in military style and sported a row of campaign ribbons above the right breast pocket. An old soldier who'd fought in the Western desert,

Italy, France, and Germany, he was not at all impressed by the warrant card Burman showed him, and answered his questions with a straight yes or no. Eventually, five pounds loosened his tongue sufficiently for Burman to learn, among other things, that Frayne had moved in fifteen months ago. It also produced the key to his apartment.

Twenty minutes later, Burman left Cumberland House and called Edmunds from a phone box down the road from Sopers' Department Store. Then he collected his Zephyr from the station yard and drove back to the training school at Gerrards Cross.

Winter opened the dossier again and gazed at the photographs of the handsome, red-haired man in army uniform on the inside cover. Lieutenant Colonel Oleg Vladimirovitch Penkovsky, born at Ordzhonikidze in the Caucasus on April 23, 1919, and currently residing in Moscow at 36 Maxim Gorky Embankment, Apartment 59. Married, October 1945, Vera Dmitriyevna, daughter of the late Major General Dmitri Gaponovitch, former member of the Military Council and chief of the Political Directorate Moscow Military District. Issue, two daughters—Galina, born 1946; second daughter, born February 6, 1962, as yet unnamed.

There was no need to look at Penkovsky's curriculum vitae; Winter knew it off by heart, from the time he'd entered the Second Kiev Artillery School in 1937 at the age of eighteen, to his current appointment as deputy chief of the Scientific Research Committee, Foreign Section. It was of little interest to Winter to know that Penkovsky had seen action against the Finns in 1940 and had commanded the Fifty-first Guards Tank Destroyer Regiment during the later stages of World War II, winning five decorations and eight campaign medals along the way. What really counted was the fact that he was a top-grade GRU intelligence officer who had spent the greater part of his service behind a desk in Moscow. Always close to the seat of power, he was the most valuable asset the SIS had ever acquired in the Soviet Union.

"You're looking very pensive, Charles." Ainsworth smiled at him from across the table in the reading room. "Mind you, I'm not surprised. Penkovsky is something of an enigma, isn't he? I mean, there he was, a professional, highly decorated intelligence officer married into the right family with friends in high places and a brilliant future in front of him, then one day he suddenly decides he can't stand the Soviet system any longer and offers to work for us."

Winter thought his motives had been far more complex than that. For one thing, Penkovsky believed Khrushchev was a dangerous, bellicose peasant whose adventurism would plunge the world into a nuclear war if he wasn't stopped; for another, he hated the Soviet leader for what he'd done to the army by dismissing Zhukov and packing the top echelons with his own yes-men. It was also a fact that Penkovsky knew his brilliant future had evaporated the day he learned the KGB had discovered that his father had fought against the Bolsheviks in the civil war and had been killed in action at Rostov in 1919.

"His career was in a shambles, Henry. His father had been branded an enemy of the people and he knew he wasn't going anywhere."

"Does it really matter why he was converted?" Ainsworth scraped out the bowl of his pipe with a penknife, then filled it with Balkan Sobranie and lit up. It didn't bother him that there was no ashtray in the reading room; he used the lid of his tobacco tin for the spent matches. "Penkovsky is still the most important asset we have," he said, drawing on his pipe.

"You think I don't know that?"

"And we should do our very best to protect him," Ainsworth continued remorselessly.

Winter gritted his teeth. Henry was steering the conversation around to McNulty again and, none too subtly, was warning him not to sell Penkovsky short. "Why don't you get on with what you're supposed to be doing?" he said coldly.

"I've finished reading the case history, Charles." Ainsworth grinned at him through a cloud of tobacco smoke. "And I'm ready to talk about George Deakin whenever you are."

"Right, let's get on with it then."

"Well, as I said before, George was morose and introspective most of the time, but who wouldn't have been in his position? George was a puppet, he didn't have a real job and saw only the files we wanted him to see. It must have been soul-destroying for him to have to sit there in his poky little office day in, day out, with nothing to do but read a book until it was time to go home again."

"You're breaking my heart," Winter snorted.

"Really? I thought I was explaining why George felt the way he did."

"Aren't you also implying that you were right all along and that there was nothing unusual about his behavior over the years?"

"You're jumping to conclusions, Charles. What I'm saying is that we've been looking for the wrong symptoms. I told you I couldn't ever remember seeing George with a smile on his face, but that wasn't strictly true. He wasn't always down in the dumps. Reading my case notes again, I see there were times when he was fairly cheerful. For instance, George was invariably affable the week before he went on holiday. Then, two years ago last Easter, there was a halcyon period lasting all of six weeks when his stepdaughter left home to set up house with Dennis Keefer."

"There's nothing sinister about that," Winter said. "Coral Hughes was the bane of his life and, in his shoes, I'd have been overjoyed to see the back of her."

"Quite." Ainsworth opened the file at the marker he'd placed between the pages. "There was another good period in April '61 which began shortly after the Bay of Pigs fiasco. At first, I thought he was secretly pleased that the CIA and the Kennedy administration had ended up with egg on their faces. George wasn't exactly pro-American, which is hardly surprising, considering Tom McNulty never made any secret of the fact that he despised him. However, a few weeks later, it transpired that he'd made a modest killing on the stock market. He showed me the check from his stockbroker; it amounted to four hundred and nine pounds, seventeen shillings, and sixpence."

"Yes, I can understand that making George cheerful; he would have considered it a small fortune."

"Well, Marjorie soon made a hole in it and his feeling of euphoria rapidly disappeared. I gather she persuaded George to buy her an automatic washing machine, and to pay for a fortnight's holiday for his stepdaughter in Rome and Venice."

Winter could see how the thought of Coral enjoying a holiday at his expense would sour George. He thought Marjorie must have exercised a great deal of charm to make him part with his money.

"The last high spot occurred a few weeks ago," Ainsworth continued. "Apparently I noticed a change in George on Tuesday the nineteenth of June, the day after he met his KGB case officer. Gorsky had asked him for information on the Iranian military procurement program and the kind of technical assistance we'd been asked to provide, particularly in the field of counterintelligence. Of course, George always enjoyed hoodwinking the Soviets, and it could be he was pleased to be in another ball game. The only thing is, I checked the diary against the case history from the time he was recruited by the KGB, and I couldn't find another instance when George had been quite so enthusiastic after meeting either Korznikov or Gorsky. With hindsight, I can see now that his behavior on that occasion didn't jell with the normal pattern."

Winter thought there was something else that didn't jell. Deakin had every reason to be morose; he and Marjorie were no longer sleeping together and, even if she hadn't told him, he must have suspected she was seeing someone else.

"I'm beginning to have second thoughts about Penkovsky,"

Ainsworth said quietly. "Maybe we should bring him into play after all."

"That's a sudden about-face, isn't it? A few minutes ago you were saying we should do our very best to protect him."

"That was purely a gut reaction, Charles. The KGB have had their eyes on Penkovsky ever since they discovered his father had fought against the Red army, and I know it wouldn't make a scrap of difference if we never contacted him again. They'd still arrest him sooner or later. He's only at liberty now because they're hoping he'll lead them to other intelligence officers in the Diplomatic Service. Naturally, I'd like to get him out, and we could do it too, but Penkovsky won't leave the Soviet Union without his wife and family."

There was one other factor Winter knew they should take into account. Where Deakin was concerned, the SIS had had complete control and had been able to dictate just how the game would be played, but those exclusive rights didn't apply to Penkovsky. Although McNulty had asked for his approval, there was no way he could prevent the CIA from contacting the GRU officer if they had a mind to. Tom only wanted his agreement to prevent the recriminations that were bound to follow should anything go wrong, and if he withheld it, the SIS would not be allowed to interrogate Korznikov.

"I believe I know what you're thinking, Charles, but no matter what you do, Penkovsky is still a dead duck."

Ainsworth was right, but even so, Winter was reluctant to go along with McNulty, at least not before they'd exhausted every other avenue of inquiry.

"This meeting Deakin had with Anatole Gorsky on the eighteenth of June," Winter said thoughtfully. "I think you should go through the subsequent planning sessions when George was present and see if you can find any pointers."

"You mean now, right this minute?"

"Why not?"

Ainsworth blinked. "Well, for one thing, everyone else has gone home."

68

Winter glanced at his wristwatch and saw that it was almost seven-thirty. "Perhaps we'd better leave it until the morning then," he said.

"Good." Ainsworth lifted the phone. "Let's hope the chief archivist remembered to give his key to the resident clerk, otherwise we'll be stuck here in this cage all night."

Somehow, Marjorie Deakin found the energy to shuffle around the crowded dance floor, her eyes closed, her head resting on Matthew Frayne's shoulder. The five-piece band was playing a slow foxtrot and, to her ears, they sounded almost as weary as she felt. Her legs ached, her calf muscles were lumps of iron, and the stiletto high-heeled shoes she was wearing felt as though they were a size too small.

"Sleepy, darling?" Matthew asked in a low voice, and squeezed her hand.

"A little." She raised her head and smiled up at him, fighting off a yawn. "What time is it?"

"I make it almost one-thirty."

Marjorie laid her head on his shoulder again. She was finding it increasingly difficult to keep track of time, but if Matthew said it was one-thirty, then it was obviously Tuesday. Or was it? They'd arrived in Paris on Friday evening and had spent the following night at the Badischer Hof in Baden Baden, before driving on to Salzburg and the Maria Theresa Schloss on the outskirts. How many nights had they stayed at the Schloss? One or two? They had arrived in time for lunch after a very early start and they had walked around the town in the afternoon taking in the sights, Mozart's birthplace in the Getreidegasse, the Hohensalzburg fortress, the Stieglkeller beer garden, the archbishop's palace, and God knows how many churches. Surely they couldn't have done all that in one afternoon? They must have stayed over, because she distinctly remembered writing a postcard to Coral, and the shops would have been closed on Sunday. No, wait a minute, she'd purchased the card from the girl in Reception at the Maria

Theresa, and had mailed it when they arrived in Vienna. It was Tuesday then; there was no doubt about that.

"How long are we going to stay in Vienna?" she murmured.

"Three, perhaps four days. There's a lot to see before we move on—the Hofburg, the Opera House, the Schönbrunn Palace, the Spanish Riding School, Saint Stephen's Cathedral, Mayerling, the Prater . . ."

The list droned on, seemingly endless, but it was a relief to know they were stopping in one place for more than twenty-four hours. The past four days had been one long whirlwind and the frantic pace was beginning to tell on her. Maybe she didn't look her age, but right now she certainly felt it and it was no use pretending otherwise.

"I don't know about you, darling, but I'm about ready for bed." Matthew patted her hip gently, then moved his hand down to rest it on her bottom as he leaned away from her. "Would you mind if we called it a night?"

"Don't you want to stay for the next cabaret?" Sheer bravado on her part, Marjorie thought, but it wouldn't do to give Matthew the impression she couldn't keep up with him. No matter how much he professed to love her, she was painfully aware that there were ten years between them and that one day she might lose him to a younger woman.

"I'm really bushed." He smiled down at her. "I also think I've drunk too much wine and that always makes me sleepy."

"Me too," she said.

"That's something else we have in common then."

Matthew steered her toward their table, draped the stole around her shouders, then led her out of the nightclub on Zirkusgasse into the chill early-morning air.

"The Danube must be that way," he said, pointing to his right.

"Surely we're not going to walk all the way back to our hotel, are we?" she protested.

"Hell, no. I'm just trying to get my bearings." Frayne took

70

hold of her arm and crossed the road. "We should be able to find a cab in Prater Strasse."

"There's one parked by the curbside behind us, Matthew."

"He's not for hire, at least not by us."

"How do you know that?" she asked.

"Well, for one thing his roof light is switched off and for another, he's already got a fare. Didn't you see that woman loitering in the shop doorway opposite the nightclub?"

"No." Marjorie frowned. "No, I can't say I did."

"Take my word for it, she's a streetwalker." Frayne turned the corner into a dimly lit alleyway. "The mobile kind," he added.

Marjorie wondered how he knew that, but didn't like to ask. Holding on to Matthew's arm, she tried to match his stride, which wasn't easy in high heels on the uneven cobblestones. "Must you go so fast?" she said irritably.

"Oh, I'm sorry, I keep forgetting you can't walk as quickly in high . . ."

A car turned into the alleyway behind them and accelerated rapidly, the deep-throated snarl of the exhaust drowning his voice. Marjorie glanced back over her shoulder and saw that the oncoming vehicle was swerving from side to side. Then a violent blow on the shoulder propelled her out into the road and she staggered forward, lost her balance, and went down on all fours, skinning her hands and knees. Frantically, she tried to crawl out of the way, but the front left wheel ran over both legs, crushing them even as the driver swerved and mounted the pavement. She heard Matthew scream, saw his body sail through the air, and heard the sickening crunch made by the impact of his skull on the cobblestones. Then the alleyway began to revolve in front of her eyes and she seemed to be floating weightless in space.

7.

The eldest of three, Diana Franklin came from an army family. Her father had retired with the rank of lieutenant general and her two younger brothers were both serving in the Brigade of Guards. At the age of twenty-one she had broken with family tradition and married an RAF pilot, who had been killed five years later when his Hawker Hunter had collided with a Cessna light aircraft over Boscombe Down. That much Burman had discovered from questioning Edmunds; that she was also slender, dark-haired, and decidedly attractive had been perfectly obvious from the moment he'd walked into her office yesterday. For Winter to keep him waiting while he took an incoming call was therefore no hardship. As far as Burman was concerned, he could spend the rest of the morning on the phone. Not that he was making much progress with Winter's PA; every conversational gambit he'd tried up to now had been killed stone-dead within a matter of seconds.

"I'm thinking of moving into town," Burman said, trying another tack. "I'm not cut out to be a commuter, it's just too much of a hassle."

"You'll get used to it." Diana looked up and smiled at him,

envelope in one hand, paperknife in the other. "That's what I was told."

"And did you?"

"No, I got tired of traveling back and forth between Haslemere and Waterloo and decided to live in town." Diana glanced at the letter she'd just extracted from the envelope and then placed it on top of the others waiting to be filed. "If you're planning to do the same, Mr. Burman, I should warn you it took me three months to find somewhere to live."

"Accommodation's that scarce?"

"It depends on what you can afford."

"I can manage fifteen to twenty pounds a week. Trouble is I don't know London all that well and I might go to the wrong agency." Burman smiled. "I don't suppose you'd like to advise me over a drink tonight?"

"I already have a date for this evening," Diana told him.

"How about Wednesday?"

"I'll think about it." She pointed to the green light which was showing above the communicating door. "And you should think about seeing Mr. Winter. He's free now."

"That's what I call lousy timing," Burman said with feeling.

The green light flashed on and off, a sign of growing impatience. Opening the communicating door, Burman walked into the adjoining office and into an atmosphere that was distinctly chilly.

"Edmunds tells me you managed to get Frayne's address from the travel agency," Winter said without preamble.

Burman nodded. "I also learned he'd rented a Peugeot from Avis for one month. It seems he's planning to motor through France, West Germany, Austria, Switzerland, and Italy. I don't know if it'll do any good, but Edmunds agreed to pass the information on to Interpol. If nothing else, it shouldn't take the French police long to discover the license number of his car."

"Quite. Do we know what Frayne does for a living?"

"I talked to the hall porter at Cumberland House. He thinks

Frayne is a partner in a firm of insurance brokers, but I couldn't find any evidence of that when I looked around his flat. He's a very anonymous person."

"In what way?"

"I went through his desk. There were the usual receipted bills from the gas and electricity boards, a wad of bank statements, and a few miscellaneous invoices, but no personal letters or photographs of any kind. The whole apartment was sterile and lacking in character, like an isolation ward."

"I don't like the sound of that," Winter said. "A man who has removed every trace of his background has something to hide."

"We could have a word with the passport office," Burman suggested. "His application form might give us a lead. Then there's the tax people; nobody can work in this country without paying taxes and National Insurance contributions."

"Yes. On the other hand, we could be making a mountain out of a molehill. I had a phone call from Ross earlier on and it appears the pathologist who did the post mortem on Deakin could find no evidence of foul play. As far as he's concerned, George slipped, struck his head on a rock, and drowned. Death occurred sometime between six and eight on Saturday morning."

"What about the bungalow Deakin rented on Fisherman's Walk? I assume the police looked it over?"

"Of course they did," Winter snapped. "Everything was just as it should be. The bungalow hadn't been broken into and there were no obvious signs of a struggle. Anyway, all the forensic evidence points to the fact that the injury to his skull occurred shortly before he was drowned."

"But you're still not entirely satisfied that was the case?"

"George could have had a visitor, somebody he knew and invited inside."

Burman mulled it over. A visitor who'd arrived after dark and stayed over until morning without anyone knowing he'd been there? It wasn't impossible, provided he left before any of the neighbors were up and about. He wondered if the police had questioned them.

"I know this may be a silly question," he began, then the phone rang and he didn't get any further.

Winter took the incoming call, his face registering annoyance. The subsequent conversation was brief, one-sided, and impossible to follow. By the time he hung up, Winter's mood had changed and he looked subdued.

"Trouble?" Burman asked him.

"You can stand Interpol down, Richard. The Foreign Office has just learned from their consular office in Vienna that Marjorie Deakin is in hospital. Apparently, she was knocked down by a drunken driver around two o'clock this morning. Both her legs were broken, but at least she was luckier than Frayne. He was killed."

"Christ, that's a turn-up for the book." Burman rubbed his jaw. "Has Coral Hughes been told yet?"

"The consular officer phoned her before he contacted the Foreign Office and the Embassy in Vienna. There are no prizes for guessing that Frayne didn't have any next of kin."

"Marjorie Deakin should be able to tell us something about him."

"Right. That's why I want you to drop everything and get yourself on a plane to Vienna. How long will it take you to pack?"

"A couple of hours," said Burman, "allowing for the round trip to Gerrards Cross."

"Good. I'll warn our people in Vienna to expect you in the late afternoon or early evening. By that time, they'll know whether or not Marjorie's in a fit state to be questioned. I know she and George were no longer sharing the same bed, but the news of his death coming on top of Frayne's is bound to shake her up."

The understatement of the year, Burman thought. Chances were the doctors would have to sedate her. "What happens if I bump into Coral Hughes?" he asked. "I mean it could be a mite difficult to explain what I'm doing in Vienna. She thinks I'm with the Civil Service Commission."

"Then you'll just have to avoid her," Winter said tersely.

75

"And you don't have to tell Marjorie Deakin who you are, do you?"

"No. I could be just another consular official for all she knows."

"That should satisfy her." Winter reached for the phone, lifted the receiver, and started dialing. "Don't let me keep you," he said pointedly.

Edmunds closed the imprest account and placed the ledger on the floor under his chair, where it would be more or less out of harm's way. He had hoped to bring the account up to date while on escort duty in the reading room, but he had figured without Ainsworth. Although two normal-sized people could sit down at the four-by-three-foot table and get on with their work in comfort, such was not the case when you were obliged to share the available space with Ainsworth. Henry liked to spread himself and his method of working was on a par with his usual untidy appearance. More in hope than expectation, Edmunds had gone so far as to divide the table in half with a strip of black masking tape, but to no avail. Inch by inch, Ainsworth had gradually encroached upon his territory with more and more files until finally the imprest account had ended up in his lap.

Ainsworth, of course, was not aware that his desire for lebensraum had been satisfied at somebody else's expense. Edmunds knew full well that once Henry became immersed in a problem, he was completely oblivious to everything that was going on around him and, as a result, was often a menace to himself and others, especially when smoking his pipe. There were any number of stories going the rounds at 54 Broadway concerning Henry's absent-mindedness, and not all of them were apocryphal. Edmund's favorite was the one about the occasion when, some years back, Ainsworth had dated a girl from the typing pool. He had taken her to see *Quo Vadis* and was sitting there, gazing up at the screen, contentedly smoking his pipe, when it suddenly dawned on him that his date was

76

holding both hands over her face. At first he'd thought she was having a nosebleed, but a solicitous inquiry revealed that she couldn't bear to watch the scene where the Christians were about to be thrown to the lions. Anxious to comfort her, Henry had knocked out his pipe, stuffed it into his jacket pocket, and encircled her shoulders with his left arm. Blissfully unaware that his jacket had caught fire, it wasn't until the girl jerked away from him with a muffled cry of pain that he discovered his smoldering pipe had burned a large hole in her dress and slip, right through to the skin.

"This isn't getting us anywhere," Ainsworth said crossly.

"What isn't?"

"Analyzing all the planning sessions with the CIA when George Deakin was present from the nineteenth of June onward. I can't find anything in the Iranian project which would have given George a great deal of satisfaction, except perhaps the SAS angle." Ainsworth removed the briar pipe from between his teeth, held it upside down over the lid of his tobacco tin, and shook the bowl violently, raining ash over the table and onto the floor. "No two ways about it, Frank, the Russians would have had a blue fit if we had succeeded in convincing them the shah had agreed we could station an SAS squadron in Azerbaijan. Think of the immense diversion of resources that would have occurred once they swallowed the story that we intended to raise at least two regiments from among the local population. Goodness me, the Kremlin would have poured troops into the Soviet republic of Turkmenskaya, built additional airfields, and improved the existing rail network as fast as they could go. George would have loved the idea of Khrushchev spending all those billions of rubles to no purpose whatever."

"I don't think you should be telling me all this," Edmunds said.

"Why ever not? You're one of the select few who are allowed inside the reading room."

"Only as an escort. Winter needed an extra body to make the

duty roster less inflexible, and I got elected. You should know that, Henry."

"I haven't committed a breach of security; the Iranian project will never get off the ground now that George is dead."

"You're still breaking the rules."

"And you're being pompous," Ainsworth told him amiably. "Just when I need your help."

"My help? You're the Soviet expert, Henry, not me."

"Maybe so, but you knew George longer than I did."

Edmunds supposed that was partly true. Ainsworth had joined the government code and cipher school straight from London University and had spent the next eight years with the intercept station at Harrogate, starting as a translator, then working his way up through successive grades to become the director of the monitoring service. He had become acquainted with Deakin in the aftermath of the Suez crisis when Winter had brought Deakin in to head the Russian desk.

"I may have met him before you did, Henry, but our paths rarely crossed. George spent the war years with the Special Operations Executive in Cairo and didn't return home until 1950. I had the Iberian desk in those days, but within six months of his arrival at 54 Broadway, I was appointed commandant of the training school at Gerrards Cross. He used to come down there once in a while to lecture the students." Edmunds clucked his tongue. "He certainly knew how to hold an audience spellbound; you could have heard a pin drop the moment George stepped up to the lectern."

"He was that good?"

"Oh, there's no getting away from it, George really knew his stuff."

"You surprise me." Ainsworth filled his pipe with tobacco and struck a match. "I mean, he only had the Russian desk for eighteen months."

"I'm talking about the time when he was in charge of the Arabian department. George was one of the greatest experts we ever had on the Middle East, which is hardly surprising when

78

you remember he was working in the Persian Gulf before the war. He was a geologist before he joined us."

"I didn't know that," said Ainsworth.

"Really? I wonder why George never told you. I've often thought those eight years he had with Anglo-Iranian must have been the most satisfying period of his life. Given his background, it's no wonder George knew exactly what went on in the oil business, especially the political infighting between the various companies. And he could put it across in a lecture. 'Friends or Enemies? The Realities of the Intelligence World'— that was the title of his course address."

"Sounds provocative," Ainsworth drawled. "What was the thinking behind it, Frank?"

"Well, George figured that the 'special relationship' between America and Great Britain always meant a great deal more to our politicians than to the people on Capitol Hill, particularly where big business was involved. He used to cite the Abadan crisis as an example. When Doctor Mossadiq decided to nationalize the Anglo-Iranian Oil Company in 1951, the Labor government of the day was all for using force to protect our vital interests, but the State Department leaned on us and we had to back off. The company's operations in Persia ceased and the British technicians at the Abadan oil refinery were withdrawn. Persia went bankrupt, there was internal disorder, and the shah left the country for a protracted holiday. Then the CIA moved in and organized a counterrevolution; Mossadiq was arrested and the shah returned to Tehran. The oil dispute was finally settled in August 1954, and guess what? British Petroleum ended up with forty percent of the shares, Royal Dutch Shell got fourteen, and Française des Pétroles was granted a measly six. The remaining forty percent went to the Texas Company, Standard Oil of New Jersey, Socony Mobil, Standard Oil of California, Gulf, and nine other U.S. companies."

"I don't see what George was beefing about." Ainsworth examined his pipe, found it had gone out, and struck another match. "After all, forty percent of something is a damned sight better than a hundred percent of nothing."

"You think so?" Edmunds shook his head. "The Yanks gave us the elbow and we've had to accept that Iran is now within their sphere of influence."

"So what, Frank? We're no longer capable of policing the Middle East; two World Wars and a sick economy have seen to that."

"Nobody would deny it, least of all George, but he felt that we'd been given a raw deal. Oh, I know the CIA organized the counterrevolution, but who do you suppose gave them all the inside dope, told them just which Iranian generals they should approach?"

"George?"

"Right," Edmunds said emphatically. "That's why the title of his lecture was so appropriate. Of course we see eye-to-eye with the Americans regarding the Soviet threat, but our mistake lies in thinking we have the same mutual interests the world over. We tend to forget the United States is primarily a mercantile nation; there are a large number of areas around the globe where big business comes first with the Americans. I've heard George expound that particular theme more times than I can remember."

Deakin's stock lecture had obviously made a lasting impression on Edmunds. The Iranian anecdote was also revealing in another direction; Ainsworth thought it showed that George was basically anti-American.

"I think you've just opened a door, Frank," he said.

"Really? Any idea where it leads to?"

"Not yet." Ainsworth went over to the safe and returned with an armful of classified documents. "However, let's hope it won't be too long before I do."

Edmunds watched him with a jaundiced eye as he stacked the files on the table. "I'll second that, Henry," he said grimly.

McNulty followed Winter across the lawn toward the summer house at the top of the garden beyond the small lily pond, and sat down on a rustic bench. Usually when Winter rang up to invite him to lunch, it was to either Claridges or his club in Pall Mall. In fact, in all the years they had known one another, he could only recall one other occasion when Charles had suggested they dine at his Edwardian house on Spaniards Road, and that had been early in February 1957, three months after the Suez debacle; Geraldine had served them clear soup followed by Aylesbury duckling with a strawberry mousse to round it off, and then they'd adjourned to the study across the hall and Charles had told him that George Deakin was working for the KGB. Another rotten apple in the barrel, he'd thought, and had waited for Winter to soft-pedal, something the British had had plenty of practice at after Burgess, Maclean, Fuchs, and Alan Nunn May. But to his surprise, there had been no embarrassed explanations; instead, Winter had informed him that the SIS proposed to use Deakin as a means of passing misinformation to the KGB and had casually asked whether the CIA would like to participate in the game. The asking price had been revealed later, after Allen Dulles and his department heads at Langley had decided they wanted in.

Five years was a long time, yet it seemed like only yesterday, perhaps because Geraldine Winter was still sniping away at her husband. They had all grown a little older but some things hadn't changed. Although Katherine Lang had died of cancer in December 1956, it seemed Geraldine could not forget that Charles and her closest friend had once been lovers, and was determined to go on exacting retribution. There was, however, one major difference between then and now: this time around, McNulty was quite certain that Winter was not in a position to spring a major surprise on him.

"You'll join me in a brandy, won't you, Tom?" Winter handed him a cup of coffee and reached for the bottle of Rémy Martin on the silver tray which he'd carried out of the house.

"There's nothing I'd like better."

"Good." Winter poured two large brandies and offered him a cigar from the engraved silver box. "They're Havanas," he said slyly. "I imagine you don't see too many of them these days?"

"Not since Kennedy fell out with Castro." McNulty trimmed the Havana with a cutter and lit up. "A woman is only a woman," he observed, "but a good cigar is a smoke."

"Who said that?"

"Kipling, I think."

"How very profound of him." Winter looked up at the sky, the sun warm on his face. "I wonder how long this Indian summer is going to last," he mused.

"You didn't invite me here just to talk about the weather, did you, Charles?"

"No, we do have more important issues to discuss."

"Like Deakin, Korznikov, and Penkovsky," McNulty said flatly.

"Yes. Well, the inquest on George will be held on Thursday. Meantime, I have it on good authority that the coroner's jury will bring in a verdict of death by misadventure."

"Do I take it you've seen the pathologist's report?"

"Let's say I know what's in it."

Through Ross, McNulty thought. He remembered Winter telling him that he'd instructed the security agent to stay on in Bembridge and keep his ear to the ground. Even so, somebody must have pulled a few strings for Ross to see a copy of the autopsy before it was made public.

"What about Marjorie Deakin?" he asked. "Any word on her whereabouts?"

"She's in Vienna, Tom. Apparently, she left George for a man called Matthew Frayne and they were touring the Continent."

"Were?" McNulty studied his cigar.

"Frayne was knocked down and killed by a hit-and-run driver during the early hours of this morning. Poor Marjorie ended up in hospital with both legs broken."

McNulty digested the news in silence for some moments, then said, "I guess things didn't quite go according to plan."

82

"What?"

"For the KGB."

"Oh, come on, Tom, it was an accident, pure and simple."

"Yeah? Next thing I know you'll be telling me it was just a coincidence."

Stranger things had happened, but despite his convincing act, he knew Winter was lying. He was equally convinced Charles would never have invited him to lunch at his house merely to break the news that the pathologist could find no evidence of foul play and that Marjorie had been injured in a traffic accident.

"I've been giving some thought to Penkovsky," Winter said casually.

"Have you now?" McNulty placed his coffee cup on one side and picked up the glass of brandy. Charles was about to show his hand and all he had to do was sit back and wait.

"I think you're right, Tom. With his connections, Penkovsky might be able to tell us what the hell is going on in Moscow."

"Does that mean you've no objections if we put him to work?"

"Yes. I think we should get as much mileage out of him as we can while he's still at liberty."

"Great." McNulty sniffed the brandy, swirled it around in the glass, and then savored it. "So's this Rémy Martin," he added.

"I knew you would appreciate it."

McNulty took refuge in silence. Five years ago, Winter had called all the shots because the SIS had had something to offer. Now the shoe was on the other foot and he was secretly enjoying it.

"So where do we stand with Korznikov, Tom?"

On the outside looking in, that was the short answer from Langley. They hadn't put it in so many words, but it was the impression he'd gotten from reading between the lines of the telex he'd received. Stall Winter, the telex had read, keep him off our backs until we've put Korznikov through a preliminary interrogation.

"There's been no change in his condition, Charles; he's still a very sick man. One of his former colleagues tried to make him even sicker."

"Do you mean the KGB took another crack at him?"

"Right. One of their hit men clobbered a hospital worker and borrowed his fatigues. He took the elevator up to the sixth floor, then backed off when he saw Korznikov was under guard. At least, that's the way Jessop sees it."

"Who's Jessop?"

"He's a vice president of the Zenith Technical Corporation. Anyway, Jessop has arranged for Korznikov to be transferred to a safer place where we can really keep him under wraps."

"He's not so sick that he can't be moved, then?" Winter said acidly.

"How would I know? I'm as much in the dark as you are; the telex from Langley wasn't exactly informative." McNulty shrugged. "Maybe I'll learn something when I'm stateside."

"You're going home?"

"The day after tomorrow, just for a week or two. I've got some personal problems to sort out with my ex. Seems our eldest daughter, Barbara, has decided she wants to quit law school and become a social worker." He shook his head. "After two years at Columbia Law. It doesn't make sense."

"I don't know what the younger generation is coming to," Winter said dryly.

"Me neither."

"So what's Lois going to do while you're away?" Lois was Tom's second wife, a petite redhead from Baltimore.

"She's coming with me; plans to do a little shopping and visit her family." McNulty glanced at his wristwatch and frowned convincingly. "I hate to rush you, Charles, but I ought to be on my way. There's a pile of work waiting for me at the office."

"Yes, of course." Winter gathered in the coffee cups and

brandy glasses and placed them on the tray. "I'll run you back to Grosvenor Square."

"I don't want to take you out of your way, Charles. You can drop me off at the nearest tube station."

"It's no trouble," Winter said firmly.

"Well, okay, if you insist. I'll just say goodbye to Geraldine and thank her for a splendid lunch." McNulty got up and followed Winter across the lawn toward the house. "I'm glad we see eye-to-eye over Penkovsky," he said, "and you can be sure I'll keep you informed about the Korznikov situation."

"Thanks, Tom. I'd certainly appreciate it if you would."

McNulty thought there was a plaintive note to Winter's voice, or was it just the distant whine of the turboprop Viscount airliner he could hear inbound for Heathrow?

Leconfield House was an anonymous white-and-red-brick building in Curzon Street and, in Winter's opinion, a visible reminder that MI5 was definitely the poor relation in comparison with the SIS at 54 Broadway. If the outside of the building was less than inspiring, Malcolm Cleaver's small back room on the top floor, with its view of slate roofs, chimney pots, and a forest of television aerials, was downright depressing. At least, most of his visitors thought so, but not Cleaver; his desk and chair were so arranged that his back was permanently turned to the window. Apart from the dreary outlook, the office was usually chilly in winter because the central heating system gave up the ghost long before it reached the top floor, and it was airless in summer because successive layers of paint had stuck the window fast. The extremes of temperature didn't bother Cleaver; an electric fire solved the heating problem when it was cold, and on a warm day, he simply removed his jacket, loosened his tie, and left the door ajar. When the messenger escorted Winter into his office that afternoon, Cleaver was sitting at his desk in shirtsleeves, displaying a pair of lurid purple braces.

"Well, I never," Cleaver said, as though surprised to see him. "What brings you here, Charles?"

"I was in the neighborhood and thought I'd drop in for a chat." Winter unbuttoned his jacket and made himself comfortable in an armchair. "You're not busy, are you?"

"No more than usual." Cleaver took the visitor's pass from the messenger, told him to leave the door ajar, then turned to Winter again. "Heard from Amanda?" he asked.

"No, but then I imagine she and Rupert are too busy enjoying themselves in Rome. Anyway, they've only been gone four days."

"And I bet you and Geraldine never sent any postcards when you were on your honeymoon."

"I can't remember, Malcolm." Winter smiled. "Actually, I wanted to thank you for fixing it so that Ross could see the pathologist's report on George."

"Think nothing of it. What are friends for if they can't do one another a favor?" Cleaver lit a cigarette and leaned back in his chair. "Have you traced Marjorie Deakin yet?"

"Yes. She's in a hospital in Vienna, the victim of a hit-and-run accident."

"I don't like the sound of that."

"You're not the only one. I had lunch with Tom McNulty today."

"Oh? What did he have to say?"

"He's flying home on Thursday, ostensibly to sort out some family problem. Tom says he expects to be away for about a fortnight, and Lois is going with him to visit her family in Baltimore."

"It's nice to know what the McNultys are doing," Cleaver said dryly.

"I'm not sure we do. That's why I'd like Special Branch to keep an eye on their house down by the river at Chiswick."

"Assuming I said okay, what would they be looking for?"

"Removal vans," said Winter. "I have a feeling that Tom won't be coming back."

86

8.

Winter had one golden rule where Ainsworth was concerned. Whenever Henry came to brief him in his office, he never invited him to sit down. Experience had taught him that once Ainsworth had settled himself in one of the leather armchairs, he was extremely difficult to budge, and his dissertation was liable to go on forever. Like most gambits, it wasn't always infallible; there were still times when expounding some theory or other, he could talk the hind leg off a donkey, and this was one of them. On the subject of Deakin and his latent hostility toward the State Department, Henry was positively loquacious. The way George had seen it, so Ainsworth would have him believe, the Bay of Pigs fiasco had been a small consolation for the double-dealing which had gone on as a result of the Abadan crisis. But just where it was all leading was far from clear to Winter, even though Henry had been holding forth practically nonstop for the past twenty minutes.

"Now hold it a minute," Winter said, interrupting him successfully this time. "Where's the connection?"

"Connection?" Ainsworth gaped at him, momentarily flummoxed.

"I'll make it easy for you, Henry. We're proceeding on the assumption that Deakin was murdered, despite medical evidence to the contrary. You're saying George was anti-American; I'm asking why the KGB should want to eliminate him on those grounds."

"I don't know—yet."

His voice sounded defiant, a sign that Ainsworth was convinced he was on the right track. Humoring him, Winter said, "What about the planning sessions we've had with McNulty since the nineteenth of June, Henry? Did you find anything in the minutes to support your contention?"

"No, but then I didn't expect to. I believe George was holding something back from us, some future operation directed against the United States which he'd learned about inadvertently from his case officer."

"I can't see Gorsky discussing Cuba with him."

"Who said anything about Cuba?" Ainsworth shook his head. "I have a feeling the projected operation was far more clandestine."

"You're letting your imagination run riot. Face the facts, Henry: no KGB officer is going to disclose a covert operation to one of his agents unless he's suddenly taken leave of his senses. And Gorsky's no fool, whatever you might think."

"Of course he isn't, but we all make mistakes. A slip of the tongue coupled with a derisive remark about the United States would be enough to set Deakin thinking, and knowing George, he'd keep beavering away until he was able to put two and two together and come up with the right answer. Whatever it is Khrushchev has in mind, you can bet it will shake the Americans to the core. That's why George was in such an amiable mood."

It was pure conjecture. Moreover, Winter thought it was based on a wholly false premise. He had known George a good deal longer than Ainsworth had and could not recall a single occasion when he'd been aware that Deakin was anti-American.

"You've given me only two instances where George seemed

88

prejudiced. Let's hear some more examples." Winter pointed an accusing finger at him. "For instance, what was his attitude toward the State Department at the time of the Suez crisis?"

"How should I know?" Ainsworth said testily. "I was still up in Harrogate then."

"You were here in 1958, the year the U.S. Marines landed in Lebanon and we flew 16 Parachute Brigade into Jordan. Did he have any harsh things to say about the Eisenhower Doctrine?"

"No, but I remember George making some pretty acid remarks about Kennedy's Inaugural Address. Remember Kennedy's 'Ask not what your country can do for you, ask what you can do for your country'? Well, George said that might have been a memorable phrase for the history books, but it was meaningless rhetoric."

"I've been pretty sarcastic about Harold Macmillan and his fond belief that we can act as a sort of mediator between the two superpowers, but that doesn't make me a supporter of the Labor party," Winter said, not unreasonably.

"I'm still convinced I'm on the right track." Ainsworth pushed a hand through his tousled hair. "I'm also damned sure I won't get anywhere unless I can listen to all those tapes we've got stored away in the basement."

"You'll be wasting your time, Henry. The minutes are an accurate record of the planning sessions."

"I disagree. They're only a summary of what occurred. Some of those meetings we had went on for hours, especially when the intelligence departments of the navy, army, and air force were represented. As I recall, the discussions were usually far-ranging, and I don't believe the secretary recorded every single point that was raised when we were considering what the Soviets would probably know from their own intelligence sources."

"And you think some minor debating point which was thought to be irrelevant at the time may now be significant?"

"Yes."

Winter raised his eyebrows. "Do you have any idea how many hours of conversation we have on tape?"

"One hundred and eighty-five," said Ainsworth, "give or take a few minutes."

At a conservative estimate, Winter figured it would take Henry close to five weeks to hear all the tapes, and that didn't allow for any replays. "It's not on, Henry. You haven't the faintest idea what to look for, and I can think of much more profitable ways for you to spend your time." He leaned forward, elbows on the desk, shoulders hunched. "For example, it would be interesting to know what trade-offs Khrushchev might have in mind should the Americans get tough with him over Cuba. He could have designs on Berlin, Turkey, or Iran."

"I assume you want me to set up a special working party to examine these problem areas?" Ainsworth said glumly.

"I certainly do. You should coopt the heads of the East European and Arabian desks, and you'd better approach the Ministry of Defense because you're going to need representatives from the three services. I want a weekly summary of the Soviet military capability in the German Democratic Republic and the Middle East. I also want to be kept informed about the state of readiness of the Warsaw Pact forces."

"That's quite a shopping list." Ainsworth edged his way toward the door. "What do I do about Deakin?" he asked.

"You can forget him for the time being."

"I think that's a mistake, a very big mistake," Ainsworth said, and closed the door quietly behind him.

It was typical of Henry, Winter thought, that he should be determined to have the last word. No argument could move him once he had a bee in his bonnet. All the same, Ainsworth was astute and had an unerring instinct for putting his finger on the crux of a problem.

Winter uncapped his fountain pen, printed Deakin's name in block capitals on his clipboard, underlined it twice, and then added a large question mark. Maybe there was a side to George he'd never seen, a facet that had only been apparent to one of his subordinates? Much as he disliked the idea of meeting Bill Turnock again, the former head of the Arabian department had been closer to Deakin than anyone else he could name. Buzzing his PA, Winter told Diana Franklin that he would be out of the office for the next couple of hours. Then he collected his Jaguar from Queen Anne's Gate and drove out to West Byfleet.

Burman studied the sketch map attached to the accident report and then started walking toward Zirkusgasse at the far end of Komodten Allee from Prater Strasse.

"The total distance is one hundred and twenty-five meters, Herr Burman," the Austrian traffic sergeant told him politely. "I measured it myself."

"And the accident occurred roughly midway?"

"As near as we can judge. The accident happened at approximately two o'clock on Tuesday morning and there were no witnesses about." The sergeant, whose English was far more fluent than Burman's German, halted outside a tobacconist's and pointed to the flat above the shop. "The proprietor says there was a loud bang and then he heard a woman scream. By the time he got out of bed and reached the window, the car was disappearing into Prater Strasse and it was too dark for him to see the number plate. He couldn't even identify the make."

The alleyway was poorly lit, with just two street lamps top and bottom, but there were no bends in the road and Burman figured the driver would have picked up Frayne and Marjorie Deakin in his headlights from a good eighty feet away.

"The driver must have seen them, and yet he didn't attempt to brake."

"We couldn't find any skid marks." The sergeant shrugged his shoulders. "He must have been drunk. Frau Deakin told me the car was swerving from side to side as it came toward her."

"She also claims that Frayne pushed her out into the road," Burman said, reading from her statement.

"It's possible she may have staggered off the pavement. We

know they had two bottles of wine at Maxi's nightclub in Zirkusgasse and the waiter who served them said he thought Frau Deakin was a little drunk. On the other hand, Herr Frayne may have been trying to save her life. He could have seen the oncoming vehicle mount the pavement and pushed her out of the way."

The last act of a gallant gentleman? Burman frowned and, turning to the end page of the folder, looked at the photographs of Frayne glued onto the back cover. Lying there stark naked on a slab in the mortuary, Frayne resembled a waxwork dummy, the blood drained from his face, the lids closed. So very different from his photograph in the passport the Embassy had recovered from his room at the Bristol. Height five foot eleven, hazel-colored eyes, dark-brown hair, no special peculiarities. Well, this one-time businessman, whose passport stated that he had been born in Manchester on May 16, 1924, certainly had a visible peculiarity now, a skull that had burst open like an overripe melon.

"I see you estimate the car was doing close on forty when it struck Frayne."

"Is that the equivalent of sixty-five kilometers an hour?"

"Near enough." Burman walked into Zirkusgasse and looked both ways. "That's a pretty tight corner," he said. "A driver turning into Komodten Allee from either direction would need to drop into second gear to take the bend."

"Unless he was either stupid or drunk, Herr Burman."

"I don't see any recent skid marks on the road."

"You think the driver negotiated the bend at a safe speed and then put his foot down on the accelerator?"

"It would seem to tie in with what Mrs. Deakin said in her statement."

"Quite so." The traffic sergeant glanced at him sideways, then hastily looked away. "We shall of course charge the driver with manslaughter."

"If you can trace him," said Burman.

"We will. The bodywork of the car will have been extensively damaged by the impact, and we know the right headlight was broken, because of the splinters of glass we found between the cobblestones. Every garage in Vienna has been warned not to carry out any repairs to a vehicle damaged in a traffic accident until it has been inspected by the police."

Burman didn't say anything, but he thought the hit-and-run driver would know that that was standard police procedure. If the man had simply been a drunk, he would probably buy some filler and do the repair job himself. If he was a KGB agent, he would dump the car, possibly in one of the abandoned gypsum mines in the Vienna Woods northeast of the city. Most of the old workings were flooded and two men could easily remove and subsequently replace the boarding nailed across the entrance to the shaft, so the local SIS head of station had told him.

"Have you seen all you want to, Herr Burman?" the sergeant inquired.

"I think so."

"Then perhaps I can drop you off somewhere?"

There was no point in going straight on to the Elizabeth Hospital when the doctors would still be making their rounds. "There a café just down the road," Burman said. "Do you have time for a cup of coffee or a beer?"

"A cup of coffee would be very nice." The sergeant fell in step beside him, then said, "What will happen about Herr Frayne? I understand the British Embassy has been unable to trace his next-of-kin."

"There are none," Burman lied. "He wasn't married and both his parents are dead."

"No brothers or sisters?"

"He was an only child," Burman said, compounding the lie.

"He must have been a very lonely man." The sergeant sounded melancholy, as though delivering the funeral oration.

"Yes, well, I daresay somebody from the Embassy will be there at the cemetery when he's interred."

"Does that mean Herr Frayne will be buried in Vienna?"

"There's no point in flying his body home." Burman pushed the café door open and stood to one side. "Don't worry, sergeant," he said cheerfully. "We'll foot the bill, we always do."

Winter parked the Jaguar outside the detached house in Heathmoor Avenue and switched off the engine. For some moments he sat there, his mind a complete blank, unable to recall the name of Turnock's wife. Jill? Jean? Jessica? Or was it Jennifer? It certainly began with a J. Josephine? Bill and Josephine? Somehow they didn't go together. Joan then? He snapped his fingers, knowing he'd gotten it right at last. Childishly pleased with himself, Winter got out of the car, walked up the front path, and knocked on the door.

He remembered Joan Turnock as a rather mousy little blonde with a turned-up nose and a hesitant smile. The woman who opened the door to him was fairly tall, decidedly plump, and had her hair tinted with ash-blond streaks. About to apologize for calling at the wrong house, the hesitant smile appeared just in time to spare him the embarrassment.

"Hello, Joan," Winter said cheerfully. "Remember me?"

"Of course I do, Charles. What a pleasant surprise."

She seemed genuinely pleased to see him, the last thing Winter had expected after the way he'd treated her husband. Either Joan Turnock was a very warm-hearted and forgiving person or else Bill hadn't told her why he'd been prematurely retired.

"How long has it been since we last saw one another, Charles?"

"It must be all of six years." He smiled. "I happened to be passing through the neighborhood, so I thought I'd drop by and see how you were." •

"How very thoughtful of you." She opened the door wider and made room for him to step past her into the hall. "I know Bill will be delighted to see you again."

"The same here." Aware that his voice was a low murmur lacking enthusiasm and conviction, Winter cleared his throat and then diplomatically admired a colorful flower arrangement in the hall.

94

"The dahlias came from the garden." She beamed at him over her shoulder and opened the door to the drawing room. "That's where you'll find Bill."

"I didn't know Bill was a keen gardener."

"He never was before he retired. Not that Bill is all that much of an expert even now, but at least it keeps him occupied and out of my way."

Winter thought he detected a slight overtone of reproach, and felt uncomfortable. There were very few openings in the business world for a man with Turnock's background, and he'd had to blackball his application for a post with the Institute for Strategic Studies. It wasn't something he was proud of, but a scapegoat was needed to keep Deakin in business, and the KGB would have smelled a rat had Turnock left the SIS to take up another sensitive appointment.

"You'll stay for a cup of coffee, won't you, Charles?"

"That's very kind of you, Joan, but I don't want to put you to any trouble."

"It's no trouble," she assured him. "We always have a cup about this time."

The hesitant smile appeared briefly for the second time, then she muttered something about giving him a call when it was ready and hurried into the kitchen. A little nonplussed by her sudden exit, Winter stepped through the French window and walked across the lawn to the greenhouse at the bottom of the garden.

Turnock had always been slightly overweight for his height, but now the spare tire around his midriff had become a pot that sagged over the waistband of his gray flannels. His face was blotchy, with a web of purple veins at either side of his bulbous nose, two obvious indications that he had become a hardened drinker.

"Hello, Bill." Winter forced a smile and extended a hand.

"Well, well, look who's here." Turnock ignored his outstretched hand and went on potting geranium cuttings. "How come you managed to drag yourself away from the office?"

"You could say I'm here on official business."

"I didn't think it was purely a social visit."

"Actually, I wondered if you'd heard that George is dead."

"What?" Turnock looked up, his eyebrows meeting in a frown.

"He was drowned on Saturday morning."

"I see."

"You don't seem very upset about it," Winter observed mildly.

"Why should I be? Of course I'm sorry for Marjorie, but I don't give a damn about George. I haven't forgotten how he dropped me in the shit over the Eisenhower business." Turnock picked up a trowel and waved it under Winter's nose. "Don't think I was the only one who was opposed to your illegal operation. I may have done all the detective work, but Deakin was there egging me on to get some really solid evidence we could present to Control. Then when I finally did get it, the sanctimonious bastard blew the whistle and you sacked me out of spite."

"It was Control who decided to retire you," Winter said coolly.

"On your bloody recommendation."

"Because he thought you weren't up to the job, and he was right. My mistake was in listening to George; if it hadn't been for his enthusiastic assessment, you wouldn't have gotten the Arabian department when he was moved to the Russian desk." Winter paused. One more twist of the knife and Turnock would lose what little remained of his self-control. He would have preferred a less abrasive approach, but with his built-in hostility, Bill would never willingly help him. "George knew you were inadequate, but you were his protégé and he had this overdeveloped sense of loyalty toward his subordinates."

"Loyalty? Jesus Christ, you've got to be joking." Turnock caught his breath, his face brick-red. A bead of perspiration detached itself from the tip of his bulbous nose and splashed onto the workbench. "Every one of us is required to sign the Official Secrets Acts, right? We solemnly pledge ourselves not to divulge classified information to any unauthorized person and we further undertake not to utilize any material as may pass through our hands for personal gain. Admirals, generals, air marshals, and former Prime Ministers can write their memoirs when they retire, but not us. Well, I've got news for you: Deakin had a book published while he was still gagged by the Official Secrets Acts."

"When was this?"

"A long time ago, soon after he met Marjorie and decided to marry her. I think Deakin wanted a bit of extra cash for their honeymoon, so he dashed off this book and got it published under a pseudonym. He told me he'd assigned the copyright to the publisher in order to preserve his anonymity."

"Do you remember the title?" Winter asked him quietly.

"What do you think I am? A memory bank?" Turnock sniffed, then wiped his nose on the back of his hand. "It was about Israel, that much I do know."

"Israel?"

"Yes. I think he called it *Birth of a Nation* or something like that."

"Are you sure you're not confusing it with the film D.W. Griffith made?"

"I may look old," Turnock said testily, "but I'm not that old."

Winter frowned. If Deakin had secretly written one book, there was nothing to prevent him from doing a sequel. The title wasn't much to go on, but with any luck, Diana Franklin could get the name of the publisher and Deakin's pseudonym from the British National Bibliography. Then Burman could do the rest when he returned from Vienna.

"What the hell does that silly cow want now?"

Winter glanced behind him and saw Joan Turnock waving to them from the French windows in the drawing room. "I think she's trying to tell us that coffee's ready."

"Shit." Turnock hurled the trowel at a bag of fertilizer.

"Don't tell me I'm going to be stuck with you for another half hour."

"I'll do my very best to make it less than that," Winter said obligingly.

Burman followed the nurse down the sterile hospital corridor and into the private room occupied by Marjorie Deakin at the far end of the passageway. Everyone who knew her had told him that she didn't look her age, but this was no longer true. Her face was drawn, the cheeks sunken and the mouth puckered as though every one of her teeth had been extracted.

"Hello, Mrs. Deakin." Burman smiled, pulled a chair up to her bedside, and sat down. "I'm from the British Embassy," he began.

"Coral tells me that George is dead." Her eyes searched his face, hoping he would deny it.

"Yes." Burman took her hand and squeezed it gently. "I'm very sorry, Mrs. Deakin. You have my deepest sympathy."

"When are they going to let me go home?"

Her question caught him unawares. "In a few days," Burman said, taking the easy way out.

Her legs were in traction, plastered up to the kneecaps and protected from the weight of the bedclothes by a steel cage. Given that she was also in a state of shock, Burman thought it likely the doctors would insist on keeping her under observation for at least another week.

He squeezed her hand again and said, "I know it must be very distressing for you to talk about the accident, but I wonder if I could ask you some questions about Mr. Frayne?"

"Matthew tried to kill me."

"You surely don't mean that, Mrs. Deakin."

"Oh, but I do," she insisted vehemently. "He pushed me out into the road." She turned her head toward the window and stared at the spire of Saint Stephen's Church in the distance. "I never want to hear his name again."

Too bad, he thought. Whether Marjorie Deakin liked it or

not, they were going to talk about him. She was the only living person who had known Frayne and could fill out his background. Recalling what the traffic sergeant had said to him, Burman set out to persuade her that Frayne had tried to save her life. It wasn't easy, but he finally managed to convince her, and from there on, she answered his questions to the best of her ability. One hour and twenty minutes later, he left the Elizabeth Hospital for the airport knowing a great deal more about the late Matthew Frayne than he had when he'd arrived in Vienna.

9.

The furrowed brow was, Burman surmised, a sign that Winter was having trouble deciphering the hand-written report he'd prepared on Frayne. At first sight, the bold upright style with its heavy downward strokes looked very neat, but on closer inspection, the middle section of most words was invariably represented by a straight line with the occasional dot or dash above it. It was a form of shorthand he'd acquired taking lecture notes as a student, and its use later was largely attributable to the fact that he could think faster than he could write. Winter had the same problem, his memos resembling a doctor's prescription, but he would never admit to it.

"What's the name of this secondary school Frayne went to in Manchester?" Winter asked, looking up.

"Gatesby Road."

"Funny, I could have sworn it was ghastly."

"Maybe he thought it was," Burman said. "He left there at the age of thirteen, when his parents emigrated to Canada in 1937."

"Then they separated a year later?"

"Right. Frayne senior took himself off to California and was never heard of again. Mother and son stayed on in Vancouver."

According to Marjorie Deakin, Frayne had worked four nights a week washing dishes in one of the local restaurants to supplement the income his mother earned from turning their home into a rooming house. A variety of jobs had then followed, when he'd quit high school at seventeen without any academic qualifications. Laundryman, waiter, bartender, storeman, sales assistant in a gentleman's outfitters—Frayne had tried his hand at them all before he finally found a niche for himself as a file clerk with the British Columbia Assurance Company. From that lowly starting point, he'd gone on to bigger things in the insurance world, progressing steadily up the ladder by changing companies whenever he thought there was a possibility of further advancement.

"How is it Frayne never served in the forces during the war?"

"He claims he was medically unfit." Burman moved around the desk to point out the relevant paragraph to Winter. "Frayne told Mrs. Deakin that he'd tried to join the Royal Canadian Air Force in May 1942, but was rejected when one of the doctors on the air-crew selection board discovered he had a heart murmur. If what he says is true, it seems his mother also had a heart condition, which led to her premature death from a coronary in January 1946."

"And he lost touch with his father twenty-five years ago," Winter said pointedly.

"Yes, that is a little disturbing. Still, his past is not a complete blind alley; it should be possible to trace somebody who knew Frayne when he was at school. I figure Ottawa can also shed some light on his background. He may not have worn a uniform during the war, but he was a temporary civil servant with the RCAF Records Office from July 1942 to November 1945."

"Assuming they haven't destroyed his personal file, which doesn't seem likely. In any case, nobody in authority would have written a confidential report on a temporary civil servant during the war."

"There's always the Canadian tax department," Burman said. "If they're anything like our lot, they never let go once they've got their hooks into you. Then there are the various insurance brokers who employed Frayne in the late forties when he was living in the States."

"I'm not exactly keen on involving the FBI in this investigation. Burgess and the rest did enormous damage to our reputation in their eyes, and I don't want them to get the impression we're in another bind. If they did, you can bet J. Edgar Hoover would make it his business to ensure we weren't allowed to interrogate Korznikov." Winter opened the passport Burman had brought back from Vienna and turned to page 4. "I see this was issued by the British Consulate in San Francisco on the ninth of April 1952."

"Yes."

"In the trade, that's known as gaining entrance by the back door," Winter observed laconically.

Burman nodded. It wouldn't be difficult for an imposter to obtain a copy of Matthew Frayne's birth certificate from Somerset House, provided he was able to supply the date and place of birth. Two fictitious referees on the application form and a signature on the back of the passport photo certifying it was a true likeness, and the little blue book with its lion-and-unicorn motif was his for the nominal sum of five pounds.

"We'll start the ball rolling in Manchester," Winter said abruptly. "Then, depending on the results of our inquiries up there, we might have a word with Frayne's business partners, wherever it is they hang out."

"Wembley," Burman said. "Their offices are in the High Street—Underwood, Vines and Frayne."

"You'd better spell it out for Diana's benefit; she won't be able to make head or tail of your handwriting."

"You want her to type up the report?"

"That's the general idea," Winter said. "Two copies should be sufficient. Then you can get down to a bit of research."

"Who with?"

"One of the librarians at the British Museum. See Mrs. Franklin on your way out and she'll tell you all about it."

Burman picked up the handwritten report he'd put together on his return from Vienna the previous evening and walked next door into the PA's office.

Diana Franklin was standing in front of the filing cabinet, her back toward him. She was wearing a navy-blue linen dress with white collar and cuffs. The narrow cloth belt emphasized her slender waist and trim hips. Very nice, he thought, his eyes traveling slowly down to focus on her shapely calves.

"Don't tell me my seams are crooked."

Burman looked up, recalling too late that Diana kept a small dressing-table mirror on top of the filing cabinet. "They look more than all right to me," he said approvingly. There was no answering smile, only an eyebrow that rose somewhat haughtily. Waving the foolscap sheets at her like a flag of truce, he said, "The man would like two copies of this report on Frayne."

"The top copy plus one?"

"I suppose so. Winter didn't make himself very clear. He seemed anxious to be rid of me."

"He has an appointment at the Foreign Office for ten-thirty." Diana closed the filing cabinet, took the report from him, and returned to her desk reading it. After a while, she sat down on the swivel chair, crossed one leg over the other, and continued reading, seemingly unaware that the hemline of the linen dress had risen above her knees.

"Perhaps it would be easier if I dictated the report?" Burman suggested tentatively.

"Why?"

"Well, I'm told it's difficult to understand my writing."

"Really? You should see the hieroglyphics I get from Charles Winter. Your longhand is almost copperplate compared to his." She placed the foolscap sheets on one side and flipped open a loose-leaf notebook. "Did he bring you up to date on the Deakin affair?" she asked.

"No, he merely said I was to see one of the librarians at the British Museum. I gathered you were going to brief me."

"I'm sure he didn't put it quite like that. However," she said, looking down at her memo pad, "it appears that some eleven years ago, George Deakin wrote a nonfiction book on the Middle East under the pen name of Morris Hughes."

"That was rather sly of him." Burman smiled. "I mean borrowing the name of Marjorie's first husband."

"Oh, he was very secretive about the whole thing. The book dealt with the termination of the Palestine Mandate and the emergence of Israel under the title of *Birth of a Nation*. It was published by Hodder and Stoughton in October 1951, at a retail price of fifteen shillings. The literary agent who negotiated the contract was Vera Ashford of Colin Porteous Limited at 15 Red Lion Square. I'm still waiting to hear if we've fixed an appointment for you to see her sometime this afternoon."

"Why should I want to do that?"

"Because Mr. Winter thinks that Deakin may have been gathering material for another book, and he would like to know if George had been in touch with Vera Ashford lately. Naturally, that's not the sort of thing you can ask her point-blank unless you happen to be an author who's been commissioned to write a book on a similar subject."

"And since her former client appears to be an authority on the Middle East, I want to pick his brains? Is that the ploy?" Burman asked.

"Yes, that's why you've got to read his book on Israel." Diana ripped the top page from the loose-leaf notebook and passed it across the desk. "The British Museum is the only place in London that has a copy, and you should ask to see a Miss Alison Shuttle. She has been warned to expect you."

"*Birth of a Nation*." Burman wrinkled his nose. "With a title like that, it's bound to be a god-awful book."

"If it's any consolation, there are only one hundred and fifty-seven pages, including the index."

"Thanks," he said, making a wry face. "Do you have any other good news?"

"Give me a call near lunchtime. I should have heard by then if we've managed to arrange anything with the Colin Porteous Agency."

"Wouldn't it be better if we met somewhere for a drink instead?" Burman suggested.

"I hardly think that's necessary."

"Oh, but it is. If it's on for this afternoon, I'll need to know who my agent is and the kind of questions I may have to field. Take it from me, you can't put a good cover story together over the telephone."

"Perhaps not." Diana followed the direction of his gaze, saw that she was showing a lot of leg, and hastily adjusted the linen dress to cover her knees. "All the same, I have a feeling I'm being hustled."

"Nonsense." Burman tried a winsome smile. "You can trust me, I'm as honest as the day is long."

"That's not very reassuring," she said, "with autumn on the way and the nights drawing in."

The manila folder contained a list of Admiralty file numbers which covered five and a half typewritten pages. The subject matter ranged from the projected navy construction program for the next decade to the development of a marine gas turbine engine. Some of the files merely had a code name, but Winter noticed that all of them were graded secret and above.

"Who compiled this little lot, Toby?" he asked, looking up.

"William Vassall." Bracecourt wrinkled his nose as though aware of a bad smell. "An Admiralty clerk with homosexual tendencies, as the KGB discovered in 1955 when he was serving with the British Embassy in Moscow. Vassall was working for the naval attaché in those days and his social life was practically nonexistent to begin with. Then one of the Russians employed by the Embassy to supervise the domestic staff discovered that he was interested in the ballet and made it his business to keep him supplied with complimentary tickets for the Bolshoi."

What followed was an old and familiar story. The Russian had invited Vassall out to dinner and introduced him to some of his friends, who had also wined and dined the Englishman. Then, one night, they had got Vassall thoroughly drunk and the militia had found him in bed with a young man.

"Of course it was a frame-up," Bracecourt continued, "but they scared the hell out of Vassall. They threatened to charge him with comitting an act of gross indecency and they had the evidence on film to prove it. Once the position had been fully explained to him by his Russian friend at the Embassy, Vassall took the easy way out and opted to work for the KGB. I don't think the material he supplied to them in Moscow was of much value, but there's no getting away from the fact that Vassall has obviously been a gold mine since he returned to London and became a clerk in the office of the civil lord of the Admiralty."

"That's very evident," Winter said tersely. "There are a hundred and seventy classified documents on this list."

"Quite. The trouble is we're only seeing the tip of a very large iceberg." Bracecourt fingered his blond moustache. "I can't help wondering whether Vassall dished your little game before it ever got off the ground."

"You mean Deakin?"

"Yes. He was the man who fed the KGB with misinformation for the past five years."

"Then you can stop worrying, Toby. The navy only participated in one black operation, and the material they supplied was authentic. Vassall wasn't in a position to warn Moscow that we were deceiving them."

"Thank God for that," Bracecourt said with feeling. "At least the press won't be able to censure the SIS for once."

"Vassall's been arrested?"

"You bet he has. Special Branch searched his luxury flat in Dolphin Square yesterday morning while he was at work, and found a camera and several cassettes of exposed film in a secret drawer in the base of a table. The police took him into custody last night."

Winter leafed through the folder. Special Branch must have worked late into the night to develop the negatives and identify the files from which the individual documents had been photographed. Bracecourt had certainly been playing it very close to his chest when he'd phoned him shortly before Burman had arrived at the office. The fact that their meeting had been set for ten-thirty suggested that he had wanted to see how the Vassall case would affect the Foreign Office before he saw him. Winter was sure of one thing: had Malcolm Cleaver been in charge of the M15 investigation, he would have warned him in good time.

"How many other people know about this business, Toby?"

"Macmillan, Lord Carrington, the first lord of the Admiralty, and the director of public prosecutions." Bracecourt frowned. "I imagine the director general of M15 will have informed Hoover by now, since the original tipoff came from the FBI."

"They actually named him?"

"Oh no, they weren't able to be as specific as that, Charles. One of their informers provided a lead and M15 did the rest."

Korznikov? After a moment's reflection, Winter dismissed the idea that he might be the informer. M15 would have kept Vassall under surveillance for some time before they decided to search his flat, and Korznikov had defected on Saturday, just five days ago. Besides, McNulty had told him the Russian was too ill to be interrogated and he wouldn't have knowingly lied to him.

"If they charge Vassall, the attendant publicity could be very damaging for us, Toby."

"I don't see how."

"You don't?" Winter shook his head. "I think you're deliberately being obtuse, Toby. You must know this affair is going to rank alongside Burgess and Maclean. Hoover already thinks our bureaucracy is riddled with Communists, and there are a number of people in the CIA who share his opinion. I have a nasty feeling they may use this latest instance as an excuse to keep us away from Korznikov."

"Nonsense. I don't remember there being an outcry in the States when the Portland spy ring were arrested last year. As a matter of fact, there was a great deal of admiration for the painstaking way M15 handled the case."

Bracecourt had a point. On that occasion, the counterintelligence service had learned from various sources that somebody from the underwater weapons establishment was passing classified information to the KGB. Subsequent investigation had pointed to Harry Houghton and Ethel Gee, two minor civil servants working at Portland, both of whom were placed under surveillance. Houghton, it was discovered, was in the habit of visiting London on the first Saturday of every month, where he met a Canadian businessman named Gordon Lonsdale at Waterloo and handed over a package. The surveillance operation was then extended to include Lonsdale who, in turn, led M15 to Peter and Helen Kroger and a wireless transmitter concealed in a bungalow at Ruislip, sixteen miles out in the suburbs of London. That M15 was later able to prove that Lonsdale was really a professional KGB officer named Konon Molody was yet another feather in their cap. In Winter's opinion, however, there was a world of difference between the two cases.

"You can't compare Vassall with the Portland spy ring, Toby. Houghton and Gee weren't at all the same. Vassall was working for a minister of the Crown and had far more scope than they did. That's why we've got to put a stop to this affair before it gets out of hand."

"It's too late, Charles. The police will have charged him by now."

"You don't know that." Winter lifted a bowler hat from the stand and handed it to Bracecourt. "You and I are going to have a word with your opposite number in the Home Office."

"Like hell we are."

"That's where you're wrong." Winter seized his arm, pulled Bracecourt to his feet, and steered him toward the door. "Whether you like it or not, Toby," he said, "you're about to become a reluctant hero."

10.

Colin Porteous Limited occupied the top two floors of a terraced house directly across the way from Cassell and Company, the publishers. As one of the senior directors of the firm, Vera Ashford occupied an office at the front of the building overlooking the small enclosed park in the center of Red Lion Square. The floor-to-ceiling bookshelves on three sides of the room were jam-packed with hardbacks and soft covers, some of which, Burman thought, must have been published just after the war, if the faded jackets and the amount of dust they'd collected were anything to go by. The four trays on the desk were full of typescripts, and the overflow, including the jacket designs of several forthcoming novels the agency was handling, occupied most of the low coffee table in front of the settee.

Vera Ashford was an elegant lady of indeterminate age. The graying hair, though cut in the latest pageboy style, suggested she was definitely the wrong side of forty; her flawless complexion, unlined face, and youthful figure contradicted that assumption. She was friendly, intelligent, and good-humored, the kind of woman most people liked instinctively. She could also be very direct, and there were times when Burman wasn't sure just who was questioning whom.

"You're with Bruce Seymour, are you?" she said.

"Yes."

"You couldn't have a better agent, Mr. Burman."

"So I've been told."

"Out of curiosity, how did you come to meet Bruce?"

"Through a friend of mine who was already one of his clients." Burman smiled. "He was also highly recommended by the producer of our current affairs program."

"Oh yes, Bruce did say that you worked for the BBC."

"Only in a freelance capacity on their overseas programs." Burman knew he was on safe ground there: television and radio were handled by the subsidiary rights director at Colin Porteous, and Vera Ashford didn't know an awful lot about the setup at the BBC, particularly its overseas service. That was one of the things he'd learned over lunchtime drinks at the Barley Mow in Tottenham Court Road, when Diana Franklin had turned up with Bruce Seymour in tow. That a busy literary agent should drop everything to brief him merely as a favor to Winter had been something of an eye-opener. Winter, it seemed, had a wide circle of friends and acquaintances in other walks of life, who were prepared to help him in any way they could, and at the drop of a hat.

"Bruce tells me you've been commissioned to write a documentary series for BBC Television?"

"Yes. I drafted a synopsis, showed it to my producer, and he liked it enough to get the television people interested in the project. It was a stroke of luck, really."

"That's often the way things happen in our business, Mr. Burman. An author produces a good theme at the right time and everybody gets enthusiastic and climbs on the bandwagon." Vera Ashford toyed with the gold charm bracelet on her left wrist, her eyes downcast but watching him surreptitiously. "Even so, you must be quite an authority on the Middle East. I mean, the BBC isn't exactly noted for going overboard with money, especially for comparatively unknown authors."

"How right you are," Burnam said. "I'm not likely to order a Rolls-Royce on the strength of a hundred and fifty pounds up front." The figure he'd quoted had been suggested by Bruce Seymour; if Vera Ashford continued her interrogation, there were other tidbits in reserve.

"Are you an expert on the Middle East, Mr. Burman?" she repeated.

"I got to know that part of the world reasonably well. I did part of my national service in Aqaba, down in the southernmost tip of Jordan. Then I spent a total of six years in Lebanon and Iraq when I was working for the Foreign Office."

"You were a career diplomat?"

"Nothing so grand," Burman said. "I was a grade B officer in administration." He could keep that line going all day if necessary, and there was no way Vera Ashford could catch him out. "Of course I saw all the guidance telegrams originated by SOSFA."

"Who?"

"Secretary of State for Foreign Affairs. It's amazing how much you can learn from a cable, but I wouldn't claim to be as knowledgeable as your Mr. Hughes. Now, he really does know his stuff."

"You've read his book then?"

"I certainly have, though it wasn't easy to get hold of a copy. Still, even when a book like *Birth of a Nation* is out of print, it's a comfort to know that either the British Museum or the appropriate regional library can produce a copy on request. My local library obtained mine from Harwich." Burman paused, wondering if he should throw in a few quotes from Deakin's book to prove he'd read it, then decided Vera Ashford might become more than a trifle suspicious if he volunteered too much information. "Morris Hughes is particularly good on the first Arab-Israeli war," he continued, "which is why I'd like to pick his brains. Unfortunately, he seems to be something of a recluse. Nobody at Hodder and Stoughton could tell me where or how I could get in touch with him."

"I'm not surprised. He's a very secretive man and really goes out of his way to avoid any kind of publicity." Vera Ashford helped herself to a king-size filtertip from the silver box on the low coffee table and screwed the cigarette into a long black holder, then lit it with the Ronson table lighter. "I'm pretty sure that Morris Hughes works for the Foreign Office and wrote the book without obtaining their permission. He didn't give any secrets away, but my guess is that he holds a very sensitive appointment."

"Why do you say that?" Burman asked casually.

"Because of the steps he takes to conceal his real identity. I've only met him twice: the afternoon he walked into my office with the typescript of his book and again three months later when I took him to lunch at the Savoy to celebrate the fact that we had sold *Birth of a Nation* to Hodders. Between times, he phoned me once to ask what I thought of the book, and I wrote him a couple of letters care of his solicitors in Hendon. Believe it or not, we even had to send the galleys via them. I've known some eccentric authors in my time, Mr. Burman, but Morris is in a class by himself."

Vera Ashford had received a nice thank-you note from him on publication day, but he'd never acknowledged any of the reviews she'd sent on to him. From then on, there had been total silence, except for the card he sent her every Christmas.

"It always arrives during the first week of December." She smiled. "There's never any message inside, apart from the usual seasonal greetings, but I think Morris mails it early to give me plenty of time to return the compliment care of Drummond, Hall and Lambert."

"His solicitors?"

"Yes." Vera Ashford moved one of the typescripts aside and handed him a plain white envelope. "You'll find their address inside."

"Thank you," Burman said. "You really have been most helpful."

"It's a pleasure. Do give Morris my fond regards if you do get to meet him."

"Oh, I will," Burman said, poker-faced.

*   *   *

Winter closed the garage doors and slowly walked round to the front of the house, deep in thought. It had been a long day, made eventful by a couple of unpleasant surprises which he believed could well have far-reaching effects on the SIS. It was a pity he and Bracecourt had been unable to persuade the Home Office that it wasn't in the national interest to prosecute Vassall, because the case would now provide further ammunition for the faction within the CIA who maintained that British intelligence had been penetrated to such an extent that it was totally insecure. Bracecourt had said he was being unduly pessimistic, but he had a nasty feeling that the CIA was determined to double-cross him over Korznikov. And that premonition had been reinforced by the cable he'd received from the head of station in Moscow, which had ended up on his desk just as he was about to leave the office. Ten groups of seven letters in a one-time cipher, which told him that the CIA had reactivated Penkovsky less than twenty-four hours after he'd discussed the possibility with Tom McNulty. Somebody in the operations department at Langley had moved fast, so fast that he was convinced they hadn't bothered to wait for his agreement.

"Are you all right, Charles?"

Winter started, and looked up to see Geraldine standing in the doorway, silhouetted by the light in the hall which cast a narrow yellow finger onto the gravel drive. "I didn't hear you open the door," he murmured.

"I'm not surprised. You've been standing there in a trance for at least five minutes."

"I was thinking."

"It's been one of those days, has it?"

Her voice was unusually solicitous and he noticed a wavering smile on her lips. "It's been pretty rough," he admitted.

"Yes, you look as though you could do with a stiff drink."

"A large whiskey and soda wouldn't come amiss." He followed Geraldine into the hall, slightly puzzled by her unfamiliar behavior; an acid greeting was about par for the course when he arrived home late. Tonight it seemed Geraldine was all sweetness and light, which was even more strange, because she was wearing the black Dior dress she kept for very special occasions. "All the same," he added, "I think I'd better change first."

"Why?"

"Well, we'll be late if I don't. We have been invited to a drinks party, haven't we?"

"Whose?"

"I don't know. Are we expecting people to dinner?"

"No." She glanced over her shoulder and smiled. "You're getting very absent-minded in your old age, Charles."

"I must be."

"You've left the front door open."

"So I have."

Winter turned about, closed the door, and this time remembered to leave his furled umbrella in the hall stand. He told himself that old age was not the cause of his absent-mindedness; he was simply preoccupied with the realization that all his hard work was about to go down the drain. For the past five years the CIA and the SIS had functioned as one; now, for some reason he couldn't even begin to comprehend, it looked as though somebody at Langley was determined to dismantle that special relationship.

"Your drink, Charles."

"Thanks." This wouldn't do at all. He'd no recollection of entering the drawing room, yet here he was with a glass of whiskey in his hand and Geraldine watching him anxiously. "Cheers," he said, then added, "What sort of day have you had?"

"Oh, so-so." Geraldine went over to the fireplace and returned with a color postcard of the Colosseum which had been propped on the mantelpiece. "This card arrived from Amanda after you'd left for the office. She and Rupert seem to be enjoying themselves."

"That's as it should be." He glanced at the brief message

on the back, full of superlatives and exclamation marks, that was so typical of Amanda.

"Did you know she was pregnant, Charles?"

"Yes." The wonder of it was that Geraldine did. Mother and daughter had never been close. "Cheer up," he said, "it's not the end of the world. These things happen nowadays, we live in permissive times."

"Is that all you've got to say?" Geraldine said quietly.

"No. Rupert loves her and Amanda's very fond of him. What more could you want?" He tucked the postcard into the inside pocket of his jacket and sat down on the couch beside Geraldine. "Besides, who cares what other people think? I could name quite a few of our friends and acquaintances who have skeletons in their cupboards." He smiled and patted her knee. "Come to that, we sailed pretty close to the wind before we marched down the aisle."

The Henley Regatta Ball, as he recalled. They'd gone for a breath of fresh air shortly after midnight and then gravitated to the back seat of his car. Their warm breath had misted the side windows and Geraldine's satin evening dress had ended up somewhere above her waist. Had there been a little more room in the back of his Sunbeam Talbot, they would have consummated their forthcoming marriage three months early. A slight tinge of color told him that Geraldine hadn't forgotten that night either.

"Lance phoned earlier this evening," Geraldine said, abruptly changing the subject.

"I suppose he's overdrawn at the bank again?" The Guards' depot at Pirbright was some distance from the bright lights of London, but that didn't seem to deter Lance.

"You're wrong, Charles. He just asked if he could spend this coming weekend at home with us."

"Then he definitely is broke."

"He's bringing a girl with him."

"I see." Winter sipped his whisky. "Do we know her?" he asked presently.

116

"No, but from what Lance said, I gather she's rather special."

"So when can we expect to see the announcement of their engagement in *The Times?*"

"Any day now." Geraldine bit her lip. "I'm beginning to feel old, Charles."

She looked and sounded vulnerable, but not old. Maybe her figure wasn't as slim as it had been, but she still drew admiring glances from other men. And her face, when it wasn't marred by a sulky expression, was still as arresting as ever.

"Rubbish," he said firmly. "You're not even in full bloom yet."

"That's the nicest thing you've said to me in a long time."

No more strife, no more bickering; Winter was sure that was the unspoken plea behind Geraldine's wistful observation. He thought Amanda's postcard and the telephone call from Lance had a lot to do with it, but the whys and wherefores weren't important. They were two lonely people and they were both too old to go their separate ways. He sought her hand, felt an answering pressure, and tentatively brushed his lips against her cheek. There was nothing tentative about her response; for the first time in over six years, she kissed him full on the mouth. A lasting peace treaty had yet to be negotiated, but Winter got the distinct impression they'd agreed to an armistice.

Oleg Penkovsky climbed the staircase to his apartment on the fifth floor of Number 36 Maxim Gorky Embankment and quietly unlocked the door. Once inside the small hallway, he removed his topcoat and hung it on a peg, and, taking care not to disturb his wife and two daughters asleep in the adjoining bedroom, he tiptoed into the living room and sat down at his desk. Slowly, and more than a little apprehensively, he reached into his pocket for the scrap of wrapping paper which his American controller had passed to him in the cloakroom of the Baku Restaurant, and smoothed it out.

The striped wrapping paper, supposedly from the GUM

Department Store, was the end result of a chain reaction that had started with the small black cross he'd observed on a lamppost while walking to the offices of the Soviet Scientific Research Committee on Tuesday morning. The cross was a sign that he should tune his innocent-looking Sony portable radio to 22.5 megacycles in order to receive a coded transmission from the American Embassy at 2342 hours that night. The message, when decoded with a one-time pad, had asked him to rendezvous with his CIA control officer at the Baku Restaurant on Neglnnoya Street on Thursday evening at eight-thirty.

Penkovsky smiled fleetingly. The Americans had obviously anticipated that he would have no difficulty rustling up a couple of dinner companions, and of course they had been right. Although only casual acquaintances, the two men he'd asked to dinner had never been known to refuse an invitation, no matter how short the notice, and he hadn't been the least bit surprised when they'd accepted with alacrity. No two individuals could have been more boring company, but they'd unwittingly provided the cover he needed.

Penkovsky rubbed the scrap of wrapping paper with his index finger, applying sufficient pressure and friction to remove the colored stripes and reveal the message underneath. Ten minutes later, having decoded the cryptogram, he knew the Americans were asking for the impossible. Policy decisions regarding future Soviet intentions in the Western Hemisphere were taken by the Council of Ministers and the Central Committee of the Politburo, and there was no way he could see the records of their deliberations.

The CIA was also breaking the rules. He was a professional intelligence officer, and nobody had to tell him what sort of information the Anglo-Americans would give their eyeteeth for. All the CIA and SIS officers he'd met had accepted that situation up to now. The records of the Politburo were untouchable, but maybe he could give the Americans something else in lieu? The ultrasecret memorandum prepared by Defense Minister Malinovsky? That would certainly give the CIA an indication of Soviet military thinking, and he wouldn't have to risk his neck either; the microdot photostat of the original document was concealed in the drawer of his desk. Penkovsky nodded to himself; the Malinovsky papers would fill the bill nicely. He would phone the two contact numbers, G3-26-87 and G3-26-94, and then deposit the material at the drop in Brusovsky Lane near the disused church. But not just yet; he would wait until he was satisfied the KGB had completed their investigation into his family background and were no longer watching him.

Penkovsky placed the wrapper and decoded message in a brass ashtray and set fire to them; then he ground the charred paper into a fine ash with his matchbox. Ordinarily, he would have flushed the waste down the lavatory but, fearing the noise from the cistern would rouse his wife and children, he carried the ashtray over to the window and emptied the contents out into the cold night air.

11.

Tired of driving around Whitehall looking for somewhere to park his car, Burman finally left the Ford Zephyr on Horse Guards Parade and started walking, a chill breeze driving the persistent rain into his face. London had been enjoying an Indian summer when Winter had sent him back to the training school at Gerrards Cross a fortnight ago, but now it seemed that the weather had skipped a season and given autumn a miss. He turned into Queen Anne's Gate and went on down the street to enter the Broadway building, opposite St. James's underground station, which purportedly belonged to the Ministry of Land and Natural Resources. A War Department constable on duty inside the main entrance checked his ID card, then, collecting a temporary visitor's pass which was waiting for him at the reception desk, he took the ancient lift up to the top floor.

A red light glowing above the door at the far end of the corridor told him that Winter had company and he dropped into Diana Franklin's office, something he'd planned on doing anyway.

"Hi," Burman said cheerily. "I'm back."

"So I see." Diana regarded his bedraggled appearance with

some amusement, then said, "How long are you going to be with us this time?"

"Seems I'm going to need that flat in town right away, according to what Edmunds told me on the phone last night." Burman removed his raincoat and hung it on a hook behind the door. "He thought I might find somewhere suitable in Bayswater."

"That's where I live."

"Really? Well, there's a coincidence. I wonder if the crafty old devil had some ulterior motive in mind?"

"The only crafty devil I know is six foot three, red-haired, and thirty-two years old." Diana pointed to the communicating door. "He's also likely to be greeted with fire and brimstone if he doesn't get a move on. Your appointment is for nine o'clock sharp. It's now one minute to."

"You can't get rid of me that easily," Burman said. "Winter has his red light on. There's somebody with him."

"I know, and they happen to be waiting for you."

"They would be." Burman snapped his fingers. "While I think of it," he said, "what time is the meeting this evening? Five-thirty or six?"

"What meeting?"

"The one you and I are having with the rental agency."

"Not that old line again," she said, smiling.

"It's got to work sometime," Burman said, his hand on the door leading to the adjoining office.

The only fire and brimstone waiting for him was a cloud of smoke from Ainsworth's pipe and a glacial look from Winter.

"I'm glad you could make it," Winter said acidly. "You've met Ainsworth, of course."

Burman nodded a greeting and joined them at the round pedestal table. Ainsworth said it was nice to see him again, and got his Christian name wrong in the process, calling him Rodney. The mistake was understandable; they'd met only once before when Henry had made his annual pilgrimage to Gerrards Cross to lecture the assembled students on the organization of the KGB. Burman recalled that it had been a very warm June afternoon and Ainsworth's sonorous voice, coupled with the stuffy atmosphere inside the lecture room, had sent many in the audience to sleep.

"It's Richard," Burman said, correcting him.

Winter said, "I'm glad we've got that sorted out; now perhaps we can move on to Matthew Frayne." He opened one of the envelopes on the table, extracted a batch of glossy prints, and distributed them to Ainsworth and Burman as though dealing from a deck of cards.

"He's not exactly a pretty sight, is he?" Ainsworth wrinkled his nose. "What are we supposed to be looking for, Charles?"

"You can ignore the head injuries," Winter told him. "Concentrate on the trunk instead."

Burman arranged the photographs in front of him, placing them side by side. One of the exposures showed Frayne in profile and obviously came from the batch the traffic sergeant had produced when he was in Vienna; the other three were a bird's-eye view taken directly above the corpse. Although Frayne had had a sedentary occupation, his lean stomach suggested that he'd taken plenty of physical exercise to ward off the sort of flabbiness common to many men of his age. Apart from that observation, Burman couldn't see anything that was especially noteworthy about the body. Then suddenly he had a hunch that the absence of any distinguishing marks could be significant.

"I'm only guessing," he said, "but should there be a scar of some kind?"

"Right," said Winter. "There ought to be one near his abdomen. Cleaver's friends in Special Branch interviewed a teacher who remembered Frayne when he was at school. It seems he managed to impale himself on a spike when somebody dared him to climb over the iron railings into the adjoining girls' playground. Another inch and the spike would have ruptured his spleen, and that would have been it. Even so, the ambulance only just got him to the hospital in time."

"Do we have any idea what happened to the real Matthew Frayne?" Ainsworth asked.

"I imagine he died from natural causes, Henry. I checked with Ottawa and they confirmed he'd been rejected by the RCAF because he had a heart condition."

"I'm surprised their records go back that far."

"Frayne was a temporary civil servant during the war; his immediate superior suspected he was either a Communist or a very left-wing socialist and submitted a report on him. That's why Ottawa still had him on file, even though they lost track of him after he went to the States."

A talent spotter had obviously kept tabs on the real Matthew Frayne, and the KGB had had a substitute ready to take his place when he died. Knowing the way they operated, Burman guessed the impostor would have waited at least a year before surfacing. That meant Frayne must have died sometime in 1951, an assumption based on the fact that the passport he'd recovered in Vienna had been issued by the British Consulate in San Francisco on April 9, 1952.

"We don't know precisely when the substitute arrived in this country," Winter continued, "but he filed his first tax return in July 1959, for the previous financial year. According to Underwood and Vines, he put up most of the working capital when the partnership was formed, on the twenty-second of March 1958. Based on that information, I think it's reasonable to assume Frayne arrived in England a few months after Korznikov recruited Deakin and spent the intervening time getting himself established."

"Are you inferring the KGB brought him over for the express purpose of keeping an eye on George?"

"I think Frayne was told to stay in the background until he was needed, Henry."

"And this happened in July last year when he introduced himself to George and Marjorie while they were on holiday in Scarborough?"

"That's the way I see it," Winter said. "I'm also betting that the necessity to bring Frayne into play arose because of something George inadvertently learned from his KGB case officer."

"Quite. I've heard you expound that theory before." Ainsworth emptied his pipe into the ashtray and then stuffed it into his jacket pocket, along with a large round tin of tobacco. "One always assumes the KGB are ultraefficient, but they really cocked it up in Vienna, killing their own man instead of Marjorie Deakin."

Winter caught Burman's eye and winked. "You don't think it was a mistake, do you, Richard?"

"No, I'm sure it was deliberate. Even if you discount Marjorie Deakin's opinion, the police found enough broken glass at the scene of the accident to show that the driver mounted the pavement. They believe he was drunk and swerved to avoid her at the last minute. I'm convinced he aimed the car straight at Frayne."

"Why?" Ainsworth blinked at him like an owl.

"Because the KGB thought we would smell a rat if there were two accidental deaths in the family." Before Ainsworth could butt in, Burman went on, "Frayne was the weak link in the chain; no matter how they played it, he was out in the cold. Had Frayne disappeared, we would have surmised that George had been murdered. Had he survived, he would have had to return to this country and they knew his cover story would fold once we started digging into his background."

"A remarkable piece of logic," Ainsworth observed, his voice skeptical. "Tell me something, Richard, have you also worked out how they killed George?"

"I could hazard a guess, but of course I couldn't prove anything."

"I wouldn't let that small consideration stop you."

"He won't," said Winter.

Burman stared at the set of photographs in front of him. There was a supercilious smile on Ainsworth's face and he longed to wipe it off. "I believe George had an unexpected visitor that Friday night," he said doggedly. "Somebody he'd met before. That would explain why the killer didn't have to break into the house and why the police could find no signs of a struggle inside the bungalow. My guess is, they had a drink or two and the killer slipped George a tranquilizer that made him feel drowsy and lethargic, the way a pre-med does before you're wheeled into the operating theater. Sometime toward dawn, the killer got George into his swimming trunks and took him down to the beach. Then he clubbed George with a rock and held him under the water until he drowned."

"I see." Ainsworth turned to Winter. "Do you agree with that explanation?" he asked.

"I wouldn't quarrel with it, Henry."

"In that case, I presume you'll ask for a second post mortem?"

"That would be a mite difficult," Winter said imperturbably. "George was cremated the day before yesterday."

"I don't understand you, Charles. You had the best part of a fortnight between the inquest and the funeral to ask for another autopsy. What stopped you?"

"It's really very simple, Henry. The KGB went to a great deal of trouble to make his death look like an accident, and I decided to accommodate them. I want them to feel they've gotten away with it, and with the Vassall affair breaking, I'm sure you'll agree I did the right thing." Winter smiled fleetingly. "We can really only afford one scandal at a time."

Ainsworth said, "You appear to have overlooked one major factor. Burman's just told us that he believes George knew the man who called on him. Hasn't it occurred to you that Ross, the watchdog from Security, is the most likely candidate?"

"You're not thinking straight, Henry. If the KGB had a sleeper in our Security Department, they would have known years ago that George was a double agent, and you've every reason to know they didn't suspect anything of the kind." Winter picked up the two remaining large envelopes in front of him and slammed them down on the table. Each manila package measured eighteen inches by twelve, and was literally bursting at the seams, so that the resultant impact made an impressive noise. "These are Deakin's private papers, Henry. I'm hoping you'll find them a damned sight more productive than our present line of conversation."

"Where did they come from?"

"His solicitors—Drummond, Hall and Lambert."

Burman rubbed his mouth, hiding a smile. In law, any communication between solicitor and client was considered privileged, but obviously Winter had not allowed a little technicality like that to deter him. He'd presumably asked somebody in Special Branch to remind Drummond, Hall and Lambert about the Official Secrets Acts, and they had seen the light.

"What do you expect me to find among that little lot?" Ainsworth asked, casting a jaundiced eye at the bulging envelopes.

"The reason why Deakin was murdered."

"That could take forever."

"I don't think so," Winter said airily. "After all, you'll have Richard here to help you."

From the resigned expression on his face, Burman got the impression that Henry was not exactly enamored of the prospect of having him as a collaborator. The feeling was mutual.

The office was on the seventh floor of the main building at Langley, and enjoyed a commanding view of the surrounding campus and its several hundred acres of forest, lawns, and gardens, enclosed by a triple fence designed to keep out unwelcome visitors and the public at large. The room gave an impression of space and was furnished without regard to expense, thanks to a generous appropriation from Congress. There were two Impressionist paintings by Utrillo on the walls, as well as something very avant-garde by Jackson Pollock, the significance of which completely escaped Tom McNulty. Four very deep, very comfortable armchairs were carelessly arranged around a low table with a marble top, and a large Persian rug covered most of the floor. If imitation was the sincerest form of flattery, then the rocking chair was an indication of just how much Melvin Zachary, the assistant director of operations, admired President Kennedy.

McNulty had known Melvin Zachary since 1944, when the latter had been running the French section of the Office of Strategic Services from behind a desk in London. On the other hand, he'd never heard of James C. Jessop before Korznikov had contacted the Zenith Technical Corporation in New York and informed the CIA duty officer that he wanted to defect. Jessop was a fair-haired athletic type in his early forties who smiled a lot, like a politician trying to woo the electorate. He had an Ivy League accent, and dressed the part in a conservatively styled gray suit, blue knitted tie, and button-down shirt. Although he knew first impressions were often misleading, nevertheless McNulty took an instant dislike to him.

Zachary placed a hand on his shoulder and steered him toward one of the armchairs. "It's good to see you again, Tom," he said. "I can't tell you how pleased I am to know you'll be working just down the corridor from me." He fetched a box of cigars from his desk while Jessop poured the coffee. "Have you and Lois moved out of the Madison yet?" he asked.

"We checked out on Tuesday morning." McNulty helped himself to a cigar from the box, trimmed the end with a cutter, and then lit it with a match. "We've rented a house on Q Street in Georgetown, a couple of blocks from the university."

"That's a real nice neighborhood," Jessop said. "Carole and I had a place on Dumbarton Street before I was transferred to New York. You want some cream in your coffee, Tom?"

"No, thanks," McNulty said, "I'll take it black."

"So how does Lois like the idea of living in Washington?" Zachary sat down in the rocker and crossed one plump leg over the other. "Any regrets about leaving London?"

"After nine years over there, I think she's glad to be home again." McNulty placed his cigar in the ashtray and reached for the cup of coffee. "Of course, Lois hasn't had time to settle down yet; she flew back to London last night. I told her our

127

people would be on hand to see the moving men didn't break any of the china, but you know what women are like. She wasn't happy about the arrangement and was convinced they would overlook some little item."

"Fine. I don't see any problems there, Tom."

"I'm not so sure. If I know Winter, he'll have somebody watching the house in Chiswick."

"So what? We're not making any secret of the fact that you've been transferred to Langley."

"Yeah, but he's going to think it very odd that I left London without saying goodbye to him."

"These things happen." Zachary clasped both hands over his stomach, as though trying to hold it in. "You flew home to sort out a domestic tangle and this new assignment suddenly came up. You can always write him a letter if you feel bad about it."

"Winter would jump to all sorts of conclusions if I didn't. He might even get the idea that my sudden departure was part of a complicated maneuver to deny him access to Korznikov." McNulty paused, hoping for some kind of reaction from Zachary, but the fat man refused to be drawn. "What exactly is this new appointment?" he asked eventually.

"Deputy assistant director of operations."

"DADO for short," Jessop said, chipping in with a smile that showed what a fine job some dentist had done capping his teeth.

"Sounds impressive, Zach. What does it entail?"

"A lot of things, but mostly you'll have special responsibility for the Caribbean, and Mongoose in particular."

"Mongoose?" McNulty queried.

"It's a blanket code name for a series of operations aimed at overthrowing the Communist regime in Cuba. There's a whole army of Cuban exiles down in Florida just itching to take a crack at Fidel Castro, and we set up an organization called JM WAVE on the south campus of the University of Miami to coordinate their activities."

JM WAVE had three hundred Americans and several thousand Cubans on the payroll, and an annual budget in excess of fifty million dollars. It supplied arms and explosives to guerilla bands operating inside Cuba and mounted commando raids against industrial and military installations, sugar refineries, oil storage tanks, road and rail bridges. In the field of economic sabotage, JM WAVE had, among other things, persuaded one German industrialist supplying ball bearings to Cuba to manufacture them slightly off center.

"I can see I'm going to spend a lot of time in Miami," said McNulty.

"Not necessarily, Tom. We pulled Theodore Shackley back from Berlin to run JM WAVE."

"What am I, then? The middleman between you and Shackley?"

"It's not that straightforward. Shackley takes his orders from a panel chaired by Bobby Kennedy; the other members are Maxwell Taylor, Rusk, and McNamara. They call themselves the Special Group Augmented."

Somehow, McNulty couldn't see himself hobnobbing with the likes of the attorney general, the chairman of the Joint Chiefs of Staff, the secretary of state, and the secretary of defense. The more he thought about it, the more this new assignment seemed like a nonevent, a job that had been created with no other purpose than to kick him upstairs.

"Tell me, Zach," he said irritably, "what am I supposed to do all day apart from twiddle my thumbs?"

"You're going to be our troubleshooter, Tom, and boy, do we need one. Believe you me, some of the independents operating out of Florida are giving Shackley a real headache, especially groups like Alpha 66 and the DRE Cuban Revolutionary Students Directorate, who are apt to go their own sweet way." Zachary laughed, a deep belly rumble that struck a decidedly false note. "Why, only last month a DRE commando took a couple of power boats across to Havana and beat up the Hotel Hornedo with a mortar and an old 20mm German cannon they'd purchased from a Mafia gun dealer in Miami."

The hard sell left McNulty unmoved. No matter how

Zachary tried to dress it up, the job still didn't amount to a hill of beans. "It's funny how you can get the wrong impression, Zach. Until a few moments ago, I thought you'd ordered me home to help debrief Korznikov." He sipped the coffee, found that it was now only lukewarm, and set the cup down on the table. "I guess that only goes to show why I've never made a killing on the stock market."

"Keep trying, Tom, you haven't done badly so far. For Christ's sake, we're not stupid; Jessop and I both realize you know more about Korznikov than the rest of the agency put together. Who else can tell us if he's lying through his teeth?"

"So when do I get to see him?"

"Soon, real soon." Zachary waved a hand. "Meantime, I figured James here could bring you up to date."

Jessop flashed McNulty another of his brilliant smiles, then in a clipped voice the media had come to associate with the New Frontiersmen surrounding Kennedy, he told him how he and Korznikov had become acquainted during the May Day reception at the Soviet Embassy on 16th Street in 1961. A little over two months later, he had bumped into the Russian again, this time at the French Embassy.

"Korznikov was very friendly, asked me all kinds of questions about the standard of living the average American would enjoy, and then said that being in Washington was giving him a taste for the good life." Jessop frowned. "I didn't attach too much significance to that remark at the time. I had a feeling he was a KGB officer and I could think of several reasons why he should want to cultivate me."

"Such as?" McNulty asked.

"Well, for one thing, Korznikov thought I was with the State Department."

McNulty had the odd feeling that the answer came out a shade too pat, as though Jessop had anticipated the question. The rest of his story sounded equally smooth and well prepared. There had been no further meetings between the two men and in November 1961, Jessop had left Washington to head the

Zenith Technical Corporation in New York. Then, one evening the following spring, Korznikov had reappeared like the genie from Aladdin's lamp.

"Carole and I were dining at Sardi's and he came across to our table. I gathered he was helping the Soviet consulate map out a program for a Russian trade delegation who would be visiting New York during the first week in September. I remember him saying that this forthcoming junket might be a good opportunity for us to really get together, then he winked at me, raised Carole's hand to his lips, and kissed her wrist. The rest you know. Two weeks ago last Saturday, Korznikov phoned the office from Saks Fifth Avenue and announced he was coming across."

"And the KGB tried to stop him."

"Right. One of their hit men pumped him full of poison."

"What kind of poison?" McNulty asked.

"Bacillus botulinus." Zachary flexed his left leg, bending and straightening it again to rock the chair gently backward and forward. "That's the fancy name of the toxin which causes botulism, a particularly virulent form of food poisoning that attacks the nervous system. He had all the symptoms—fits, double vision, and creeping paralysis starting in the face."

"I didn't realize botulism could act so fast, Zach."

The pendulum motion of the rocking chair ceased abruptly, and with it, the distinctive creak of seasoned wood under stress.

"What are you getting at, Tom?"

"The way Korznikov fainted on the sidewalk. Kind of odd, wasn't it?"

"Not when you've also had a shot of pentothal." Zachary curled the thumb, third, and little finger of his right hand into the palm. "The way we figure it, the assassin had two spring-loaded syringes taped one on top of the other."

We? McNulty wondered just who else besides Zachary and Jessop shared that opinion, wondered too why the KGB should have hit Korznikov with both barrels. Somebody had ordered his execution and provided an unusual weapon, yet despite this degree of premeditation, the assassin had chosen the wrong place and the wrong time to eliminate him.

"They bungled it then," he said, voicing his thoughts aloud.

"They sure did," Zachary agreed. "Twice over. On Saturday, and then again forty-eight hours later, when that intruder broke into the Roosevelt Hospital. That's why we've got Vasili under wraps."

"Where are you hiding him?"

"Ah, now that would be telling," Zachary said, and winked at Jessop.

The house the McNultys had rented in Chiswick was situated in Hearne Road, some three hundred yards downstream from Kew Bridge. The Special Branch officer assigned to watch their residence that afternoon waited just long enough to satisfy himself that the moving van had called at the right house and then made his way to the public call box in Spring Grove.

Twenty minutes later, Winter sent a telex to the head of station in Washington. It read: "Our tame eagle has fled the eyrie and is thought to be orbiting in your area. Request you ascertain and inform me soonest exactly where he is nesting."

12.

Although his colleagues had always known that George Deakin had been an introvert, nobody had fully appreciated just how complex a character he'd been until Ainsworth and Burman began to examine his private papers. Apart from being recognized as one of the foremost experts on the Middle East, Deakin had enjoyed a reputation for being ultraefficient. He was, it was said, highly organized, a description which implied that his whole way of life had been one of fastidious tidiness. The contents of the two large manila envelopes, however, provided abundant proof that this impression was not entirely correct. The papers, clipped together in haphazard order, were a collection of notes, theses, essays, and personal reminiscences of events Deakin had witnessed, some of which had taken place long before World War II. Spectroscopic analysis of the ink had shown that some of the material had been written as far back as 1954, and in some instances, certain geopolitical theses had either been subsequently amended or completely revised at a much later date.

The reason for such diligence was not readily apparent. In a moment of extreme vexation, Ainsworth had tartly remarked that it looked as though Deakin had entertained the notion of writing another *Seven Pillars of Wisdom*, despite the fact that George lacked both the literary talent and erudition of T.E. Lawrence. Whether accurate or not, Ainsworth's observation did not explain why Deakin had been murdered. Nor did a careful scrutiny of every sentence, every paragraph, and every page produce anything tangible, other than the comforting knowledge that at least George has not infringed the Official Secrets Acts by regurgitating classified information. Undaunted by this setback, Ainsworth and Burman had gone through the papers again and extracted those theses which he had amended or rewritten in the hope that, buried in the subject matter, they might find something which would indicate why the KGB had considered it necessary to eliminate him.

The written word alone was insufficient. To be absolutely sure no possible innuendo was overlooked, the theses were then compared with the tapes of those sessions of the Joint Intelligence and Planning Committee which Deakin had attended, for three months either side of the time it was thought he'd written the paper. The tapes were selected by Ainsworth; Burman was the man who had to listen to them for hour after hour, locked inside the top security room in the basement. It was the kind of job that could induce hallucinatory side effects, and some days Burman fancied he could still hear their voices long after he'd removed the headphones and switched off the Grundig recorder.

The division of labor was far from equitable. On Winter's instructions, Ainsworth had formed a working party to study possible Soviet countermoves against Berlin, Turkey, and Iran in the event of a major confrontation with the United States, and this provided him with a ready excuse to absent himself from the reading room whenever he felt like it. As a result, this meant that Edmunds did more than his fair share of escort duty, a thankless task which he accepted with phlegmatic resignation. It had become such a regular occurrence that he now made sure he had sufficient files to keep himself gainfully occupied until they either broke for lunch or Burman decided to call it a day. Completely engrossed in their work, they rarely spoke to one another, so that when Edmunds jogged his elbow, Burman assumed it was lunchtime, until he looked up and saw that Winter had entered the cage. The thick transcript which he placed on the table suggested that he intended staying some time and Burman switched off the tape recorder and removed his headphones.

"What are you working on this morning, Richard?" Winter asked him, after Edmunds had left them alone together.

"Deakin's favorite thesis, 'The Destablization of the United States.'" Burman stretched both arms above his head and fought off a yawn. "He figured that was Khrushchev's prime objective."

"George could be right. Penkovsky sent us a photocopy of the lecture Lieutenant Colonel Ivan Prikhodko gave to the Military Diplomatic Academy in May 1960, which would tend to support his contention."

"I wish Ainsworth had thought to tell me that," said Burman. "We could have saved ourselves a lot of time and effort."

"If Henry told you to examine that paper in detail, you can be sure he thought it was worthwhile."

"I suppose so." Burman shrugged. "All the same, there's nothing very original in it. I get the impression Deakin lifted most of his material from the *Times*. He has a lot to say about the strengths and weaknesses of the American economy, and I doubt if he carried all those facts and figures around in his head."

"It's what he argues from those facts and figures that is important," Winter said evenly.

"Yes, well, Deakin needed three attempts and fifteen thousand words to give us a glimpse of the blinding obvious. 'The United States is the richest and strongest nation in the world, therefore the Soviet Union either has to live with this fact and toe the line or else they have to find some way of undermining that power base without provoking an all-out war.' That's the gist of his thesis."

135

"Did George indicate how the Kremlin might achieve this aim?"

"He thought they would seize every opportunity to destroy the morale and confidence of the American people."

There were several ways the Soviets could do this, Deakin had argued. They could encourage the oil-producing countries to increase the price of crude, which, in time, would lead to inflation and a major recession in the American economy. They could also step up the propaganda war against Western Europe and the Third World, asserting that the arms race between the two superpowers was entirely the fault of the United States. When the Kremlin judged the time was ripe, they would table an agenda for a conference aimed at limiting the proliferation of strategic weapons, but not before the Soviet Union achieved nuclear parity or better.

"Some problems they don't have to create. Race riots, increases in crimes of violence: they're the kind of factors which could make a lot of Americans look inward and wonder if their society was coming apart at the seams."

"You're getting to be quite a philosopher," Winter said.

"I'm just voicing Deakin's opinion. Mind you, he also said that only some really traumatic event could produce the kind of moral decay the Kremlin was hoping for."

"What sort of traumatic event?"

"Vietnam was a possibility, he thought. An extension of American involvement to such a point that they became embroiled in a counterrevolutionary war they coudn't hope to win. And in an earlier paper, he considered what effect it would have on the Americans if their president were assassinated."

"When was this?" Winter asked, his voice suddenly razor-sharp.

"A long time back. About three months after Eisenhower was reelected for a second term, as near as we can tell."

"Does he discuss this possibility again in subsequent papers?"

"No. He must have had second thoughts and decided it wasn't on."

136

"Damn right. Kennedy may not be riding high in the opinion polls, but even in his wilder moments, Khrushchev would never authorize the KGB to assassinate him. He knows that would anger Americans too much—the same way Pearl Harbor did."

It occurred to Burman that there might be a very different reaction if the president were killed by a fellow American. He could imagine the mind-numbing effect that would have, the sense of shock and grief, the collective feeling perhaps that somehow they were all guilty.

"What about the JIAP committee meetings?" Winter pointed to the Grundig. "Have you heard anything on the tapes which might lead you to think Deakin was holding something back?"

Burman shook his head. Although he'd never met Deakin, his voice had become so familiar that he felt he knew him as well as any man could. He had learned how to read his every mood, to know when George was up or down, when he was sulking, angry, or excited, and there was nothing, absolutely nothing on this tape to indicate that Deakin was being secretive about some matter of which he alone knew.

"Pity." Winter rippled the transcript. The pages were stapled together inside a soft yellow cover and resembled a film script, except for the security classification and reference number in the top right-hand corner. "Korznikov's preliminary interrogation," he said, answering Burman's unspoken question. "Got it special delivery from Tom McNulty's replacement."

"That was very decent of him."

"Yes, wasn't it? Of course, our friends at Langley sat on it for long enough." Winter sniffed. "Korznikov has been telling his interrogators how he recruited George and what a valuable source of information he's been."

"Then the joke's on him."

"So it would seem." Winter rippled the pages again. "The transcript is all right as far as it goes, but I wish they'd sent us an invitation to join the party instead."

Burman knew what he meant. The written word had its

limitations; it could not reflect Korznikov's tone of voice or the hunted look in his eyes which might have appeared had a question caught him off guard. You needed to be there, sitting across the table from Korznikov, to know whether or not he was lying.

"Maybe it's time Harold talked to Jack. They're supposed to be the best of friends and you never know, the old boy might be able to wangle us an invitation."

"I suppose there's no harm in trying," Burman said, when it dawned on him that Winter had been alluding to Macmillan and Kennedy.

"Quite." Winter pushed his chair back and stood up. "Meantime, you'd better keep plugging away. I'd prefer not to arrive empty-handed when I call on Tom McNulty."

Burman nodded, picked up the headphones, and clamped them over his ears. Then he depressed the play button on the Grundig to set the spools revolving at their predetermined speed.

McNulty glanced at the odometer and saw they had covered just over twelve miles since Jessop had picked him up from his house on Q Street. From Washington Circle they'd driven east on K Street to Mount Vernon Place, and then swung into New York Avenue to head out of town on Route 50. Roughly five minutes ago, they had crossed the Beltway and Interstate 495 and turned off on to Palmer Highway. Still heading east into Maryland, they were now on Annapolis Road, a narrow, hilly two-lane street.

Jessop was dressed in Air Force blue, the chevrons on his sleeve indicating he was a T4. The sedan he was driving also bore USAF plates, part of the camouflage he and Melvin Zachary had dreamed up. As Jessop had explained it, the safe house where Korznikov was being held had been selected because it was well off the beaten track, was reasonably close to Washington, and, more important, was only six miles from the U.S. Air Force transmitter station near Patuxent River Park. As far as the outside world was concerned, the CIA officers guarding the Russian defector were merely Air Force person-nel and their dependents, who happened to be sharing the same large rented house. A casual visitor like McNulty could be passed off as one of the civilian technicians working at the transmitter station.

"What do you make of Korznikov?" Jessop asked, breaking a long silence. "Do you think he's leveling with us, Tom?"

"I'm not sure. When did he tell you about the missile sites at San Cristobal?"

"Doesn't it give the date in the transcript you received?"

"No," said McNulty, "that's why I'm asking."

"We must be slipping." Jessop drummed his fingers on the steering wheel. "Let's see now," he mused, "it must have been last Thursday. Yeah, that's it, Thursday, October eleventh."

"You're positive about that?"

"Absolutely. I know it was Thursday because that's when Zach told me the president had sided with McNamara, and ruled that all U-2 missions over Cuba henceforth should be flown by Air Force pilots and not our guys. Zach said the director was hopping mad about it."

"I bet he was."

The CIA had lost control over their own planes as a result of a bureaucratic interdepartmental squabble which made very little sense to McNulty. The secretary of defense had argued that should a U-2 be shot down over Cuba, there would be less hassle all round if the pilot were a regular Air Force officer, and not a civilian who would automatically be regarded as a spy by Castro. But the men who flew the U-2 planes for the CIA were not civilians in the strict sense of the word; they were USAF personnel seconded to and paid by the agency. To McNulty's way of thinking, it would have been a simple matter for them to put on a uniform, but the brass had wanted a tidier solution.

"You still haven't given me a straight answer to my question, Tom." Jessop glanced his way, prompting him with a toothy smile.

"The Air Force was over San Cristobal on Sunday; I saw the

results of the mission at the National Photographic Interpretation Center yesterday evening."

"So?"

"So I'm inclined to believe Korznikov is on the level. Provided you're certain of the date, it means he told you about the missile sites three days before the Air Force confirmed their existence." McNulty picked up the transcript which was lying between them on the bench seat. "Do the British have a copy of this?" he asked.

"No. Zach didn't see any reason why we should pass it on to them. After all, Cuba is our ball game, not theirs." The toothy smile appeared again, white and gleaming like an advertisement for a dental mouthwash. "Hell, Winter's got nothing to complain about. We sent him the transcript of the initial debriefing and there's enough material in that to keep him occupied for weeks."

"You don't know Winter," said McNulty. "He'll ask for more, just like Oliver Twist."

"Yeah? Well, I doubt that will cut much ice with our people." Jessop put the wheel over and turned right into a narrow dirt track, which led to a small grove of trees about half a mile back from Annapolis Road. "Korznikov defected to us and we're calling the tune for once."

McNulty said nothing, merely stared through the windshield at the grove ahead. Most of the trees were evergreens, but there were three or four maples, their leaves turning red and gold, the way they always did in the fall. Although there were cattle grazing in the fields on either side of the track, he couldn't remember seeing any farm buildings before they turned off Route 450. Then suddenly they were in the grove and Jessop braked to a halt outside a large timber-frame house.

"This is it," he said unnecessarily.

"So I see."

The house had five upstairs rooms and looked as though it hadn't had a lick of paint in years. As they got out of the Ford sedan and trudged across the clearing, a burly figure dressed in jeans and a checked shirt opened the door and then backed off, still holding a .28-gauge, pump-action Remington shotgun at the point of balance in his left hand. Exchanging a few words with the guard, Jessop led McNulty through the hall to a small room at the back of the house, where two men were seated at a table playing checkers. Sneakers, denim pants, and a plaid shirt seemed to be the standard garb, but although both men were dressed alike and were roughly the same angular build, Korznikov was instantly recognizable. He had a lean, Asiatic-looking face, and he reminded McNulty of the photographs he'd seen of Lenin.

"This is Mr. Smith, Vasili," Jessop said, introducing him, "but you can call him John."

"How very original." Korznikov stood up and shook his hand, squeezing it in a viselike grip. His thin lips ghosted a smile. "Quite a change from John Doe."

"Vasili has a terrific sense of humor," said Jessop.

"He certainly has." McNulty flexed his numbed fingers and managed a broad grin for Korznikov's benefit. "A real joker."

"It would seem you are also a comedian," Korznikov observed icily.

"You're wrong there," Jessop said. "John's one of the best Soviet analysts we have. Which is why we decided he should talk to you about the missile sites at San Cristobal."

"John is an expert Soviet analyst, is he?" Korznikov looked skeptical.

"You'd better believe it." McNulty waited until the guard had cleared the checkerboard and left the room, then took his place at the table and motioned the Russian to sit down. "About these MRBMs you plan to install," he said, "they have the same range as our Jupiter missile. Right?"

"Give or take a hundred kilometers."

"So what's wrong with your fifty-megaton intercontinental rockets Khrushchev is forever boasting about?"

Korznikov hesitated for just a moment, then, folding his arms, he leaned both elbows on he table and in a low voice began to tell McNulty just why the Soviet High Command believed they were singularly vulnerable to a first strike.

Burman left the tube station at Lancaster Gate and walked along Bayswater Road, toward Marble Arch and Diana Franklin's ground-floor apartment at 27 Hyde Park Gardens. The old rental agency ploy had worked a couple of times, and she had had a celebratory drink with him after he'd acquired a flat in South Kensington, but so far he hadn't managed to get past her front door. Burman wasn't entirely sure he'd progress any farther tonight; Diana wasn't expecting him and it was possible she already had a date, but he was the persistent kind and not one to give up easily.

He turned into the quiet cul-de-sac on the left-hand side of the road that was part of Hyde Park Gardens, and went on down the street until he came to an Austin Healey parked between a Mercedes and a vintage Bentley. Then, wheeling into the portico, he walked up the short flight of steps and pressed the buzzer to Diana's apartment. There was no reply, but he knew she was in; there was a chink of light between the drawn curtains in the room to the left of the portico, and he jabbed the button again. This time a breathless voice, distorted by the amplifier, asked him what he wanted.

"It's me—Richard," Burman said into the mike. "Can you spare me a few minutes? Something's cropped up and it's rather urgent."

A rushing noise which sounded like an exasperated sigh came through the amplifier; then the lock tripped with an electric buzz and he pushed the door open and stepped inside the entrance hall, to find Diana waiting for him at the door to her apartment. He noticed she had changed out of the navy-blue suit she had been wearing at the office into a pair of well-tailored dark-brown slacks and an equally expensive-looking cashmere sweater.

"Something tells me I've called at an inopportune moment," Burman said apologetically.

"Why's that?"

"I thought I heard a loud sigh."

"Purely one of relief." Diana closed the door behind him and ushered him toward the living room at the far end of the narrow passageway. "My mother was on the phone trying to persuade me to come home for the weekend, and I was glad of the excuse to hang up."

The living room was perpendicular to Hyde Park Gardens and was, Burman estimated, about thirty feet by twelve, with a ceiling so high that the crystal chandelier hanging from a chain in the center cleared his head by at least a yard. Apart from the fact that the sheer size of the room made his place seem like a walk-in cupboard, the elegant antique furniture and the two nook cabinets filled with Meissen ornaments were also visual reminders of a lifestyle way beyond his means.

"I was about to have a drink. Care to join me?" Diana opened a cupboard and crouched in front of it. "Whiskey, gin, or dry sherry? I'm afraid the choice is very limited."

"I'd like a whiskey, please," Burman said. "With just a splash of soda if you have it."

Diana reached inside the cupboard for the siphon and held it up to the light to see if there was any soda left. "A splash is about all you will get," she murmured.

"What about you? I mean, I'm happy to take it neat."

"I'm going to have a large gin and tonic."

Burman left her to it and moved away, drawn to the photographs in silver frames displayed on the open bookshelves on either side of the marble fireplace. The family gallery, he thought; an enlarged snapshot of her parents taken in the garden of their Surrey manor house three miles from Haslemere, two formal portraits of her younger brothers looking resplendent in full-dress uniform, and an appealing picture of a small, round-eyed, very serious little boy.

"That's Giles," Diana said, coming up behind him. "It was taken on his eighth birthday, a few weeks before he went off to prep school."

"I didn't know you had a son."

"Why should you?"

No reason, Burman thought, except that he wondered why Edmunds had neglected to mention it when he'd questioned him about Diana Franklin.

"He's a very nice-looking boy. You must be very proud of him."

"Oh, I am." Diana placed a Waterford tumbler in his hand and then raised her glass. "Cheers," she said.

"Cheers." Burman savored the whiskey, his eyes still on the small boy and ignoring the photograph of her long-dead husband smiling jauntily from the cockpit of a Hawker Hunter. "How old is Giles now?" he asked.

"Eleven. He likes to think he's very grownup and I have to watch my step on visiting days. He hates me fussing over him in front of the other boys, but it's a different story when he's home from school."

"You must have your hands full during the holidays. How do you manage?"

"We cope. Giles spends part of the time with my inlaws at Aylesbury and I commute to and fro from the office on the Metropolitan Line. And of course Charles is very good about letting me have leave whenever I want it."

"That's very considerate of him," Burman said dryly.

"Yes, well, we've known each other for longer than I care to remember." Diana pointed to a black-and-white snapshot that had faded in the constant exposure to sunlight. "This was taken in the summer of forty-six when I was eighteen, and that's a very long time ago."

A mixed doubles posing at the net. Her father was partnering an attractive brunette in a pleated tennis skirt, who looked a trifle sulky, possibly because Winter had an arm round Diana's waist and she was smiling up at him like an infatuated schoolgirl.

"I presume that's the Honorable Geraldine Winter?" he said, pointing to the brunette.

"Yes."

A momentary frown told him the two women were not the best of friends, but her expression changed when she talked of Winter, and Burman got the impression he could do no wrong in her eyes. He was kind, generous, thoughtful, and a loyal friend. He'd been a good soldier too, she had her father's word for that. They'd fought together in the same Guards battalion during the long retreat to Dunkirk, when the general had been second in command of the Third Coldstreams and Winter a lowly platoon commander with less than a year's service behind him. His coolness under fire had been quite remarkable; the sole surviving officer in his company, Winter had marched his men down to the bomb- and shell-torn beaches as though they were on Horse Guards parade, Trooping the Color on the king's birthday. Then, as if to prove to the other units awaiting embarkation that there was more to the Guards than mere ceremonial, he'd deployed his small force among the sand dunes and had exhorted his men to such an extent that they'd shot down two marauding Stukas with their rifles and light machine guns.

"Sounds like I've got a bad case of hero worship, doesn't it?"

"Just a little," Burman admitted.

Diana stared at her gin and tonic. "What don't you like about him?"

"Well, for one thing, he's completely ruthless and doesn't hesitate to use people." Burman saw her eyes narrow but ignored the warning sign. "Take Deakin, for example. Winter doesn't really give a damn who killed him, he only wants to know the reason why. That may be the professional approach, but it's a sight too cold for my liking."

"You think he should be breathing vengeance?" she snapped.

"It would make him seem more human."

"It would also be hypocritical. One man died and another was severely wounded because of what George did six years ago."

145

The evening was full of surprises, and now it seemed that Winter hadn't been entirely frank when he'd briefed him. "I didn't know that," he said lamely.

"Well, you do now." Diana smiled, her sudden anger dissipated. "Sorry about that," she said. "I didn't mean to sound like a cantankerous schoolmarm."

"You don't look like one, either," Burman told her.

"There's no answer to that." Diana finished her gin and tonic and left the empty glass on the mantelpiece. "Isn't it time we were on our way?"

"Where to?"

"The office, I presume." Her eyebrows rose fractionally. "You did say that something rather urgent had cropped up."

"That was just an excuse to get past the front door. It so happens I can get a couple of theater tickets for *Chips with Everything* at the Vaudeville and thought you might like to come with me."

"Tonight?"

"Not necessarily," said Burman. "I'm very flexible. How about Saturday?"

"That could be too late. Charles is flying to Washington the day after tomorrow, and I have a hunch he'll send for you before the week is out."

Winter obviously hadn't wasted any time after he'd left the reading room. Control, Bracecourt, and then the Cabinet secretary: Burman figured it was logical to assume Winter had seen them in that order and had enlisted their support before he'd seen the PM and persuaded him to call Kennedy at the White House.

"You've got to hand it to Charles, he's certainly a fast worker."

"He's not the only one," Diana said with a laugh.

13.

Winter paid off the cab and stood there on the sidewalk, gazing up in the gathering dusk at the clapboard house on Q Street. Although no lights were showing in the front other than the one in the porch, there was a Lincoln convertible parked in the driveway, and from somewhere in the backyard came the smell of a bonfire of autumn leaves. Smiling to himself, he walked up the front path into the porch and pressed the luminous button by the left side of the door. As the melodic chimes died away in the hall, a light came on and high heels clacked on a wood floor; then the door opened as far as the security chain would allow and a petite redhead peered at him through the gap.

"Hello, Lois." Her eyes popped and she gave an excited squeal, half pleased, half surprised. "Good God," Lois repeated, "isn't this just wonderful?"

The security chain came off in double-quick time and the door swung open. As he stepped inside the hall, Lois raised herself on tiptoe, gripped his shoulders, and planted a firm kiss on his mouth.

"What are you doing in Washington? Where are you staying?" The questions were fired at him with machine-gun speed.

Before Winter could answer either of them, Lois grabbed him by the hand and led him toward the kitchen. "Tom." Her voice carried through the open window. "Tom, will you look who's here?"

McNulty appeared at the window, did a double take, then scurried around the side of the house and entered the kitchen, his lean face creased in a broad smile. The same questions were fired at Winter again, but unlike his wife, Tom allowed him to get a word in edgeways.

"It's purely a fleeting visit," Winter said. "Three, perhaps four days at the most. The head of station is putting me up."

"You'll stay to dinner, won't you?" Lois interjected.

Winter protested that he wouldn't dream of imposing on their hospitality, but Lois refused to take no for an answer. They were having a pot roast, she said, and it was no problem to lay an extra place at the table; meantime, Tom would take him into the den for a drink.

The den was off the hall to the left and directly opposite the dining room. Definitely a man's room, Winter thought, his eyes taking in the pennants, trophies, and athletic cups McNulty had won at high school and Cornell University. Some of the memorabilia, like the photograph of Tom with Eisenhower's headquarters staff at Algiers, he'd seen before at their house in Chiswick, but not the souvenirs from the North African campaign. The camel saddle, the divisional shoulder patches of the Big Red One mounted on green baize in a picture frame, and the brass 20-mm cannon shell he used as a holder for pens and pencils, had obviously been stored in a local warehouse, along with some of the household furniture.

"How about a dram of Southern Comfort?" McNulty opened the liquor cabinet. "Or would you prefer a bourbon and water?"

"Southern Comfort," said Winter. "I'm feeling mellow."

"You and me both." McNulty poured two large shots, handed Winter a glass, and waved him to a comfortable leather-upholstered armchair. "How are things in London?" he asked casually.

"The Indian summer came to an abrupt end; weatherwise, I think we've skipped autumn. You're well out of it."

"Yeah." McNulty stared at his glass, plainly embarrassed. "I'm sorry I left without saying goodbye. I'd no idea I was going to end up at Langley."

"It's not your fault, Tom. These things happen."

"You got my letter?"

"Yes. What's it like to be deputy assistant director of operations?"

"How do you know about that? I don't remember mentioning it in my letter."

"I expect a little bird told me," Winter said blandly.

"Then you already know what the job entails."

"Not really. All I heard was that this appointment had been tailor-made just for you. Of course, your title sounds very impressive."

"I've got a nice office too, down the corridor from Melvin Zachary."

"Keeps you busy, does he?"

"I get to see all the intelligence reports on Cuba and I've made a couple of trips to Miami to liaise with Shackley, who's running the Cuban exiles down there." McNulty laughed derisively. "If nothing else, it's done wonders for my suntan."

He sounded bitter, Winter thought, and with good reason. The appointment was obviously a sham, a job that had been created to facilitate his removal from London.

"Never mind, Tom," Winter said cheerfully, "I daresay you'll soon have more than enough on your plate. Nobody in London is very happy about the way things are shaping up in Cuba. Perhaps we ought to get together and pool our information."

"Is that why you're over here?"

"More or less. There's a feeling in Whitehall that Khrushchev might be tempted to follow Stalin's example and put the squeeze on Berlin if you get tough with him over Cuba. Anyway, Macmillan thought it would be a good idea if I were on hand in case of trouble, and apparently President Kennedy was inclined to agree with him." Winter smiled. "It seems I'm considered to be something of an authority on the hawks and doves within the Kremlin."

"Thanks to Korznikov and Deakin."

"Yes. By the way, how is Vasili? Have you met him yet?"

"The day before yesterday," said McNulty. "Zachary asked me to check him out and we talked about the Saddler SS7 missile and its limitations. He didn't tell me anything we hadn't already got from Penkovsky."

"So what's strange about that? The preliminary interrogation didn't yield much of a dividend either; for the most part, it was a blow-by-blow account of how he recruited Deakin."

"Korznikov also named a considerable number of KGB officers who were masquerading as embassy officials around the world."

"Most of whom, Tom, are now safely back inside the Soviet Union. It makes you wonder why the KGB were so anxious to eliminate him."

"Perhaps they were worried he could destroy the entire Soviet espionage network in the United States."

"There is that possibility."

"Except that you don't believe it for one moment." McNulty poured himself another drink and topped up Winter's glass. "I can tell that from your tone of voice, but I think you're prejudiced. Maybe Korznikov is a big disappointment as far as British intelligence is concerned, but he blew the whistle on the missile sites at San Cristobal three days before the Air Force confirmed their existence."

"The first reconnaissance mission by a U-2 took place on the fifteenth of August," Winter said calmly. "Korznikov was merely establishing his credentials; he knew it was only a question of time before the CIA discovered the facts for themselves."

"What are you suggesting, Charles? That he was ordered to come across?"

"Why not? His defection was somewhat dramatic; one might almost say it was scripted by Hollywood."

The frantic telephone call from a booth in Saks and the way Korznikov had just made it to the sidewalk before going into a coma were reminiscent of a Hitchcock movie. Then, less than forty-eight hours later, a mysterious intruder had tried to nail him while he had been under guard at Roosevelt Hospital, and the CIA had been obliged to transfer him to a safe house for better protection.

"This poison the KGB are alleged to have pumped into him," Winter continued. "Has anybody identified the toxin yet?"

"Sure they have. Korznikov was injected with bacillus botulinus, plain old food poisoning in our language. They also gave him a shot of pentothal for good measure."

"Why would they do that?"

"Search me." McNulty shrugged. "Maybe they hoped it would lower his powers of resistance and make him more susceptible to the toxin."

"Or it could be they were anxious to ensure that he received the best of medical attention in time. That would make sense if Korznikov had deliberately taken the poison."

"What?"

"In a soluble capsule," said Winter.

"Jesus." McNulty closed his eyes briefly and sighed. "That's the most fantastic thing I ever heard. You don't really believe that claptrap, do you, Charles?"

"It isn't claptrap. I think Korznikov is a plant who was sent across to spread misinformation."

"Such as?"

"Your guess is as good as mine, Tom. Who knows, we may see Vasili emerging as a dove should your president get tough and demand to have those missile bases dismantled. It could be that he'll suggest some sort of compromise to save Khrushchev's face, like the removal of your Jupiter missiles from Turkey."

"We might just buy that," McNulty said thoughtfully. "Those liquid-fueled rockets are obsolete, and the Polaris submarines are a much more effective deterrent. But where does Deakin fit into the picture?"

It was a good question and there was no way Winter could

answer it satisfactorily. One man had defected, the other had been eliminated. He still thought there was a connection, but the Cuban problem was not one of the matters Deakin had considered in the papers he had deposited with Drummond, Hall and Lambert.

"I wish we could sit in on the interrogation," Winter said, abruptly changing the subject. "I can't understand why the agency is so dead against it."

"To tell you the truth, Charles, some of our people think that British intelligence is about as leakproof as a colander, and the Vassall affair has only hardened that opinion. Then there's the hard bargain you drove over the Deakin-Korznikov angle; the entrance fee certainly raised anguished protests around Washington and made you some bad enemies."

"And now the shoe is on the other foot?"

"Except you don't have anything to offer us," said McNulty. "Of course, personally I happen to think you're getting a raw deal, but that's the way it is."

"You've had a pretty raw deal too," Winter reminded him. "Someone made it his business to ensure you were shunted off to a dead-end job. Who was behind that? Melvin Zachary?"

"Don't be ridiculous. Zach and I have known each other for years and he'd never stick a knife in my back. Besides, it isn't his style, Charles. You should know that."

Tom had a point there, Winter thought. He had first met Zachary in July 1945, when the SIS had dressed him up as a major and sent him into Berlin with the Seventh Armored Division. The American had arrived in much the same guise attached to the United States Eighty-second Airborne Division, and they had gotten to know one another fairly well in the following eighteen months. He'd always found Zachary to be absolutely straight, the kind of uncomplicated man you liked and trusted on sight.

"You're right, Tom, he's not the least bit devious."

Zachary had his faults, though. A bitter opponent of the puppet Communist regime the Russians had installed in East

Berlin, his judgment had been seriously at fault when he'd backed the Gneisnau Abteilung, a bunch of neo-Nazis who claimed they controlled a network of agents in the Soviet zone. They also ran a thriving black market in cigarettes, nylons, and food supplies, which they bought from the occupying forces and then sold at a vast profit to their fellow countrymen. It had taken Zachary some considerable time to discover that the Gneisnau Abteilung were using the funds they'd obtained from him to finance the operation, and although he'd subsequently put the entire organization behind bars, the whole sorry business had shown that he was open to manipulation.

"How about Jessop?" Winter asked. "Is he another friend of yours?"

"I hardly know the guy. We were introduced to each other in Zach's office a little over two weeks ago. Since then, I've only seen him once, and that was the day before yesterday, when I was allowed to interrogate Korznikov."

Winter smiled. "I get the feeling you don't like Jessop."

"I must be slipping, I didn't realize it showed." McNulty leaned back in his chair and hooked one leg over the arm. "James Jessop is one very ambitious man and I'm told he has the ability to go right to the top. Believe me, he's a smooth operator; the subtle way he handled Korznikov when Vasili started making overtures proves that."

"Korznikov approached him before he came across?"

"Several times," said McNulty. "According to Jessop, they bumped into one another at various functions here in Washington. I guess he must have nursed Korznikov along, because Vasili definitely went out of his way to contact him after he was transferred to Zenith."

"Why rely on guesswork, Tom? Wouldn't Jessop submit a report each time they met, detailing exactly what had passed between them?"

"Sure he would, that's standard procedure."

"Then why couldn't you take a look at those reports? I doubt they'll reveal just who is taking who for a ride, but you never know, you may come across a few gray areas that would bear checking out."

"I don't see how I can pull those files from Central Registry unless I go through Zach." McNulty rubbed his jaw. "Convincing him I need to see them shouldn't be too difficult, but from there on I'd have to keep a low profile. That means somebody else would have to handle the follow-up, somebody whose face isn't known around town, and that rules you out."

"Quite," said Winter. "I thought we might use Burman as a front-runner."

"And who else?"

"A young woman named Diana Franklin. She can act as your go-between."

"Your PA?"

"She's very attractive," Winter said persuasively.

"Then I guess I'm about to become a philanderer," McNulty said with a wry smile.

Zachary checked the rearview mirror to make sure the road behind was clear, then, killing the main beams, he turned off the John Hanson Highway into Patuxent River Park, half a mile due east of the U.S. Air Force transmitter station. Driving on sidelights, he went down a narrow track which eventually led to a small clearing in the wood, where he parked the car and switched off the ignition. Moments later, Jessop appeared out of the darkness and got in beside him.

"How long have you been waiting?" Zachary asked him.

"Less than five minutes. What you might call perfect timing."

"Yeah. Well, I hope you can be equally slick with our Russian friend because we need some grade-A information on the Soviet Council of Ministers and the Central Committee of the Politburo. Who's for Khrushchev, who's against him—that kind of thing."

"Is this another test?" Jessop asked quietly.

"Test?" Zachary turned to face the other man. "What the hell are you talking about, James?"

"McNulty was pretty hostile the other day. As a matter of fact, his approach was downright crude. Korznikov is no fool; he knew Tom was trying to trip him up."

"That's not like Tom, he's one of the best interrogators I know."

"Then he must have had an off day. Hell, Zach, he didn't even try to disguise the fact that he was comparing everything Korznikov told him about the Saddler missile system with another source. I tell you, he really got under Vasili's skin." Jessop shook his head. "I sure had my work cut out smoothing his ruffled feathers."

"This is no test, James. We need that information, and fast."

"How fast is fast?"

"Like yesterday," Zachary told him.

"That might be risky. Korznikov is very cooperative, but if we push him along too fast, it could be counterproductive."

Zachary knew what he meant. In his eagerness to please, Korznikov might be tempted to tell his interrogators what he thought they wanted to hear. There was a very real danger that his assessment of the political scene could be misleading, but the alternative source was no longer available. Penkovsky had had it; he hadn't been arrested yet, but the cable Zachary had received from Moscow earlier in the day had stated categorically that it could happen at any moment. Penkovsky had contacted his control all right, but somebody else had collected the microfilm from the drop near the disused church in Brusovsky Lane. And that somebody else could only be the KGB.

"We're getting evidence of other missile sites at Guanajay, Sagua La Grande, and Remedios."

"Shit." Jessop gave a low whistle, then said, "We can't let them get away with that."

"The president doesn't intend to. He's formed a special executive committee to decide just what action we should take. McGeorge Bundy, Maxwell Taylor, Rusk, McNamara, Lyndon Johnson, Ros Gilpatric from Defense, George Ball from State." Zachary ticked their names off on the fingers of both hands.

"Ed Martin, the expert on Latin America, Dillon from Treasury, Bobby Kennedy . . ."

"Stop there," Jessop said dryly, "you've run out of fingers. In any case, does it really matter a damn who's on the committee and who isn't? We both know what happens when you get a bunch of high-powered officials around a table. There's a lot of talk, but nothing gets done."

"This committee is split down the middle. The hawks want to obliterate the missile sites and invade Cuba, while the doves prefer some kind of naval blockade."

"It's still talk."

"You're wrong, James. This time we're going to the brink. That's why we have to know how sure Khrushchev is of his power base."

"Forget what I just said. I can see we've got to pull out all the stops." Jessop ran a hand over his short blond hair. "Are you going to sit in on the interrogation, Zach?" he asked. "Two heads are better than one, and it's essential Vasili doesn't give us a bum steer."

"You'll have to manage without me, I'm afraid. I'll be too busy protecting your rear."

"My rear?"

"Charles Winter's in town," Zachary told him laconically.

"Aw, for Chrissake," said Jessop, "that's all we need."

14.

It was a cool, sunny morning, the sky an azure blue without a wisp of cloud cover. Seven stories below McNulty's office, an overnight dew had made the campus lawn seem a lusher green against the yellow and browning leaves of the massive oak and elm trees bordering the perimeter fence. In sharp contrast to the idyllic view beyond the window, the atmosphere inside the building was charged, with a localized storm still rumbling three doors away along the corridor. A slim buff-colored folder was the root cause of the adverse conditions and, considering how innocuous the contents were, McNulty wished he'd never listened to Winter.

He flipped through the pages again, his face scowling as he reread the director's comments at the end of each report. "I find this rather intriguing"—an enigmatic observation in green ink after Jessop had described how Korznikov had approached him during the May Day celebrations at the Soviet Embassy in 1961. And then, just over two weeks later, there was a more personal note which said, "We may be on to something here, Zach, but Jessop will need to play it cool." There were other remarks, ranging from, "This ongoing situation looks very promising," to a cryptic, "Good. Keep me informed," but in

McNulty's opinion there was nothing in the goddamn reports which in any way justified the acrimonious exchange he'd had with Melvin Zachary before he'd been able to obtain them from the Central Registry.

Jessop had told him he'd only met Korznikov on two occasions before being transferred to New York, but he'd neglected to mention that there had been a supposedly chance encounter between his wife, Carole, and Vasili in Kann's Department Store at Eighth Street and Pennsylvania Avenue, on July 25, 1961, ten days after the reception at the French Embassay. That, plus the subsequent phone calls to his house on Dumbarton Street, could have constitued the gray areas Winter had been on about, except for the fact that Jessop had been wired for sound and their conversations were recorded on tape. There were no question marks against Carole Jessop either; as far as the agency was concerned, it seemed she was a model wife, and the director had written a letter commending her for the way she had handled the situation.

Although McNulty thought there was little point in holding on to the folder, he was reluctant to return it to the Central Registry on the second floor. Zachary would get to hear about it and would want to know what conclusions he'd drawn, if any. Another shouting match this early in the day was something he wished to avoid, but the heavy footsteps in the corridor suggested he was going to be unlucky. Stay cool, McNulty told himself, but the advice was unnecessary; the casual way Zachary strolled into the office, both hands deep in his pockets and a file wedged under his left arm, told him that peace had been declared.

"You read those reports yet, Tom?" Zachary asked, as though there had never been a difference of opinion.

"Yeah. They were very interesting." McNulty tried to sound equally casual. "You've got to hand it to Jessop, he did a great job."

"Maybe you should tell him so, Tom."

"That would seem kind of patronizing, wouldn't it?"

"Depends on how you put it." Zachary moved toward the

window and stood there, gazing into the far distance. "I know I can rely on you to be diplomatic."

"Sure you can."

McNulty wondered why he wanted him to give Jessop a pat on the back. Had Jessop sensed that he'd disliked him on sight? Winter had guessed as much when he'd mentioned his name last night, but that could just be Charles stirring the pot.

"James is one hell of a fisherman, Tom. He's got a lot of patience." Zachary rocked backward and forward on his heels, still facing the window. "I guess that's why he managed to hook Korznikov."

"But only after he'd moved upstream to New York. Whose idea was that, Zach? I mean, why transfer him before the fish took the bait?"

"There's no mystery, Tom. Everything was looking good up to mid-October sixty-one, then Korznikov's eagerness began to wane and we got the impression he was having second thoughts. Jessop suggested that in view of this, we should post him elsewhere and put in a new man. He thought there was a chance it would prod Korznikov into making up his mind one way or the other. We knew a Soviet trade delegation was scheduled to visit Washington and New York the following September, because State told us that Vasili was making all the necessary arrangements. That clinched the argument as far as the director was concerned and we found a niche for Jessop at Zenith."

"And hit the jackpot."

"Right." Zachary turned away from the window, removed the file from under his arm, and placed it in the in tray. "If you're through reading those case notes, Tom, you might like to cast your eye over this telex we've received from Shackley in Miami. Eight of our Cuban exiles made a commando raid last night, hoping to blow up the cable car system in Pinar del Rio. They were spotted by a militia patrol before they could lay their charges, and there was a fire fight. Two of our guys are missing, the others made it back to the beach."

"You think Castro's people were tipped off?"

"No." Zachary shook his head. "No, they would have ambushed them as they came ashore if there'd been a leak. Castro has mobilized his forces because he expects us to invade Cuba, and our guys simply ran out of luck. That's the bottom line as I see it."

"And?" McNulty prompted.

"Well, I'm just wondering if we shouldn't impose a temporary embargo on all these commando raids. Bobby Kennedy won't like the idea, but we both know an amphibious landing is one of the contingency plans the Joint Chiefs of Staff are considering and there's no point in alerting Castro."

"That makes sense to me."

"The attorney general may take some convincing." Zachary ambled over to the door, then glanced back over his shoulder and smiled. "You're pretty good at expressing yourself on paper, Tom," he said. "Think you could knock out a memorandum to Kennedy?"

"Give me an hour and it'll be ready for your signature."

"Good. Just be sure you don't pull any punches," Zachary said, and closed the door behind him.

McNulty reached for the file lying in his in tray and flipped it open. Tucked inside was another, much slimmer folder from the Personnel Department which contained a summary of James Jessop's career and his annual assessments from 1952 onward. If he hadn't known Zachary better, McNulty would have said it was an error, that the two files had become intermingled because Zachary had started to read Jessop's record of service while the other folder was still lying open on his desk. But he was sure that wasn't the way it had happened; Zachary was getting devious in his old age and had wanted him to see the file, because it contained something which was beginning to make him feel a little uneasy. Convinced his assumption was correct, McNulty started to go through the confidential dossier on Jessop, making notes as he went along.

Lunch had consisted of fruit juice, a huge T-bone steak, French fries, and a green side salad, followed by apple pie and ice cream and two large cups of coffee. Too much to eat, too little exercise, that was the American way of life, Korznikov thought, and it was small wonder so many of them become obese when they reached middle age. James Jessop was still in his early forties, with the body of an athlete, but give him a few more weeks cooped up in this isolated house and even he would start to go the way of the shorthand writer, a short tubby man with thinning hair and an asthmatic wheeze. How anybody could hope to keep in trim by taking a ten-minute stroll around the grounds after such a lunch was beyond his understanding. In the circumstances, Korznikov thought it was a good thing he was blessed with a frugal appetite and had the strength of will to resist temptation.

Jessop flashed him one of his brilliant smiles. "Okay, Vasili," he said, "let's talk some more about Khrushchev."

Korznikov stifled a sigh. They had talked about no one else all morning, and there was little more he could tell Jessop about the man. They had discussed his standing in the party, and his friends and potential enemies. They had dwelt at length on his private life, his drinking habits, his womanizing, and the dachas he was reputed to own at Kiev and in Yalta on the Black Sea, as well as the fine country house off the Rublevskoye Highway outside Moscow, but apparently there was no satisfying the Americans.

"I'm ready when you are, James," he said politely.

"Great." Jessop pulled out a chair and sat down, facing him across the table. "A purely hypothetical question," he said. "Who in your opinion is most likely to replace Nikita? Mikoyan or Brezhnev?"

"I've already told you, Nikita Khrushchev is secure, his enemies are weak and divided among themselves. Besides, they would need to have the army on their side, and Khrushchev has the generals in his pocket; his promotion list on the ninth of May 1961 saw to that. Those three hundred and seventy-two generals he plucked from obscurity overnight owe him everything and they are not likely to forget it. The marshals who might have rallied the army against him have gone: Zhukov has been sacked, Koniev and Sokolovsky retired. There's no one left."

"Do you mind taking it a little slower, Vasili?" Jessop pointed to the shorthand writer punching away at his machine in the far corner of the room. "Max is having a hard time keeping up with you."

"I'm sorry." Korznikov glanced over his shoulder. "My apologies," he added, then turned to face Jessop again. "Marshal Bulganin is a prestigious figure whose face is well-known; as one of the Old Guard who survived Stalin and his successors, he's respected by the people and commands a good deal of support in the Politburo. Unfortunately, he's not liked by the officer corps, so you can forget him."

"Suppose we got tough with Khrushchev over Cuba and he was forced to back down? Wouldn't those self-same generals lose confidence in him?"

"They might. However, it would be more realistic to look to the Central Committee of the Communist Party; they would certainly be howling for somebody's head. Anastas Mikoyan would be my first choice to replace Khrushchev in those circumstances. Mikoyan is an astute politician, calm, intelligent, and flexible, but he's a sick man and I doubt if he will run for the leadership.

"Which leaves us with Leonid Brezhnev."

"Yes." Korznikov paused. The interrogation had reached a critical point and he needed to have his wits about him. The room was undoubtedly wired, and somewhere in the house, his every word was being recorded. During the next few days, those tapes would be played over and over again and his voice analyzed by experts. It was essential to strike exactly the right attitude; if he sounded too glib or too confident, the Americans might suspect that he'd been primed and was repeating everything parrot fashion.

"I believe you served together during the war?" Jessop said quietly.

"In the same sense that millions of Americans served with

162

General Eisenhower. Brezhnev held the rank of colonel and commanded the political section attached to the Eighteenth Army, while I was a junior lieutenant in the NKVD security battalion. I met him twice: once at army headquarters in October 1943, and again during the Crimean campaign, when we were trying to break out from the narrow bridgehead we'd established at Kerch. I doubt we exchanged more than a dozen words all told."

"You got to know him better after the war." Jessop made it sound more like a statement of fact than a question.

"Through my wife," Korznikov said, responding to the cue. "She was elected to the Supreme Soviet in 1950, the same year Leonid Brezhnev was chosen to represent the Lenin District of Dnepropetrovsk."

"Why the grimace, Vasili? Don't you like him?"

Korznikov blinked. Was there also a hidden camera somewhere behind Jessop? If so, it wasn't only his tone of voice he would need to watch. "I was thinking of my wife, Olga," he said, recovering quickly.

"It's a bit late in the day to be having second thoughts about her, isn't it, Vasili?"

Jessop was going off at a tangent, but he knew there was a purpose to the sudden diversion. A defector who left his wife and children behind in the Soviet Union was always suspect and it was necessary to clear the air once and for all.

"I've no regrets about leaving Olga. She is a very ambitious woman and we ceased living together as man and wife long before I was sent to London."

The enforced celibacy hadn't bothered him. Olga came from peasant stock, and although she had not been unattractive when he'd married her, she had allowed her figure to go to pot after the birth of their second child in 1951, and one look at her coarse features and lumpy body was enough to cool the ardor of a rampant stallion. It had even put Beria off in the end, and that was saying something, because the KGB chief had been noted for his distinctly odd sexual tastes.

"Fainna is Beria's daughter, not mine."

163

"I bet you found that hard to stomach."

"I learned to live with it." Korznikov shrugged. "I had no desire to end up in one of those slave-labor camps in the Gulag Archipelago and, distasteful as it may seem to you, certain advantages sprang from their relationship. It's unlikely Olga would have been elected to the Supreme Soviet if she hadn't been sleeping with Beria, and their long-standing affair obviously furthered my career."

"And damn near put an end to it when Beria was executed?" Jessop suggested.

"I had no reason to suppose so at the time. I wasn't the only officer who was promoted to major when Beria was in power, there were thousands of others. Men like Bulganin and Malenkov remembered how the show trials of 1937 had almost destroyed the Red Army as an effective fighting machine after fifty percent of the officer corps had been liquidated, and I knew there would not be another purge like that."

"What about Olga? Surely she must have been in jeopardy?" Korznikov recognized the question for what it was, another cue. "Olga's no fool," he said. "With her peasant cunning, she sensed Beria wouldn't be long for this world when Stalin died, and made sure she was on the winning side. I've even heard it said that it was she who'd assured Beria that his fears were groundless, and then persuaded him to leave the safety of his headquarters in Dzerzhinsky Square and make that short, fateful journey to the Kremlin."

"Are you telling us that everything was sweetness and light from then on?" Jessop asked.

"I stayed with the First Chief Directorate and was promoted to full colonel, if that's what you mean."

"That was in 1954, before you were posted to the Soviet Embassy in London. Right?"

"Yes."

"And just under two years later you recruited George Deakin, the crowning achievement of your career."

"Yes." Korznikov projected a note of weariness into his voice.

"Your star was in the ascendancy, but then you threw it all away. Why?"

Korznikov had lost count of the number of times he had answered that question, but clearly there were some people at Langley who still weren't satisfied with his explanation. He wondered if Jessop was equally annoyed by their skepticism.

"What's the matter, Vasili? Why don't you answer my question?"

Korznikov pushed a hand through his graying hair. "Because I was just thinking that it's impossible for you Americans to understand the corruption and rank hypocrisy which exists in the circles I moved in. You are right to say that recruiting Deakin was the crowning achievement of my career, and there were grounds for believing it had been recognized as such when I was recalled to Moscow in July 1959. Everybody wanted to shake my hand, a prestigious appointment with the Foreign Ministry awaited me, and Khrushchev made me a Hero of the Soviet Union, though for reasons of security, the citation never appeared in *Pravda*. I was also given to understand that accelerated promotion to the rank of major general would follow in due course, but nothing ever came of it."

"They passed you over?"

"Twice," Korznikov said vehemently. "When my name did not appear in the 1960 list, I was informed that I was to be posted as trade counselor to the Soviet Embassy in Washington, and that my promotion to major general would be suitably backdated when I took up the appointment in October. When my name was omitted again the following May, I demanded an explanation in writing. One month later, the Embassy security officer took me aside and explained why I had been blacklisted and would remain a colonel until the day I retired."

"This is the first time we've heard about a blacklist, Vasili." Jessop stared at him, eyes narrowing thoughtfully. "How come you never mentioned it before?"

"I was accused of moral turpitude. Do you think that is something to boast about?" Korznikov goaded himself into a fury,

165

knowing that only a convincing display of anger would impress the Americans. "There was this secretary who worked for me in Moscow—Lydia Fedorovna Golkin. She was young, attractive, and very friendly, but had I been aware she was sleeping with Viktor Krasin, I would never have invited her into my bed."

"Who's Viktor Krasin?"

"A professor of law at Moscow University." Korznikov raised his right hand and crossed two fingers. "He and the present chairman of the KGB are like that—bosom friends. That's why I was posted to Washington and put on the blacklist. The rest you know."

"I guess we do." There was a long pause, then Jessop said, "About Brezhnev—is he another hard-liner like Khrushchev?"

It was, Korznikov thought, a moment to be savored. Jessop had decided his story was no longer open to doubt and he would never again be called up to answer those skeptics at Langley who questioned his motives. Masking his elation behind an air of indifference, he told his interrogator why he thought it would be in America's interest to throw Khrushchev a lifeline, then answered every question that came his way with equal conviction. Three hours later, with the evening shadows stealing across the room, Jessop finally called it a day.

Winter answered the phone, read out the number on the dial, and then heard a loud clacking noise in his ear followed by a high-pitched warble. A two-hour delay on the transatlantic submarine cable had already detained him long after the resident SIS officer and the diplomatic staff had left the Embassy on Massachusetts Avenue, and now, just when the call he'd been expecting from London had finally come through, it seemed there were a bunch of bloody gremlins on the line. Venting his spleen on the receiver, he slammed it down on the cradle; moments later, the phone rang again and Diana Franklin came through loud and clear.

"That's better," she said, her voice sounding as though they were in the same room. "We were cut off."

"So I gathered," Winter lied. "Let's hope we can finish our conversation this time. How did you make out with the people at the Trans-Globe Travel Agency?"

"They've booked me on a Pan Am flight to New York departing from Heathrow at 2315 hours tonight, our time. It was the best they could do at short notice, and that was entirely due to a last-minute cancellation. They couldn't get me a seat on a plane to Washington for love or money. Apparently, every flight is booked solid with Americans wanting to return home; the agency thought the situation in Cuba was to blame."

"I daresay they're right. What time do you expect to arrive in Washington?"

"Nine-thirty tomorrow morning. My plane arrives at Idlewild around midnight your time, and I've got six hours to kill before the train leaves from Penn Station."

"Book yourself into a hotel and stay the night in New York," Winter told her. "There's a train every hour to Washington."

"I think I'll take your advice. Do you have any idea where the Ambassador Hotel is in Washington?"

"It's on K Street, three blocks northeast of the White House." Winter paused to listen to some faint clicks on the line, then said guardedly, "I bumped into Tom McNulty the other day and told him you were coming over. He asked to be remembered and hinted he'd like to hear from you."

"Did he now?"

Winter thought Diana sounded cool, and got the impression that the idea of acting as a go-between didn't exactly appeal to her. He wondered in passing if Burman had tried to warn her off. "Why don't you give him a ring after you've settled in? You can reach him any time after seven P.M. on 555-6001."

"What was that number again?" Diana asked, her voice still offhand.

"555-6001. You'd better make a note of it."

"I already have," she said.

"Good." Winter cleared his throat. "I hope you have a safe journey," he said, and put the phone down.

15.

The conversation between Ainsworth and Deakin ended abruptly and the tape ran silent, except for a slight hissing noise as it transferred from one spool to the other. Burman stopped the machine, rewound the tape to its original starting point, then switched off the Grundig and removed the headphones.

"Well?" Ainsworth looked up from doing *The Times* crossword. "What do you think?"

"It's pretty obvious, isn't it?" Burman said. "The tape is a record of two entirely separate conversations you had with George on the subject of radar. For some reason you had them spliced together without a noticeable break."

"Go on."

"In the first conversation, Deakin was anxious to know how much he could tell his Russian case officer about the type of radar installation the Americans were positioning at Laconbury. It's apparent he'd been asked a number of specific questions and felt he was being tested. If that assumption is correct, then I figure your conversation with George must have taken place shortly after he was recruited by the KGB."

"You're right about it being a test, but your deduction is

hopelessly inaccurate." Ainsworth reached for his pipe and filled it from the round tin of tobacco he'd left on the table. "That conversation actually took place on Wednesday the twenty-second of July 1959, a few weeks after Anatole Gorsky had taken over from Korznikov. I imagine Gorsky was instructed to run another check on him to see if he was still a reliable source of information. The KGB do that sort of thing from time to time."

"I know. That's something I learned in basic training."

"Oh, did you?" Ainsworth struck a match and lit his pipe, drawing on it contentedly. "Care to put a date on the second part then?"

"You were talking about the Iranian military procurement program and how you might hoodwink the opposition."

"So?"

"So the operation was still in the planning stage and there's no record of it being put into effect. That means your discussion must have occurred just over three months ago, some time toward the end of June."

"Any other conclusions?"

Ainsworth was like a preparatory schoolmaster questioning his pupil to see if he really understood a passage in Virgil he'd just translated from the Latin. The impression was reinforced by the way his tufted eyebrows arched into his forehead.

Burman smiled and said, "Deakin seemed enthusiastic about the project, but he sounded a cautionary note. There was to be no attempt to deceive the Soviets about the type of sophisticated radar equipment the Iranian air force could expect to receive from the Americans. They already knew too much about Parrot." Burman frowned. "Whatever that might be," he added.

"Parrot is the code name for a complex electronic machine which can identify friend from foe. When a plane is picked up on the radar, the pilot is requested to squawk on one of three selected channels and a series of lines appear on the screen against the image of the aircraft. Should the pilot not comply with the request, he is of course automatically regarded as hostile."

"You learn something every day," Burman said dryly. "Who's this 'Alec' Deakin referred to?"

"You're anglicizing the name. If you listen to the tape again, I think you'll find the last syllable is *ik*." Ainsworth smiled, his manner condescending. "As you might suppose, Alik is the source of their information."

"That thought had occurred to me, Henry."

The bushy eyebrows signaled Ainsworth's mild astonishment as he stood up and moved around the table to switch on the Grundig. Selecting the appropriate button, he wound the tape forward, stopping and starting the machine until he found the fragment of conversation he wanted. Then he switched to broadcast, turned the volume all the way up, and depressed the play button. Deakin's voice boomed through the speaker and said, "I have a feeling that one of these days, Alik will stop our American friends dead in their tracks."

"For Christ's sake." Burman reached out and turned the volume down. "What are you trying to do? Rupture my eardrums?"

"That wasn't the object of the exercise. I just wanted you to hear the intonation of his voice."

"My ears are still ringing."

"Sorry." Ainsworth switched off the recorder. "But surely you noticed how pleased George sounded? I thought he was almost smacking his lips with pleasure."

"Because of what Alik might do to the Americans?"

"Precisely. Remember those theses he wrote on destabilization?"

"I'm not likely to forget them in a hurry," Burman said.

"Yes. Well, I think George had reason to believe that Alik is the cataclysm who's going to make it all happen. That's why we've got to identify him."

"How?"

"It shouldn't be too difficult," Ainsworth said airily. "The equipment Deakin referred to is designed and manufactured in the United States. Therefore our defector is almost certainly an American, and a highly skilled radar technician who may have served with either a USAF or Marine Corps air-control unit."

"Or he could have been in the RAF, the Luftwaffe, the Armée de l'Air, the Dutch air force, the Belgian, Danish, Greek, Norwegian, Turkish, or whoever else was supplied with that type of equipment."

"You're making difficulties."

"No, I'm not," Burman said patiently. "I'm merely pointing out that we're faced with a number of possibilities. You're also assuming that Alik is a defector, but for all we know, he or she may still be amongst us."

"She?"

"I don't see why Alik can't be a woman." Burman shrugged. "Still, we've got to start somewhere, so I'll check the international card index and list every radar technician who's skipped behind the Iron Curtain. Then you'll have to decide which one is Alik."

"We," Ainsworth corrected him. "We'll have to decide."

"You'll have to manage on your own, Henry. This is my last day in the office."

"What?"

"Didn't Edmunds tell you? I'm off to New York first thing tomorrow morning. Seems I'm to approach Washington by the back door."

"First Winter, then Mrs. Franklin, and now you." Ainsworth snorted. "What am I supposed to do while you're all away?"

"You could try doing some of the work for a change," Burman said.

"Tom." Lois called to him through the kitchen window, her voice razor-edged. "The phone."

McNulty propped the garden rake against the fence and

171

turned about. "Any idea who it is?" he asked as casually as he knew how.

"Some woman with a fancy English accent. She said her name was Diana Franklin."

"So what's eating you? You know she's Winter's PA."

"Yeah? Well, she sounds a darn sight too sexy to me for anyone's secretary." Lois glared at him, then slammed the window shut, rattling the glass in the frame.

McNulty sighed. Lois was a terrific woman, but if he lived to be a hundred, he would never understand the convoluted machinations that occasionally went on in her head. He had told her that Winter had arranged for his PA to get in touch with him on a purely business matter, but the way Lois was acting, you'd think he was having an affair with the woman. Still pondering on the injustice of it all, he walked around the side of the house and let himself into the kitchen, to find Lois stirring a pan which was gently simmering on the stove.

"That smells good." McNulty came up behind and peered over her shoulder. "What are we having? Spaghetti Bolognese?"

"Yes."

"My favorite," he said.

"Is that a fact." Lois sniffed. "Better not keep your girl friend waiting, she might get impatient and hang up on you."

"I keep telling you, this is business." McNulty moved sideways and picked up the phone on the countertop.

"I'd sooner you took it in the den, Tom."

"Why? I've got nothing to hide."

"I don't like eavesdropping on private conversations. Anyway, I'm busy preparing dinner and I don't want you getting in my way."

There was, he knew, no arguing with Lois when she was in a contrary mood. Leaving the extension off the hook, McNulty went into the den and snatched the receiver out of the cradle.

"Yes?" His voice was sharp and drew a startled gasp from Diana Franklin.

172

"I haven't called at an inconvenient moment, have I?" she asked.

"No," McNulty said, and winced as he heard Lois slam the phone down in the kitchen. "No, I was just sweeping up the leaves in the backyard."

"Only Charles did say it would be all right to call you any time after seven P.M."

"Sure." He thought Winter had a nerve. It simply didn't occur to him that he might have something better to do than hang around the house every night waiting for a phone call. "When did you get into town, Diana?" he asked.

"Early this afternoon," she told him. "I'm staying at the Ambassador Hotel, Room 426."

"Fine," he said. "I'll come by as soon as I can."

McNulty said goodbye and put the phone down, wondering how he was going to explain the situation to Lois. In her present mood, he was tempted to skip it tonight and call on Diana Franklin tomorrow, but, on reflection, he decided that would only make his wife even more suspicious. Before or after dinner then? It would take him less than twenty minutes to brief Winter's PA, and they usually dined at eight, a habit they'd acquired from the British during the nine years they'd lived in London. Glancing at his wristwatch, McNulty saw that it was only five past seven and calculated he could just about do it in the time available.

Never one to leave anything to chance, he opened the liquor cabinet and fixed Lois a very dry martini, lacing the vermouth with a generous measure of Gordon's gin, in the hope that a good stiff drink might mellow her a little. Then he went into the kitchen to explain why he had to go into town.

Samarin thought there was no point in hanging on. More than an hour had passed since McNulty had parked the Lincoln convertible in the driveway, and with a bonfire smoldering in the backyard, the American wasn't likely to be going anywhere tonight. He was also beginning to feel a mite conspicuous. Q Street was a residential area and even though the girl sitting beside him in the Chevrolet was supposed to be his date for the evening, there was a limit to the amount of time they could spend parked by the curbside without drawing attention to themselves.

The surveillance plan left a lot to be desired, which was hardly surprising, considering how rapidly it had been put into effect. This time yesterday, he had been in New York, sitting at his desk in the Soviet Consulate, censoring the outgoing mail; then just as he was about to leave the office and retire to his room on the seventh floor, a phone call from the Embassy had brought him posthaste to Washington.

Samarin could understand why he had been summoned from New York. Apart from the fact that he'd played a leading role in Korznikov's defection, his face wasn't known in Washington, but all the same, with so much at stake, he thought the resident KGB officer should have waited until one of his "illegals" had bugged McNulty's house and attached a homing device to the Lincoln convertible. First thing tomorrow, he would make it his business to see that was done; then they would be able to keep the American under surveillance with minimum risk to themselves.

"Look." The girl sitting next to him nudged his elbow and pointed to the clapboard house twenty yards down and across the street from where they were parked. "Look, he's on the move."

It was something of an understatement. The Lincoln convertible skidded in reverse out of the driveway, the steering wheel locked hard over to the right, and braked to a halt. Then, shifting into forward drive, McNulty put his foot down on the accelerator and took off, the rear tires screaming on the road surface until they got a firm grip.

"He seems to be in a hurry," Samarin observed calmly.

He switched on the ignition, cranked the engine, and, shifting into gear, pulled out from the curb. He was some two hundred yards behind the Lincoln when it reached the T junction at the top of the street and turned right.

"He's heading south on Wisconsin Avenue," the girl told him.

Samarin grunted an acknowledgment, waited for a break in the oncoming traffic, and then made the turn. The convertible was now too far ahead for his liking and, putting his foot down, he overtook a station wagon and a delivery truck to close the gap between them. A few minutes later, McNulty turned left and drove east on Route 29, before branching off into Pennsylvania Avenue. At Washington Circle, he changed direction again and headed south toward the Lincoln Memorial, his speed fluctuating from twenty to thirty-five miles an hour.

"He's checking to see if he's being followed," Samarin said, voicing his thoughts aloud.

"Do you think he's spotted us?"

"I doubt it."

"Even so, we mustn't take any chances." The girl leaned forward and peered through the windshield. "That's the State Department up ahead," she said. "You'd better turn left just beyond it."

Samarin flicked the traffic indicator and eased out on to the crown of the road. "I hope you know what you're doing," he said.

"Stop worrying. There's only one direction he can go now and that's east on Constitution Avenue. We'll stay parallel with him as far as the National Academy of Sciences, and then cut down Twenty-first Street to come in behind him again."

Her directions were crystal clear, but she talked him through the diversion, her right hand shooting out like a traffic signal when she wanted him to turn right. When they swung into Constitution Avenue, there was no sign of the Lincoln convertible and for a while, Samarin thought the American had eluded them and was heading north on one of the side roads. Then, shortly after passing the Washington Monument, he spotted him again and the girl sighed with relief.

"There's always one bad moment," Samarin told her.

McNulty turned left into Fourteenth Street, crossed Pennsylvania Avenue, and continued on north over New York Avenue. Two blocks farther on, he turned into Franklin Square and found a parking space opposite the Franklin Park Hotel. Samarin continued on north, turned right at the next intersection, and pulled into the curb.

"This is where we start walking," he said. "You'd better double back to the crossroads and I'll cover the northeast side of the square."

"What about the hotel back there?"

"Forget the Franklin, that's just a blind." Samarin glanced into the side mirror, saw the road was clear, and, unlatching the door, scrambled out of the Chevrolet.

McNulty left Franklin Square, walked up to K Street, and made his way toward the Ambassador Hotel. He'd told Lois he would be back inside of an hour, but the roundabout route had added a good ten minutes onto the journey and it was a little optimistic to think he could brief Diana Franklin in under half an hour. The diversion had been a complete waste of time; he hadn't spotted anyone on his tail, but of course his mind had been elsewhere, dwelling on the difference of opinion he'd had with Lois. The truth was, he'd merely gone through the motions of observing a procedure which had become second nature over the years, and that was plain stupid because it had served no useful purpose.

The doorman at the Ambassador Hotel cast a disapproving eye over his windbreaker, but McNulty ignored the implied criticism and strode through the lobby. Three hotel guests were still checking in at Reception when he joined them at the counter, and it was several minutes before one of the desk clerks apologized for keeping him waiting and then asked if he could be of any assistance. By the time the desk clerk had phoned Diana Franklin in Room 426 and relayed her message inviting him to come on up, the number of people clustered around the desk had been swollen by the arrival of a honeymoon couple and a young woman in a dark-brown suit and shapeless felt hat.

Backing out of the throng, McNulty moved to his right and tagged on to the small crowd filing into one of the elevators. The young woman in the brown suit followed him into the cage, squeezing past the attendant as he was about to close the gate. An anonymous voice at the back remarked that he now knew what it was like to be a sardine and drew a faint ripple of laughter, then the cable jerked and the car began to move upward.

There were no takers for the first and second floors, and only a bellhop and a middle-aged business executive got out at the third. Two very old ladies, an Air Force sergeant, McNulty, and the dowdy young woman alighted at the fourth. Room 426 was directly opposite the elevator and the other hotel guests were still ambling along the corridor, when Diana Franklin opened the door to him.

Room 426 was larger than he'd expected and was furnished with a divan bed, a chest of drawers, a dressing table and stool, two easy chairs, a small writing desk, and a low occasional table. A fitted wardrobe with sliding doors took up the whole of one wall and a full-length mirror disguised the entrance to the bathroom. A twenty-one-inch television set mounted on a chromium pedestal faced the single bed.

"Can I offer you a drink?" Diana asked him.

"Another time." McNulty smiled apologetically. "I don't mean to sound unfriendly, but I promised Lois I'd be home by eight."

"Yes, of course. I quite understand."

She was very polite; the cool reserve of the English, McNulty thought. Reaching inside his jacket, he took out an envelope and placed it on the occasional table.

"I don't know how much Winter has told you," he said, "but this envelope contains some notes I made concerning James Jessop. It's all background stuff, like an entry for *Who's Who*—date and place of birth, education, his wartime career in the navy—that kind of thing."

"I see." Her eyebrows met in a brief frown as though she didn't understand what all the fuss was about.

"The rest is up here," McNulty said, tapping his forehead. "You can get your memo pad out, but don't take anything down unless I say so."

He expected questions, but none came. With a barely perceptible shrug, Diana opened her handbag, took out a small notebook and a gold pencil, and sat down in one of the easy chairs.

"I'm ready when you are," she said quietly.

"Okay." McNulty pushed a hand through his wiry hair. "The story goes like this. Jessop was a freshman at Princeton when the Japs bombed Pearl Harbor. The following April he enlisted in the navy, completed his basic training as a seaman, and went on to become an officer, one of the ninety-day wonders we were busily churning out. When he returned from the Pacific Theater of Operations to be mustered out of the navy in October forty-six, he stayed on in California and enrolled at Stanford to complete his education under the GI Bill of Rights."

Jessop had opted for business studies, majoring in English, but halfway through the course he had dropped commerce in favor of learning Russian. After graduating from Stanford in the summer of 1949, he had taken an administrative job with Standard Oil of California, only to find himself back in uniform again on the outbreak of the Korean War less than a year later.

"Jessop had made the mistake of joining the U.S. Navy Reserve," McNulty continued. "Anyway, somebody in the Department of Defense must have thought his Russian would come in handy, because he was assigned to Naval Intelligence and ended up behind a desk in the Pentagon. It wasn't a top-grade appointment, and but for Senator McCarthy, he would never have come to our attention. The senator from Wisconsin was turning this town into a three-ring circus then with his Senate subcommittee. The longer the witch hunt for Communists went on, the wider McCarthy cast his net, until the time came when nobody was safe. I guess some of the hysteria finally rubbed off on Jessop."

In the spring of 1951, Jessop had approached his commanding officer to seek his advice on a matter of national security. He had been concerned to know what he should do about a man called Steven Yarrow, who'd been a lecturer in the English Department when he was at Stanford.

"Yarrow ran one of the drama groups on the campus, and it was a well-known fact among the students that any pretty but untalented girl who appeared in one of his productions had only gotten the part because she'd auditioned for it in bed. The one exception was a singularly determined young woman whose radical views had earned her the nickname of Red Rosa. Jessop told his CO that this girl had Yarrow wrapped around her little finger and that within a very short space of time, he had swung around to her way of thinking. His political conversion was regarded as something of a joke at the time, and Jessop said he'd only raised the matter now because he'd just heard from a friend in California that Yarrow had changed occupations and gotten himself a job with the Internal Revenue Service. The navy referred Jessop to the FBI, and they subsequently discovered that Yarrow was a member of the Communist party. As a result, Yarrow was fired by the IRS and one of our talent spotters in the Pentagon suggested the agency might consider employing Jessop when he left the service, which we did."

"I don't think I like your Mr. Jessop," Diana said.

"A lot of people would say he was only doing his duty."

"Is that your opinion, too?"

"No. I think the way he joined the CIA could be the kind of gray area Winter had in mind." McNulty pointed to her small notebook. "You'd better make a note of this address." He waited for Diana Franklin to adjust the lead in the gold pencil, then said, "As of now, Mrs. Carole Jessop is residing at 631 Chadwick Road, White Plains, New York."

"I don't understand." Diana looked up, frowning. "Why should Charles be interested in knowing her address?"

"Because I think he'll arrange for Burman to call on her," said McNulty. "That's how I would set out to spook Jessop."

Samarin glimpsed the girl in the felt hat in the rearview mirror and leaned across to open the far door as she came toward the Chevrolet. Ducking her head, she got in beside him and slammed the door.

"Well?" he grunted. "How did you make out back there in the hotel?"

"McNulty called on a Mrs. Diana Franklin in Room 426. She's a dark-haired woman, English I think, judging by her accent."

"You followed McNulty up to her room?"

The girl nodded. "You needn't worry, he didn't suspect anything. The elevator was crowded."

"You're sure her name is Diana Franklin?" Samarin asked.

"Yes. Do you know her?"

"In a manner of speaking. She happens to be the personal assistant of Charles Winter." Samarin switched on the ignition and started up. "That's one of the items of information about the British SIS we got from Comrade Korznikov."

16.

Burman paid off the cab at the corner of Sixtieth and Fifth, then walked down the avenue toward Grand Army Plaza before crossing the road at the next set of traffic lights to enter Central Park. Branching off to his left, he followed a footpath which led him to the bridge at the north end of the pond, where he found Winter leaning against the guardrail, staring at some ducks perched on a rock above the murky water.

"Unsightly, isn't it?" Winter said. "You'd think they'd remove the litter once in a while."

Burman eyed the rusting beer cans, empty Coke bottles, and crumpled cigarette packs that had been tossed over the railing into the bushes. "The ducks don't seem to mind."

"They're probably used to it." Winter straightened up and moved away, drawing Burman with him. "Are they looking after you at the British Consulate?" he asked.

"I've been getting the four-star treatment."

"Good. I presume you got my little parcel?"

"It was waiting for me when I arrived on Saturday evening." The little parcel had consisted of a brief letter attached to some notes on the career of James Jessop, and a copy of the official *History of the British Pacific Fleet 1944–1945,* which Burman assumed Winter had borrowed from the naval attaché at the Embassy in Washington. "Reading the book helped to pass the time over the weekend," he added.

"I'm sure it did."

Burman waited, hoping for an explanation. When it didn't materialize, he gave Winter a gentle prod. "I see Jessop served in the Pacific, but what's he got to do with the Royal Navy? There has to be a connection somewhere, but right now, I don't understand why you wanted me to read those passages you marked in the official history."

"Jessop is very much an unknown quantity as far as we're concerned; when it comes to Korznikov, I'm not sure who has who under his thumb."

They walked on toward the Heckscher playground, Winter silent and seemingly brooding on his own private thoughts. Away over on Central Park West, a prowl car headed uptown, its siren warbling on two nerve-jangling notes.

"About Korznikov," Burman said tentatively. "Ainsworth's working on a new line of investigation. He believes Deakin was killed because he knew too much about a radar technician called Alik."

"Yes, I know. I received a long telex from him the day you left London." Winter smiled. "What's your candid opinion, Richard? Do you think Henry is on to something or is he just chasing rainbows?"

"It seems a pretty long shot to me." Burman shrugged. "I pulled him some names from the international card index—a cipher expert, a radar mechanic, and a couple of U.S. Army sergeants who'd served in the Counterintelligence Corps and who might have had access to the kind of information Alik supplied to the KGB, but I don't see how Henry is going to identify him. All we've got to go on is Deakin's hunch that Alik has a nasty surprise in store for our friends. Still, you never know, he might come up with something we could trade for the right to interrogate Korznikov."

"There was a time when I'd have given my right arm to do that, but not any more." Winter shot him a sidelong glance. "Does that surprise you?"

"I'm lost for words," Burman said.

"Yes, I imagine you would be, after all the work you've put in. It's just that the more I learn about the manner of his defection, the more I'm convinced Korznikov is a plant. That is why I want to discredit him."

"I doubt if the CIA will thank you. No one likes to be told they've made fools of themselves, even if it happens to be true."

"I'm sure you're right, but we're on the brink of war, Richard, and I can't sit back and do nothing."

Looking around, Burman found it hard to believe Winter's assertion. The two young mothers watching their children bumping up and down on the seesaw didn't appear to be preoccupied with thoughts of a possible war. Nor did the woman exercising her Great Dane or the couple walking hand in hand across the grass beyond the playground. But the threat of a head-on collision between the two superpowers was there all right. According to Winter's information, the First Armored Division had left Fort Hood in Texas for the East Coast to prepare for a possible invasion of Cuba, and would be joined by four more army divisions. The Strategic Air Command had also been placed at Defense Condition Two, which meant that every unit was fully mobilized for war, ready to go at a moment's notice.

"Kennedy has despatched Dean Acheson as a special envoy to brief Macmillan and De Gaulle." Winter pursed his lips. "The president's anxious there should be no dissenting voices from America's allies when he goes on television to announce that the U.S. Navy will be blockading Cuba effective Wednesday the twenty-fourth of October."

"A naval blockade," Burman mused.

"Quarantine is the word he'll use," said Winter, "but it amounts to the same thing, and the risks are just as great. Nobody knows whether the Russians will allow their merchantmen to be stopped and searched, and even if they do, there's no guarantee they'll take the hint and remove their missiles from Cuba."

"Where are the nearest Soviet vessels now?"

"The *Gagarin* and the *Komiles* will enter the quarantine zone two hours after the blockade has been officially imposed."

"The next few days are going to be very interesting," Burman said quietly.

"Yes, the president is bound to be inundated with advice from all quarters. My one aim is to make sure Korznikov doesn't get in on the act."

"How?"

"By attacking Jessop."

In Winter's view, it was a matter of simple logic. Jessop was the supreme manipulator; from the moment Korznikov had defected, he had taken steps to ensure the Russian was not exposed to a hostile interrogation. Excluding the SIS would have been a relatively easy task to accomplish; although unaware that Deakin had been a double agent, Jessop had only to imply that British intelligence was not entirely reliable, for people like Melvin Zachary to use it as an excuse to settle old scores. Admittedly, McNulty was more difficult to neutralize; as the man who knew Korznikov's background better than anybody at Langley, it was obvious that the agency would recall him from London. The trick therefore lay in persuading his superiors that McNulty should be employed as an adviser rather than as an active member of the interrogation team.

"I imagine he convinced Zachary that Tom McNulty was too pro-British and was likely to insist the SIS be given equal access to Korznikov." Winter changed direction again, leaving the footpath to head across the grass toward Central Park West. "There are two alternatives," he continued. "Either Jessop is a very ambitious man, who sees Korznikov as his personal stepladder to the top and is determined nobody else should get a chance at him, or else he's bent."

"I think I can guess what's coming," Burman said. "You want me to apply a little psychological pressure in order to see which way he'll jump?"

"How very perceptive of you."

"Not really. I knew you hadn't sent me all that reading material for nothing."

"Right. You're going to need every bit of that information when you call on Carole Jessop this afternoon."

" 'We've never met, but I know your husband from way back.' Is that the general idea?"

"Almost," said Winter. "Your elder brother met Jessop when his ship was attached to Admiral Halsey's Third Fleet. He also met him again when he was attending a postgraduate course at Stanford in 1948, and suggested you look Jessop up while you were in the States on business. Embroider the story as much as you like, but make sure you tell her that your brother was somewhat amused when he heard James had accused Steven Yarrow of being a Communist. Leave her with the impression your brother also thought they were two of a kind, politically speaking."

"And then what?"

"You drive down to Washington, check in at a motel, and telephone Mrs. Franklin to let her know you're in town. She's staying at the Ambassador Hotel, Room 426."

"Diana is a sort of cutout, is she?"

"Diana?" Winter glanced at him quizzically, one eyebrow raised. "I hadn't realized you were on such friendly terms with my PA."

"You're ducking the question," Burman told him.

"Mrs. Franklin is the link between you and Tom McNulty. Naturally, I shall be hovering somewhere in the background."

"Naturally."

"Two other small points," Winter said crisply. "First, it's possible the consulate will offer to lend you one of their chauffeur-driven limousines when you call on Carole Jessop this afternoon. If they should do so, thank them very politely, but don't take them up on it. Get a car from a rental agency, it'll be less conspicuous. And secondly, we'll have to change your surname." He smiled fleetingly. "How does McNulty strike you?"

"That should put the cat among the pigeons." Burman hesitated, then said, "I hope Diana's going to be all right. I mean, she's not likely to find herself in the firing line if the shit starts flying, is she?"

"Give me credit for some sense, Richard. I can't afford to lose Mrs. Franklin, she's far too valuable."

"That's a comforting thought."

"I thought it would be. Do you have any other questions before we go our separate ways?"

"Only one," said Burman. "Suppose Mrs. Jessop isn't at home this afternoon . . ."

"She will be," Winter said, cutting him short. "Read the notes again. The Jessops have two little girls in the second and third grades."

Burman watched him walk away, then turned about and strode off in the opposite direction. When he looked back, Winter was standing by the transverse road, waiting for a cab in the passing traffic.

Chadwick Road, White Plains, was a secluded tree-lined avenue, the kind of up-market real estate development depicted by Hollywood as typical of suburban life in America. The Jessops owned a split-level house fronting a large, neatly trimmed lawn which sloped gently to meet the road. Beneath the picture windows of the rooms on either side of the porch, standard fuchsias in garden tubs were still in bloom, and a tangled forest of geraniums spilled over the narrow flower bed onto a strip of crazy paving that started near the front door and wandered around to the back of the house. One of the up-and-over doors of the adjoining double garage was in the raised position, and Burman could see a Volkswagen parked in the left-hand bay. Conscious that he was being watched from one of the rooms

186

downstairs, he collected the gift-wrapped packages lying on the seat beside him, got out of the Chrysler, and walked up the drive. The woman who opened the door for him was younger than he'd expected; her light-brown hair was in a bouffant style, and she wore a pair of bright-red toreador pants and a black turtleneck.

"Mrs. Jessop?" Burman said politely. "My name's Richard McNulty. I phoned you about half an hour back to say I would be passing through White Plains on my way to Danbury."

"You surely did and I'm pleased to meet you, very pleased." She smiled and pumped his free hand. "My name's Carole, okay?"

Burman nodded and handed over the gift-wrapped packages. "This is just a little something," he murmured. "A box of candy for each of the children and some perfume for you."

"Ah now, Richard, you shouldn't have done that."

She thanked him again, several times over and very effusively, then showed him into a spacious living room that resembled a showroom for Ideal Homes. The Indian rug was hardly worn, the three-piece suite looked brand-new, and the mahogany occasional table had been French-polished until you could see your face in it. A log fire had been laid in the grate, but the pristine state of the hearth suggested that this particular room was rarely used by the Jessops. It also occurred to Burman that they couldn't have done much entertaining at home during the eleven months they'd been living in White Plains.

"Would you like a cup of coffee, Richard?" She waved a hand toward the tray on the occasional table. "Or perhaps you'd prefer something stronger? Scotch, bourbon, a dry martini?"

"Coffee is fine." Burman smiled. "I make it a rule never to have a drink before sundown."

"How about a beer?" Two small frown lines appeared above the bridge of her nose. "I think there are a couple of cans in the fridge."

"A cup of coffee is just what I need," he said firmly.

"Well, if you're really sure." The slim hand waved again,

directing him toward an armchair. "So your brother, David, is a friend of Jimbo's?"

"Jimbo?"

"A family nickname." Carole poured the coffee and handed him a cup. "But of course your brother wouldn't know that. Do help yourself to cream and sugar."

Burman stirred his coffee and sipped it thoughtfully. His phone call had taken Carole Jessop by surprise, but she'd recovered now and had had time to reflect on what he'd told her. Although outwardly pleasant, it was obvious she viewed his story with considerable suspicion.

"No." Burman frowned and shook his head. "No, I can't recall David ever mentioning that nickname to me. My brother was the air-strike liaison officer on board the carrier *Indefatigable* and he met James when his ship was attached to Task Force 38 in July 1945. James held a similar appointment in the United States Navy and was serving on the *Shangri La*, Vice Admiral McCain's flagship. They were seated next to one another when the admiral held a planning conference before the air strikes on Kure, Tokyo, and Yokosuka."

"That's really fascinating." The bright accompanying smile was intended to show that she really meant it, but Burman thought there was a noticeable edge to her voice.

"Didn't you say they met again when Jimbo was at Stanford?"

"That's right. David joined British Petroleum when he came out of the navy and they sent him on a postgraduate course. He'd read mathematics at Cambridge before the war, and they thought a year on management and business studies would give him a greater perspective."

Burman knew he was on relatively safe ground. Jessop hadn't met his wife until 1952, and as long as he stuck to generalities, Carole was unlikely to trip him up. The background notes Winter had supplied were short on raw material, but he embellished Jessop's prowess on the tennis court, making him seem a potential champion. He was, however, sparing with names, saving the one he did have until she began to throw a few at him.

"Herbie Klingman?" Burman shook his head. "That name doesn't ring a bell with me. The only fellow I remember David talking about was Steven Yarrow."

"Who?"

"Steven Yarrow. He was a lecturer in the English Department and ran one of the drama groups on the campus."

"Oh yes, I remember him now." The smile was there again, but it was definitely uneasy and her eyes looked wary.

"I believe Yarrow found himself in hot water when he left the university for a job with the Internal Revenue Service. Didn't your husband have to appear before some congressional subcommittee?"

"Yes." Carole avoided his gaze and cleared her throat nervously. "Yarrow was a member of the Communist party," she said faintly. "Jimbo was subpoenaed to appear before Senator McCarthy and had to testify against him."

"That must have been very embarrasssing for your husband."

"Jimbo said it was the worst thing that ever happened to him."

"I bet it was." Burman leaned forward and placed his empty cup on the table. "According to David, your husband was pretty much of a radical when he knew him, always on about civil rights and how government and big business exploited the blacks."

"That doesn't sound at all like Jimbo," Carole said, frowning.

"People change."

"I suppose they do . . ." Her voice trailed away and she craned her head to one side, listening to the distant sound of a musical jingle. "That'll be the Good Humor man."

The raucous jingle grew louder, disturbing the quiet street. Glancing over his shoulder, Burman saw an ice-cream van drive slowly past the house.

"Your Good Humor Man doesn't appear to be doing much trade," he murmured.

"It's the wrong time of the day. He should have waited another half hour, until the kids were home from school." Carole eyed him thoughtfully, then said, "Are you related to Tom McNulty by any chance? He's one of Jimbo's business associates."

"Not as far as I know," Burman said. "There are a lot of McNultys in Ireland."

"You're Irish?"

"My grandfather came from County Meath to settle in England. My brother and I were born in Southampton."

The opening was there and she seized on it, plying him with questions about his background. Was he married, what line of business was he in, and what was he doing in the States? Burman fielded them effortlessly and turned the conversation around to her children, trotting out the names of both girls and when they were born, using every scrap of information he had with telling effect.

"You say your brother has been corresponding with Jimbo all these years?"

"Off and on."

"That's funny, I don't ever remember seeing a letter from England." Her teeth sought out her bottom lip and nibbled at it, a nervous habit that had become more and more frequent the longer they talked.

"I believe David always wrote to him care of his business address." Burman glanced at his wristwatch and feigned surprise. "How time flies," he said. "I really ought to be on my way. I have an appointment in Danbury at four-fifteen."

There was no audible sigh of relief from Carole Jessop, but the prompt way she stood up and steered him toward the hall was a sure sign that she would be glad to see the last of him.

"I'm sorry I didn't get a chance to meet your husband." Burman smiled. "Still, maybe I'll run into him when I'm in Washington next week."

"Where are you staying?"

The obligatory question, he thought, and moved out of her way so that she could step past him and open the door. "I'm not sure yet, but I'll phone you as soon as I know. Then perhaps James and I can get together."

190

Carole nodded, shook his hand, said how much she had enjoyed meeting him, and thanked him again for the presents. When Burman was halfway down the drive, she called after him to have a nice day and be sure to drive carefully. Then she went back inside the house and closed the door.

The bartender at Everard's Toll House on Route 29 was used to seeing Jessop on alternate nights of the week. Every Tuesday, Thursday, and Saturday he arrived at seven-fifteen on the dot, and ordered a large Scotch on the rocks as he strolled through the bar to call his wife from the phone booth opposite the hatcheck counter. Ten minutes or so later, he would return to the bar, drink his Scotch, and talk a little, mostly about what it was like to be in the U.S. Air Force these days and the problems he was having trying to persuade his wife to leave their house in upstate New York and move to a rented apartment near the base. Tonight was different though; tonight was Monday, it was six-thirty, and he walked straight through the dimly-lit bar, looking neither left nor right.

"Hey, sarge," the bartender called after him. "You want your usual?"

"What?" Jessop halted in his tracks and turned about.

"You forgot to order a Scotch on the rocks."

"So I did. Make it a triple tonight."

"Nothing wrong, is there?"

"Just a minor domestic problem." Jessop stretched his mouth in a tight smile. "There's always something with kids."

He went on through toward the restaurant, wheeled into the phone booth, and closed the door behind him. Feeding a coin into the slot, he dialed and waited. The number rang out just once before the receiver was snatched from the cradle. Carole must have been sitting by the phone waiting for him to call her, he thought.

"Hi," he said. "What's this message I got from Zach about Katie being sent home from school with the mumps?"

"That was just an excuse, the only one I could think of."

He heard Carole laugh, but there was no merriment in it,

and it was apparent that something was very wrong. "What's eating you, hon?" he asked softly.

"I had a surprise visitor from England this afternoon, a man called Richard McNulty. That's what's eating me."

"McNulty?" Jessop swallowed, his mouth suddenly dry. "Are you sure you got the name right?"

"Of course I did, I'm not stupid." Her voice cracked at him like a whip. "He said his brother, David, knew you from way back when you were serving on the *Shangri La*."

"I don't know any David McNulty."

"Don't lie to me, Jimbo. You've been writing to him secretly ever since the war."

"This is crazy," Jessop said, "absolutely crazy."

"I'm the one who's going crazy," Carole told him in a harsh voice. "This David McNulty was at Stanford when you were there, and knows just about everything there is to know about us—when we were married, the names of our two daughters, where and when they were born. He also knows about Steven Yarrow and how you were subpoenaed to testify before the Senate subcommittee."

"For Chrissake," Jessop exploded, "how many more times do I have to tell you that I've never heard of David McNulty?"

"A thousand times and I still won't believe you. I learned things from this Englishman I never knew before—the way you were always championing the underdog when you were at Stanford."

"So now I'm supposed to be a Communist—is that what you're implying?"

He was wrong; the mysterious stranger had done the insinuating, feeding Carole with half-truths until she didn't know fact from fiction. But it was important to make her believe the assumption was hers and that it was unjust.

"He said you were a radical, that's the same thing, isn't it?"

"It depends on how you slant it." Jessop found a handkerchief in one of his pockets and wiped his face. The booth was airless and he could feel the sweat oozing from every pore.

"Somebody's running a test on me," he said, blurting out his thoughts.

"What?"

"A security check." The suggestion sounded plausible, even to his ears, and he began to enlarge on it. "Don't you see, the goddamned agency is running one of their periodic security checks on us."

"Yes?" Her voice sounded doubtful and he could picture Carole chewing her bottom lip as she mulled it over. "I'd like to believe that, Jimbo, really I would, but how come they sent an Englishman to interview me?"

"He was probably faking the accent. What did he look like?"

The description came haltingly and he could tell from the catch in her voice that Carole was close to tears. He let her ramble on, his brain groping for a convincing explanation, while he listened to a long and involved account of the conversation she'd had with the stranger.

"You've just described Pearson," Jessop told her calmly. "He always did think of himself as an actor."

"Pearson?"

"Amos Pearson from Internal Security. I don't think you've met him."

He was very sure of himself now and the lies came smoothly. Feeding another coin into the slot, he went on talking, gradually easing her fears. Then, changing tack, he steered the conversation around to their daughters, and somehow he even contrived to make her laugh along the way.

"Are you feeling better now, hon?" he asked her presently.

"Much better."

"Good, that's my girl." Jessop wiped his face again and put the handkerchief away. "I'll call you again tomorrow, the usual time. Okay?"

"Yes."

"Meantime, give my love to the girls."

Jessop blew a kiss into the mouthpiece and put the phone down. Moments later, he picked it up again, fed yet another coin into the slot, dialed a number, and was connected to an answering machine. Waiting until the recorded voice had stopped talking, he said, "This is Bird Dog. We've got another intruder on the scene, an Englishman—six foot three, about one-eighty pounds, reddish-brown hair, in his early thirties, and passing himself off as Richard McNulty. He called on my wife this afternoon and from what he said to her, it's obvious he'd been primed by our mutual friend. I don't know what you're doing about the real McNulty, but I want him taken out of the game."

17.

The Rapid Domestic Plumbing Service operated out of a lockup shed on Seventh Street, a dead-end road off New York Avenue which backed on to a slip line belonging to the Baltimore and Ohio railroad. A one-man business, the Domestic Plumbing Service was owned by a Mr. Ralph Oster and controlled by the KGB resident officer at the Soviet Embassy. Armed with a spare key, Samarin arrived shortly after nine-thirty, parked the Ford sedan he'd rented that morning on the pavement alongside the shed, and let himself in through the back door.

The office was separated from the supplies by a hardboard partition, which left barely sufficient room for a worm-eaten table that looked as though it had been salvaged from a rubbish heap, and a battered filing cabinet. The old-fashioned portable typewriter was covered with ash, and there were cigarette burns along the entire length of the table facing the upright wooden chair. The only piece of office furniture which looked reasonably new was the answering machine connected to the telephone.

Samarin pulled out the chair, turned the greasy cushion on it upside down, then sat down at the table and switched on the answering machine. A woman living at 1122 Benning Road had called at five forty-five the previous evening, asking Oster to fix a leaky radiator, and another housewife in Orden Street wanted him to take a look at her dishwasher, which was acting up again. The third message on the tape was from a man calling himself Bird Dog who sounded very tense. Playing the track again before he wiped it clean, Samarin thought Bird Dog had every reason to be on tenterhooks.

Thomas McNulty, Diana Franklin; he wrote their names on a scrap of paper and linked them with an arrow. Then he drew two more arrows against Diana Franklin, one leading to Winter, the other to the mysterious Englishman who had called on Bird Dog's wife. The tape had confirmed what he'd suspected all along; McNulty was using the girl to pass on information to Winter and the newcomer who'd suddenly entered the scene. The clandestine setup was also further proof that the American was acting without the knowledge and consent of his superiors at Langley. Remove him and the girl, and the whole undercover operation would collapse like a house of cards.

How, where, and when? Those were the questions he would have to answer before they could be eliminated. Obviously it would have to be accomplished in such a way that neither the police, the FBI, nor any other agency would suspect the KGB had been involved. No problem there, Samarin thought; from what he'd read in the *Washington Post* or seen on TV, hardly a day went by without somebody being knifed, strangled, shot, or bludgeoned to death. Where and when depended on the victims themselves, and he would have to bide his time until they saw one another again. One thing was certain; he was sure it was McNulty's intention to choose a less conspicuous rendezvous than the Ambassador Hotel next time they met. Why else would Diana Franklin have rented a Dodge from Hertz on Saturday if that wasn't the case?

Samarin lit a cigarette. The surveillance plan was no longer the slipshod arrangement it had been five days ago, and he could afford to sit back and wait for something to happen.

McNulty's house on Q Street had been bugged, one of the KGB's illegals had fixed a homing device to his Lincoln convertible, and the Ambassador Hotel was being kept under observation. The Soviet Embassy knew where to reach him, and they'd get in touch the moment they had something for him.

Nothing to do and all day to do it in. Samarin reached inside his jacket, took out a street map, and slapped it down on the table. He could study that again, but after five days, he had it photographed in his mind and knew every street, every avenue. Frowning, he went over to the file cabinet, opened the top drawer, and found it contained a jar of instant coffee, an electric kettle, a can of evaporated milk, several plastic cups, and a dog-eared paperback. It seemed Ralph Oster had thought of everything, except sugar for the coffee.

Until McNulty moved in, the office had been occupied by the executive supervisor in charge of the typing pool on the seventh floor. In accordance with his status as deputy assistant director of operations, the room was still in the process of being refurbished to the appropriate scale, and the intercom was the most recent and unwelcome addition to the furniture. Before the night maintenance staff had installed it on Monday evening, Zachary had been obliged to walk down the corridor or use the phone whenever he wanted to talk to him; now all he had to do was depress the appropriate button on the squawk box to summon him to his office. Zachary had done so twice already: once, soon after he'd arrived, to update him on the Cuban situation, then again around eleven-thirty to receive a transcript of the latest interrogation which Jessop had conducted over the weekend. The sudden blowing noise in the speaker was, McNulty thought, a sure sign that he was about to call him for the third time in a row.

"Tom?" Zachary's voice boomed at him and made the amplifier vibrate.

"Yes, Zach?"

"You finished reading that transcript yet?"

"Almost," said McNulty. "I've just gotten back from lunch and opened the safe. Give me another ten minutes and I'll come and talk to you about it. Okay?"

"Sure," Zachary said. "Drop into my office any time you're ready."

McNulty said he'd do that, then opened the transcript on his desk to read the last few pages and the summary of conclusions Jessop had listed in the final paragraph. Not content with underlining each major point in red, McNulty also found that he'd had the Graphic Arts Department produce a template illustrating the maximum range of the SS4 missiles based at San Cristobal. Anyone looking at the curving line from New York which dissected Cincinnati, embraced Little Rock, Arkansas, and ran on down to Galveston on the Gulf of Mexico could see just how vulnerable the eastern seaboard had suddenly become. Depressed by the thought of what a twenty-kiloton nuclear warhead could do to places like Philadelphia, Baltimore, Washington, and Charleston, he picked up the transcript and left the office.

Three doors along the corridor, he found Zachary comfortably settled in his rocking chair, imitating his hero, Kennedy, while gazing at the Jackson Pollock original on the wall.

"Come on in and sit yourself down, Tom." Zachary waved a plump hand toward one of the armchairs grouped around the low marble-topped table. "You know something?" he said. "I still don't see what he's getting at."

"Who are we talking about?" McNulty asked. "Jackson Pollock or Korznikov?"

"I guess they're both a little obscure."

"Yeah? Well, one of them's definitely a faker."

"What are you suggesting, Tom? That we should dump the transcript in the shredder?"

"That's the best place for it."

"You're prejudiced." Zachary wagged a finger at him. "What Vasili had to say makes a lot of sense to me. Khrushchev has a twofold aim: he wants to achieve some sort of nuclear parity

198

and split NATO down the middle. And I think he's got an even chance. Why should we expect our allies to go to the brink with us just because those medium-range ballistic missiles in Cuba threaten our easternmost states? Hell, the British have lived for years with the knowledge that every one of their towns and cities is wide open to attack."

"Korznikov would have us believe that's a good argument for doing nothing."

"Balls. He never said anything of the kind."

"The implication's there in black and white." McNulty went through the transcript looking for the place he wanted, then placed the document on the table where Zachary could see it, his forefinger marking the appropriate paragraph. "Jessop asks him if the Soviets intend to supply Castro with nuclear warheads for the SS4 Sandal missiles and Korznikov says he doesn't know and starts talking about their use in a conventional role, which is pure, unadulterated crap. Can you see the Russians spending billions of roubles to install a battery of peashooters?"

Zachary shook his head. The Sandal was an improved version of the old German V2, with an inertial guidance system. Approximately seventy feet long, with a maximum diameter of five and a quarter feet, the liquid-fueled rocket could deliver two tons of high explosive over a range of eleven hundred miles, or so weapons experts at the Pentagon had calculated.

"Neither can I," said McNulty. "But, in a very roundabout way, Korznikov is urging us to adopt a policy of wait-and-see."

"Then his timing is lousy, Tom. He should have gotten the message across before we decided to blockade Cuba."

"I wonder? Suppose the Russians comply with the quarantine order, recall their dry cargo vessels which have military hardware on board, and allow us to stop and search the rest? We'd have made our point, but the missiles would still be in place. What do we do then? Bomb the sites and invade Cuba?"

"I doubt it." Zachary smiled lopsidedly. "We'd find ourselves out in the cold if we did. No friends, no allies."

"That's terrific. You've just repeated one of the points

Korznikov made. Of course, I realize Vasili is only telling us how he thinks the Kremlin played this particular war game before they tried it for real, but he's not above doing a little brainwashing on the side."

"You don't approve of the way Jessop is handling the debriefing?"

"I don't go for his soft approach," McNulty said bluntly. "He's allowing Korznikov to make all the running and decide just what information should come our way. I'd have said he was little more than our mouthpiece for Korznikov but for the template he attached to the end page. It's the only goddamned thing in the whole transcript which shows the other side of the coin."

"His soft approach usually pays off in the end," Zachary observed calmly. "Check the Baltic file, S-214, and you'll see what I mean."

"S-214?" McNulty repeated.

"That's the one. Jessop spent three years in West Germany with the Gehlen organization, from 1956 to 1959, and was in charge of the S-boat division, running agents into the Baltic states. The boats were supplied by the British and crewed by former officers and men of the German navy. One of Jessop's petty officers was a man called Fritz Briesemeier, whose ability to continually avoid detection by the Soviet patrol boats operating in the Gulf of Riga struck him as too good to be true. Jessop didn't believe anybody could be that lucky all the time, so he kept his ears and eyes open, and strung Briesemeier along until he'd acquired enough circumstantial evidence to indicate the German was playing for the other side. Then he pounced, grilled Briesemeier unmercifully, and finally cracked him, to bust wide open the biggest Soviet espionage ring operating in the Federal Republic. The trail even led to Lieutenant Commander Horst Heinz Ludwig, who was attached to the Royal Navy station at Lossiemouth in Scotland."

"That's interesting."

"Very interesting," said Zachary. "You should read the file sometime."

Like now, McNulty thought. Jessop was a high-flier destined for the top and Zachary didn't trust him, but was too unsure of his own position in the agency to do anything about it, and needed a surrogate to pull the rug from under Jessop. That was the message behind the bland invitation. "Do you want me for anything else, Zach?" he asked.

"I don't think so."

McNulty nodded, got up, and moved toward the door.

"One other thing," Zachary called after him. "What do you suggest we do with this transcript?"

"File it," said McNulty. "Don't show the damn thing to anybody. The best advice we can give the president is to urge him to release the aerial photographs of those missile sites at San Cristobal. That way we beat the Russians to the punch and convince our allies we're not just flexing our muscles for the sake of appearances."

"Great minds think alike." Zachary grinned. "That's exactly the same advice I got from Jessop when he called me before lunch."

McNulty walked out into the corridor and made his way to the elevators near the staircase. A feeling that he was on the wrong track and was about to make a fool of himself was dispelled when he strolled into the Central Registry on the second floor and discovered the chief archivist had already been warned to dig out the Baltic file. Signing the receipt docket, he returned to his office on the seventh floor, fully expecting it would take him the rest of the afternoon to wade through the bulky folder. Zachary, however, had made things easy for him; clipped to the back of the cover was a typewritten note which told him exactly where to find the relevant material on Horst Ludwig and Fritz Briesemeier.

Horst Heinz Ludwig had begun his military career as a young conscript in Hitler's Wehrmacht toward the end of World War II. Following his release from an American POW camp, he'd returned to his parents' home in the Soviet Zone and enrolled as an engineering student at Jena University. In 1951, he'd fled to West Germany and got himself a job with the

American-controlled labor unit employed on minesweeping in the port of Bremerhaven, where he'd met and made friends with Fritz Briesemeier. Four years later, Ludwig had joined the newly formed Bundeswehr and, after being commissioned, had been trained as a pilot at the U.S. Air Force base at Pensacola, Florida. Although seriously injured when he'd attempted to land his plane on the deck of an aircraft carrier, Ludwig had made a full recovery and had been transferred to the naval air arm on his return to West Germany. Rapidly promoted to the equivalent rank of lieutenant commander, he had been sent to Lossiemouth in the early summer of 1958 to train on the de Havilland Sea Vixen and the Supermarine Scimitar, a brand-new all-weather fighter which was then still on the secret list. At his subsequent trial, an officer from Gehlen's organization told the court that Ludwig had built up an amazing mosaic of British air and sea dispositions in NATO.

While Jessop had not been called to give evidence against Fritz Briesemeier, Gehlen had written a letter to his old friend, Allen Dulles, describing in some detail the major role he'd played in the successful counterespionage operation. Given that glowing testimonial, McNulty could see why Jessop had been earmarked for stardom. The only question mark against a seemingly brilliant achievement was the fact that Jessop had only started to interrogate Briesemeier after he'd learned the S-boat division was to be disbanded. He wondered if it was just a co-incidence, then smiled, knowing Winter certainly wouldn't think so.

McNulty glanced at the phone. Contacting Diana Franklin from the agency was asking for trouble, but there was no harm in warning Lois he would be working late. Lifting the receiver, he dialed his home in Georgetown and got her on the line.

Twenty-nine laps; Korznikov closed his left hand, leaving only the thumb extended. One more to go and then Jessop would turn about and they would walk round and round the timber frame house in the middle of the copse, until they had completed thirty laps in an anticlockwise direction. Over the weeks, the morning and afternoon exercise periods had become a mindless routine as soul-destroying as a treadmill. Usually, he could rely on Jessop to break the monotony, but for once the American was strangely subdued.

"You're very quiet this afternoon," Korznikov observed, breaking the long silence between them.

"What's the point of talking?" Jessop said tersely. "We're not making any progress."

"Oh? I thought I'd answered all your questions to the best of my ability."

"I know some people who don't think so. They say you haven't told us a damn thing we couldn't have gotten from the State Department or the newspapers."

"Can I help it if my assessment of the Cuban situation does not meet with their approval? I can only tell you what I know."

"And that's not an awful lot, is it?"

"I'm sorry you're disappointed, James," Korznikov said acidly. "Unfortunately, Chairman Khrushchev did not confide in me. He did not take me on one side and say, Now see here, Vasili, our five-year plan is coming to grief, which means I've got to do something spectacular, otherwise I'll be out on my ear. That's why I intend giving that bearded wonder in Cuba a few missiles to play with, knowing the Americans will get all steamed up about it. There's nothing like an international crisis to distract the proletariat and keep the Council of Ministers in line."

"Cut it out, Vasili, I'm not in the mood for jokes."

Jessop glared at him, then turned about and strode off in the opposite direction, leaving Korznikov to follow suit. The guard with the Remington pump-action shotgun stepped off the path they'd worn in the long grass and allowed them to pass, before tagging on behind, a good ten yeards to their rear.

"I gather I'm in your bad books," Korznikov murmured.

"It's not me you have to worry about, it's my superiors." Jessop stooped, picked up a stick lying in the grass, and hurled it high into the air. "They don't think you're worth a plugged nickel."

"A plugged nickel?" He shook his head. "I'm not sure I understand the meaning of that expression, James."

"It means you're worthless. In their opinion, you're just one big pain in the ass."

The honeymoon was over. Somebody had told Jessop it was time he toook the gloves off and leaned on him. There was nothing unusual about that; it had happened sometime during the course of every interrogation Korznikov had sat in on back in Moscow, but he thought the American could have chosen a more opportune moment. In his shoes, he would have waited until they were back inside the house in the room wired for sound and in front of the hidden camera.

"I don't see what your superiors are complaining about," Korznikov said mildly. "After all, I must have betrayed at least twenty high-ranking intelligence officers, five of whom are still at our Embasssy in Washington."

"Oh sure, and how long do you suppose they will remain there? Another month or two and they'll be recalled to Moscow. Meantime they'll close down whatever operations they're running and adopt a low profile."

"Five out, five in; the FBI should be able to identify their replacements, James."

"Bullshit." Jessop rounded on him, his face white with anger. "It won't happen that way and you fucking know it. Your people will reshuffle the deck; chauffeurs, filing clerks, typists, information officers—you name them, they'll all be going home for one reason or another. A year from now, we'll have twenty or more new faces to deal with."

"There's no pleasing you, is there?" Korznikov said plaintively.

"You're not even trying.'"

"I gave you Deakin."

"Big deal." Jessop snorted derisively. "He's dead."

"What?"

"He was drowned on Saturday the eighth of September, the day you came across."

Korznikov stared at the ground in front of his feet, his mouth suddenly bone-dry. Could it have been an accident? The manner and timing of the Englishman's death suggested otherwise, but on the other hand, he couldn't think of a single reason why the KGB should have considered it necesssary to eliminate him. Moscow had given him the green light to blow Deakin in order to establish his credentials with the CIA, and they had also told him they expected the British to expel Gorsky once the facts became known. The situation hadn't changed since his briefing. Or had it? What if something had gone wrong and Moscow had been forced to take urgent remedial action? The possibility didn't bear thinking about, and it was no use asking Jessop; the American knew only what he'd told him about the setup.

"Have you ever thought what would happen to you if we sent you back, Vasili?"

Korznikov looked up slowly. "Is that meant to be a joke?" he asked in a hollow voice.

"If it is, the laugh's on you." Jessop glanced over his shoulder at the guard trailing on behind, then lowered his voice. "Right now, you're bottom of the popularity poll, but you can change all that."

"How?"

"By giving me something my superiors can get their teeth into. What we need is a name, a really big one that will make them sit up and take notice."

Korznikov smiled. "I can give them yours," he said.

"Jesus Christ." Jessop looked over his shoulder again. "That's not even halfway funny."

"Really?" Korznikov clucked his tongue. "I thought you said I had a terrific sense of humor."

205

18.

McNulty returned the Baltic file to the clerk on duty in the Central Registry, then went on down to the ground floor, where the security guard in the main hall checked his ID and noted the time of his departure in the log. Zachary and the other department heads on the seventh floor had left some time ago, and the Lincoln convertible was now the only vehicle in the small executive parking lot outside the main entrance to the building. Opening the offside door, McNulty got in behind the wheel and inserted the key in the ignition. He glanced into the rearview mirror, saw the security guard reach for the telephone, and watched him dial out. Forewarned is forearmed, he thought, and started the engine. Then, shifting into gear, he drove out of the parking lot, turned right, and headed toward the exit for State Highway 193.

His ID and time of departure were checked and logged again at the gatehouse a mile back from the main road. Although this was standard procedure, McNulty couldn't recall a previous occasion when anybody had bothered to compare the license plates on the Lincoln with the vehicle register before raising the barrier, and he wondered if there was an ulterior motive. The way Zachary was acting lately, it was just conceivable that good old Melvin had arranged for him to be kept under surveillance. With several exits to cover, the prolonged security check at the gatehouse could have been a delaying tactic to enable a shadow vehicle to move into position.

McNulty reached the highway, turned left, and headed north on 193. Maybe he was being paranoiac, or was he? What if Zach were gunning for him and not Jessop? The quickest way to get rid of him was to prove that he was passing information to the British. No problem there, he thought; a few infra-red camera shots showing him in conversation with Diana Franklin and the agency would have all the evidence they needed.

Idiot, he told himself, you're not thinking straight. If Zachary was trying to set him up, the chief archivist and at least one other person were involved in the conspiracy. The note telling him where to look in the Baltic file for the material on Briese-meier and Ludwig was unsigned, but somebody had typed it out. The more people there were involved in the conspiracy, the greater the risk of it falling apart. Zachary would know that, would also know it was possible to identify which typewriter had been used. Okay then, he'd been right the first time; Zachary was simply using him as a surrogate to undermine Jessop. All the same, he couldn't afford to take any chances.

McNulty glanced into the rearview mirror, saw the head-lights of another vehicle a hundred yards or so behind him, and eased his foot up off the accelerator. The headlights grew larger, then dipped, seconds before the Porsche pulled out and overtook him. Two miles farther on, he turned off Route 193 on to the Capital Beltway and crossed the Potomac into Mary-land. Still wary of being followed, he continued to dawdle along at a steady twenty-five miles an hour and was overtaken by everything on the road. Shortly after passing under Bradley Boulevard, he pulled into a filling station and told the attend-ant to fill the tank and check the oil while he made a phone call.

There were three other vehicles in the service area, a Volks-wagen, a '59 Dodge Custom Royal with raised tailfins and organ-stop rear lights, and a Pontiac coupe. When McNulty left the phone booth, the Volks and the Pontiac had gone, their places taken by a Chrysler 300c, a customized Ford Mercury, and a gray van.

The phone rang twice, stopped, then rang again exactly thirty seconds later. Recognizing the coded signal, Samarin laid his paperback aside, disconnected the answering machine, and lifted the receiver.

The caller had a hoarse voice which sounded as though he had a throat infection. He said, "Our friend left the office at six forty-five and drove north as far as the interchange on the Capitol Beltway. He then pulled into a filling station the other side of the Potomac and made another phone call."

"Another phone call?" Samarin queried.

"He rang his wife just after four to tell her he'd be working late."

"What about the Franklin woman?" Samarin asked.

"She went to the Smithsonian Institution this morning, but hasn't left the hotel since then."

Samarin told the caller to hold on and cupped a hand over the mouthpiece. He thought it likely McNulty had rung the Englishwoman and arranged to meet her somewhere out of town, but there was another posssibility. It could be that McNulty suspected he was being followed and the diversion was simply a blind. Either way, the surveillance team had made an error. The transmissions from the homing device attached to McNulty's automobile could be monitored from a distance of two miles, but the gray van must have followed him into the filling station to know he'd stopped to make a phone call.

"Forget our American friend," Samarin said. "Get in touch with the van and tell them to back off. We'll concentrate on the Franklin woman instead; she's not in the same league as her contact. If we play this right, there's every chance she'll lead us straight to him without knowing it."

"Right."

"Meantime, I'll drive into town. Call me on the two-way radio the moment she leaves the Ambassador Hotel."

Samarin put the phone down and reconnected the answering machine. A methodical man, he returned the paperback to the file cabinet, folded the street map and slipped it inside his jacket, and burned the diagram which showed Diana Franklin as the connecting link between McNulty, Winter, and the mysterious Englishman. Then he switched off the light and left the office, locking the door behind him.

Burman punched the buttons, tried all eleven TV stations one after the other, then came back to Channel 5 and a repeated episode of *I Love Lucy*, before switching the set off to silence Lucille Ball in mid-sentence. He had checked into the Travelodge Motel on New York Avenue late on Monday evening and phoned the Ambassador Hotel to let Diana Franklin know he was in town. Since then, he'd read everything at hand, from the *Washington Post* to *Life* magazine, and worn the pile off the carpet pacing up and down the room. He'd also chain-smoked his way through a pack and a half of Lucky Strikes, which was a retrograde step for someone who had supposedly kicked the habit.

For the umpteenth time that day, Burman wondered how much longer he would have to stay cooped up in the motel room waiting for something to happen, wondered too who would be the first to make the next move. Winter, McNulty, or Jessop? Winter could hover in the background and pull all the strings he liked, but unless McNulty produced some really incriminating evidence for him, there was nothing more he could do. In the end, everything depended on Jessop, and the way he reacted to the news that a total stranger from England had called on his wife. The American would certainly be perturbed by the knowledge that a man he'd never heard of knew so much about his personal life, and it would soon dawn on him that the stranger must have obtained his home address from somebody at the agency. Jessop was also intelligent enough to guess who was behind it. If Winter had gotten it wrong, Jessop would probably report the incident to his superiors, which would do McNulty no good at all. On the other hand, it could be a very different story if the American had anything to hide and felt he had to do something about the potential threat to himself before the situation got out of hand.

A loud trilling noise interrupted Burman's train of thought and he got up from the chair to answer the phone on the bedside table. Lifting the receiver, he heard the switchboard operator say, "One moment, please," and then Diana Franklin came through on the line to tell him McNulty had been in touch.

"When did this happen?" he asked.

"About five minutes ago. I'm to meet him in Rock Creek Park, one hundred yards north from the junction of Beach Drive and Wise Road."

"Why there?" Burman opened the drawer in the bedside table and removed the road map he'd gotten from a filling station on the way into Washington. "What's wrong with your hotel?"

"Nothing. He's just being cautious."

"So should we." Unfolding the map with his free hand, Burman spread it out on the bed. "Where exactly is Rock Creek Park?"

"You don't have to come with me. I can look after myself."

"I'm sure you can."

"Anyway, Charles said you weren't to approach our mutual friend."

"I don't intend to," Burman said patiently. "But I'd still like to find this place on the map."

"Oh, very well, it's near the Reed Army Medical Center on Route 29." There was a brief pause, then in an apologetic tone, Diana said, "Look, I'm sorry to rush you but time's running on and I've got to go. I'll call you again, soon as I return. Okay?"

Burman heard her put the phone down and slowly replaced the receiver. Locating Rock Creek Park on the map, he traced the highway south until it merged with New Hampshire

Avenue and Sixteenth Street, then turned the sheet over to look at the street plan on the reverse side. Scott Circle to Mount Vernon Place and on up New York Avenue to the Travelodge Motel, making a total distance of roughly eight miles in all. With the rush hour over, it should take him less than twenty-five minutes to reach the rendezvous McNulty had chosen. Folding the map, he stuffed it into his jacket pocket and left the room.

The Chrysler was parked on the gravel drive outside Reception; handing his key over to the desk clerk, Burman got into the car and drove up to the main road. He flicked the direction indicator down to show he intended to turn left into New York Avenue, glanced right, saw the road was clear, and started to move out.

A horn blared a warning, tires screamed on the road, and he shifted into reverse and stamped on the accelerator in a desperate bid to avoid the vehicle coming at him from the left. The oncoming headlights told Burman the other driver was swerving toward the crown of the road, and for a brief moment he thought they would manage to avoid a collision, but luck wasn't with him and the station wagon clipped his left fender. There was a loud crump, a grinding squeal of tortured metal, and the wheel shuddered in his grip as the impact shoved the Chrysler around to the right. The station wagon careered on, fishtailing from side to side, then came to a stop twenty yards up the road, its red brake lights still glowing angrily.

Burman scrambled out of the Chrysler and walked toward the stationary vehicle. The driver of the station wagon wasn't in an amiable mood and wanted to call the cops the moment Burman produced his passport and international driver's license. His temper didn't improve when he saw the insurance certificate and realized the Chrysler had been rented from an agency in New York. After a long and heated discussion, it transpired there was a clause in his policy which required him to pay the first hundred and fifty on any repair bill, and he didn't see why the hell he should be out of pocket. Anxious to get the matter settled and be on his way, Burman said he agreed with him and extracted two hundred dollars from his wallet, which almost cleaned him out. The American didn't want to take the extra fifty, but he pressed it on him, and after exchanging addresses, they parted almost on friendly terms.

It then took Burman another twenty minutes of tugging and heaving with a jack to separate the left fender from the front tire.

McNulty left the Capital Beltway at Interchange 21 and headed south on Georgia Avenue. Of the vehicles he'd observed back at the service area, the Custom Royal, the Chrysler 300c, and the customized Ford Mercury had all passed him long before the interchange, but he'd seen no sign of the gray van in the side mirrors. Tripping the right indicator, he pulled off the road on to the hard shoulder and stopped. The odometer showed he had covered 6.3 miles since leaving the filling station and he estimated his average speed had been around twenty-five miles an hour. Computing time, distance, and average speed, he decided fifteen minutes should about do it.

McNulty pushed the release catch, got out, walked around to the front, and raised the hood to its fullest extent. The cops were never around when you wanted them, but they had a nasty habit of materializing from nowhere when they were the last people you wanted to see. Questions and answers were part of their way of life and he thought it advisable to be ready for them. Now, if a patrol car should stop to inquire what he was doing there, he could tell them the engine had overheated.

As it happened, the precautionary measure proved unnecessary; the cops didn't come by, nor did the gray van. When the fifteen minutes was up, McNulty closed the hood, got back into the car, and drove on. Two hundred yards farther up the road, he forked right on to Route 410, then turned right into Wise Road and headed toward the rendezvous he'd arranged with Diana Franklin in Rock Creek Park.

* * *

Samarin relaxed and leaned back in the driver's seat. He had recognized the license plates on the sedan in front and knew the Franklin woman was therefore only a short distance ahead, heading north on Sixteenth Street in a Dodge Polara. His eyes still on the vehicle in front, Samarin took his right hand off the wheel, picked up the two-way radio which was lying on the seat beside him, and depressed the transmit button. Acting like a cab driver, he called up the despatcher and told him he had picked up his fare from 3225 Sixteenth Street and was proceeding to Silver Spring. The despatcher acknowledged and went off the air; two minutes later, the vehicle in front signaled it was turning off on to the slip road leading to Missouri Avenue. Keeping within the speed limit, Samarin gradually closed on the Dodge Polara, until the distance between them was down to fifty yards.

Sixteenth Street merged with Interstate 29 and a notice board by the roadside warned Samarin that he was approaching the Walter Reed Army Medical Center. As he drove past the hospital grounds, the right indicator on the Dodge started winking and, reacting swiftly, he eased his foot on the accelerator and gently applied the brakes, allowing the other vehicle to draw farther ahead. Branching off to the right, he followed Diana Franklin into Alaska Avenue where, after covering approximately a mile, she then turned left into a narrow side road leading to Rock Creek Park.

His quarry must be nearing the rendezvous McNulty had arranged with her. They were off the beaten track, driving west along a narrow, little-used country road, and there were dense-looking woods on either side. Looking about him, he knew it was the kind of place he would have chosen for a meet.

He came around a long looping bend, saw the Dodge was no longer in sight, and glanced anxiously left and right. For a few pulse-racing seconds, Samarin thought he'd lost the Franklin woman, then he spotted her tail lights up a track to his left, and guessed she was heading toward a picnic area in the woods. Continuing on past the track, he looked for another clearing where his car wouldn't be seen from the road, and found one just two hundred yards beyond the point where the Dodge had turned off.

He drove off the road into the woods, doused the headlights, and cut the ignition. Leaning across the seat, Samarin opened the glove compartment, took out a yellow handkerchief and a nine-cylinder .22 rim-fire Sentinel revolver, with a two-and-a-half inch barrel. He stuffed the handerchief into the left pocket of his jacket, the fifteen-ounce handgun into the other, then got out of the car and slowly closed the door, depressing the catch with his thumb to minimize the noise.

The Franklin woman was somewhere two hundred yards to his rear. Stealthily as a hunter closing in for the kill, he moved through the woods, his eyes downcast to avoid any dry twigs lying on the ground that might betray his presence if he stepped on them.

19.

Diana Franklin drove into the clearing, flashed the headlights twice, then made a ninety-degree turn and backed up toward the trees before switching everything off. Unfamiliar with the controls, she was still fumbling with the handbrake when McNulty appeared from the shadows and got in beside her.

"Hi," he said. "Having trouble?"

"A little," she confessed. "This car is twice the size of my Austin Healey and it's like driving a tank. You haven't been waiting long, have you?"

"I just got here," McNulty told her.

"That's a relief, I thought I was late. I don't suppose I did much above twenty all the way here."

"Yeah? Well, I doubt you'll be needing the Dodge again after tonight."

"Oh?" Diana glanced at McNulty, thought he looked tense and preoccupied.

"It's a crazy world," McNulty said slowly. "A few hours from now and this planet may cease to exist. By this time tomorrow morning, the first Soviet vessels will be nearing the quarantine line, and it won't do any good to hold your breath if

215

they don't stop. The lights are burning in the Pentagon and the White House, and the agency has been dealing out pink evacuation cards to the chosen few who've been selected to go to some underground bombproof refuge." He shook his head. "And here we are, you and I, sitting in the middle of a wood on a dark night because of something that happened years ago."

"I'm here because you phoned me," Diana reminded him gently.

"Yeah, that's right." McNulty leaned his left shoulder against the door and half-turned to face her. "Horst Heinz Ludwig," he said. "Does that name mean anything to you?"

"No, I've never heard of him."

"I'm pretty sure Winter has," McNulty said and began to explain the reason why.

Samarin froze. The Dodge Polara was about eighty feet away, directly in front and facing him. Studying the lie of the ground, he decided to move around to his left, where there was more cover, and approach the vehicle on the driver's side. That meant the Franklin woman would be between him and McNulty, but on the whole it was better that way. If he shot the American from the other side, she might just be sharp enough to drive off before he could nail her. He would have to keep well down, though, when he broke cover the far side of the sedan, otherwise they might catch a glimpse of him in either the rearview or the side mirror.

Samarin pulled the yellow handkerchief out of his left pocket, folded it in half diagonally, and tied it over his nose and mouth. Still watching the car, he reached for the Sentinel revolver in his other pocket, withdrew it slowly, and curled his finger around the trigger. Then he moved back deeper into the woods and headed toward the road, before crossing the track some distance below the clearing. Testing the ground before putting his full weight on it, he began to work his way back to the Dodge Polara. Halfway there, he heard the distant sound of a vehicle on the road behind him and stopped to listen intently until the noise was no longer audible. Then he moved on again, silent and purposeful.

Burman hit the brakes and skidded to a halt at the fork in the road. Beach Drive to the right, Wise Road straight on. Diana had told him McNulty had arranged to meet her one hundred yards north of the junction, but he hadn't seen either the Dodge or the Lincoln convertible since entering Rock Creek Park.

He switched on the courtesy light and studied the road map. North could mean one of two things, depending on which way you happened to approach the junction. If you were heading toward State Highway 29, the spot McNulty had in mind was beyond the fork, but if you were traveling in the opposite direction, the rendezvous had to be somewhere on the right-hand side of the road. It was also a fact the compass direction could apply either before or after reaching the junction, depending again on whether you were going east or west.

Burman wished to God he'd been more forceful and kept Diana on the phone until she had told him exactly how to find the RV. "I'm sorry to rush you, but time's running on and I've got to go." Diana's words, and in her haste she had given him imprecise instructions, that was the top and bottom of it. Should he go on or turn back? She had obviously turned off somewhere along the way, but there were no tracks marked on the small-scale map and he hadn't noticed any on his side of the road. In the circumstances, he thought it best to go on for another hundred yards, then, if he didn't find anything, he would turn round and search the woods on the opposite side. Throwing the map aside, Burman switched off the light and drove on.

Samarin crouched low and moved forward, legs bent like someone performing a Cossack dance. He could see their silhouettes in the rear window, McNulty on the right, the Franklin woman on the left, both of them too engrossed in their conversation to notice him. Crouching lower still to avoid showing himself in the side mirror, he crept down the driver's side of the sedan until he was within reach of the front door. Then he stood up, snatched the door open with his left hand, and covered them both with the revolver as the roof light came on to illuminate the interior.

Diana Franklin reared back, her mouth open and working to summon a scream. McNulty just stared at him, eyes taking in the improvised mask and the small revolver pointed towards his head.

"Jesus." McNulty smiled weakly and fluttered his hands. "I guess you want our money? Right?"

It was the last thing he said. Ice-cool and showing no emotion whatever, Samarin shot him between the eyes, into the gaping mouth and through the heart, the .22 rimfire pistol cracking like a tinder-dry branch each time he squeezed the trigger.

Diana heard herself cry out, then a thumb jabbed into her windpipe and the scream died in a gagging choke. The fingers of the same hand pressed against her cheek and forced her head around to the right to face McNulty.

"Look at him," a harsh voice commanded her. "Look at him and remember the same thing could happen to you."

Tom McNulty had fallen back in the seat, his head tilted up toward the roof. His light topcoat and jacket were unbuttoned and the whole of his shirtfront from necktie to waist was already stained with blood. Another trickle oozed from the neat round hole in his forehead and ran down his nose to the upper lip, where it divided to form a drooping moustache. Two front teeth were missing from the upper jaw and the open mouth was a bubbling red fountain.

"No more noise, not even a whisper. Understand?"

Diana nodded, felt the pressure ease on her windpipe and breathed in, retching as she did so.

"Now take off your coat and dress."

"What?" She looked up, mouth slack, eyes incredulous.

"You heard me," he said. "Take off your coat and dress. I want to see what you've got underneath."

218

Her hands shook, fumbled with the buttons of her navy coat, and slowly undid them one by one. Richard, Richard, Richard; his name was in her mind as she slipped her arms out of the sleeves. Then, Help me, help me, as she leaned forward, reached behind her back, and unzipped the dress to the waist. One shoulder bare, now the other, the straps of the nylon slip down to her elbows.

"Come on, come on, I haven't got all night."

Diana felt the bile rise in her throat when a hand grabbed her bra and jerked it up to free her breasts. Her flesh crawled at his touch, but she bit her bottom lip and suffered it in silence, letting him pinch the nipples, tweaking them painfully between forefinger and thumb until they were rigid stalks. Bastard, bastard, but the revolver was still pointed at her head and there was a dead man at her side.

"That's the style," he told her. "Why bother to resist? It won't do you any good."

His voice was flat and disinterested, and there was something very clinical about the way he reached down and peeled her skirt and slip up above her stockings. It was as if she were an inanimate object, like a tailor's dummy in a shop window. And suddenly it dawned on her that that was exactly how he saw her—a tailor's dummy to be arranged this way and that until he had achieved the desired effect. Then he would squeeze the trigger again, and hours, perhaps days later, some stranger would find her lying there with Tom McNulty, a married man and his girl friend, robbed and killed while they were busy petting.

The stage was set, so what was holding him back? The distant sound of a car back there on the road? Why should he worry, the driver had already gone past the track leading into the woods. Or had he? Diana turned her head, saw the twin beams veering toward them, and also noticed the gunman had stepped back a pace. Reacting instinctively, she reached out, grabbed the door and pulled it to, then threw herself sideways and rolled off the bench seat onto the floor. There was a numbing pain in her right hip which spread to her back; milliseconds later, she heard two loud cracks and realized the gunman had fired through the window, the bullets splintering the glass before they struck her.

The track jinked to the right and led to a small clearing in the forest. The headlights were on full beam and, fifty yards ahead, Burman saw a masked figure fire two shots into the stationary Dodge even as he pushed his foot down on the accelerator and sounded the horn, in a last-minute effort to distract him. In one fluid motion, the gunman switched targets, aimed his revolver at the Chrysler, and put two bullets through the windshield.

The zone-toughened glass exploded like a bomb to become a solid mass of opaque fragments. Burman swung the wheel hard over to the left to avoid ramming the Dodge, then, steering one-handed, he punched a hole in the windshield with a clenched fist. A tree loomed up in front of him and he swerved to the right, stamping on the brakes as he did so. A low branch caught the windshield, showering his lap with glass before it snapped off and gouged the bodywork all down the side, with a loud squealing noise that set his teeth on edge.

Making a U-turn, Burman came around the Dodge, his rear wheels sliding on the damp grass. The headlights picked up the gunman again, this time running hard for the belt of trees on the far side of the clearing, and accelerating rapidly, Burman aimed the Chrysler straight at him. Twenty yards out from the tree line, the gunman knew he wasn't going to make it and turned to face the oncoming vehicle. He fired just one more shot at Burman, then tried to jump clear, but he left it too late and the left fender caught him a glancing blow and hurled him out of the way.

Burman stamped on the brakes, tried to steer the Chrysler between what seemed a narrow gap in the trees, realized he wouldn't be able to squeeze past the oak directly ahead, and braced himself for the inevitable crash. Still traveling at fifteen miles an hour, he ploughed into the massive tree and was thrown forward over the steering wheel into the shattered windshield, the jagged edges lacerating his hands and face. The impact buckled the front end, springing the hood which reared up like a startled horse. Both headlights blew out, the coolant spewed from the fractured radiator, and the horn short-circuited to blare a strident requiem for several thousand dollars' worth of twisted machinery.

Burman collapsed back into the seat. His chest felt as though it had been caved in and he knew there was a minute particle of glass embedded in his left eye. For some moments he sat there nursing the damaged optic, then, as the shock began to wear off a little, he willed himself to ignore the intense pain and, reaching for the door handle with his right hand, opened it and got out. That much was easy, the rest wasn't. In his own mind, Burman knew what he had to do, but his legs weren't inclined to carry him toward the Dodge and threatened to give way with every step.

The horn's resounding blast dropped an octave and, above the noise, he heard the gunman grunting like a pig somewhere over to his right. Drawn to the sound, Burman found him lying on his back, one hand outstretched, scrabbling for the revolver lying in the grass. Just what he intended to do with the firearm when both his legs were broken was somewhat perplexing, but his fingers were only inches from the butt when Burman grabbed the revolver and shot him in the head. Still functioning like a robot, he dropped the pistol and moved on toward the Dodge. Any regrets he had about killing a man in cold blood vanished the instant he opened the door and saw the carnage inside.

One glance at McNulty told him there was nothing he could do for the American, but Diana was still alive, though her pulse beat was slow and very erratic. As gently as he could, Burman lifted her up off the floor onto the seat and wrapped the navy coat around her. Then, just in case she regained consciousness, he draped a handkerchief over McNulty's face and turned his head away from her. That done, Burman got in behind the wheel, slammed the door shut, and started the engine. Blind in one eye, he drove on down the track, taking it steadily until he reached the road, where he turned right and put his foot down. Two miles and three minutes later, he pulled up outside the guardhouse at the Walter Reed Medical Center.

From then on, the army took care of everything, one of the enlisted men directing him to the casualty department, while the sergeant phoned ahead to warn the hospital staff they had an emergency on their hands. There were other phone calls, to the provost marshal, the Washington Police Department, and the British Embassy on Massachusetts Avenue. A lieutenant from Homicide took a brief statement from Burman before a nurse gave him a pre-med, and one of the third secretaries from the Embassy showed up in a dinner jacket to tell him that Winter had been informed and was expected to arrive at any minute. Throughout it all, Burman never stopped asking after Diana Franklin, but nobody was saying much, and the last thing he remembered was being wheeled down a long corridor toward the operating theater, the lights in the ceiling merging to form a continuous train.

Zachary had been an elusive man to run down. Minutes after the resident clerk at the British Embassy had phoned him, Winter had called Langley, only to discover he'd left at five-thirty to attend a meeting at the State Department. From there he had traced Zachary to the Pentagon, then back across the Potomac River to the FBI building on Pennsylvania Avenue, where Hoover's secretary had informed him he'd just departed for the Justice Department before going on to the White House. At that point, a chauffeur-driven limousine from the Embassy had arrived to pick him up and Winter had left for the Walter Reed Medical Center. Two hours and several phone calls later, he eventually learned that Zachary had been to see Lois McNulty before returning to his home in Aurora Heights.

During the drive from the Walter Reed—across Dupont Circle, Washington Circle, over the Francis Scott Key Bridge, and on through Rosslyn and the Wilson Boulevard to the

Dutch Colonial house on Wayne Street—Winter had had plenty of time to consider how he ought to handle the situation. In the end though, everything depended on what sort of mood Zachary was in. Uncertain of what sort of reception awaited him, Winter got out of the car, walked up the front path, and rang the bell.

Zachary didn't keep him waiting; the prompt way he answered the door suggested he'd heard the limousine drive up to the house and had been watching him from one of the downstairs rooms.

"You've heard the news?" Winter said quietly.

"Yeah." Zachary gazed at him, eyes cold and unblinking like those of a dead fish. "I don't think we've got anything to say to one another except maybe goodbye."

"I disagree."

"That's your prerogative," Zachary told him and started to close the door, only to find that Winter had a foot in the jamb. "Jesus," he said wearily, "what does it take to get rid of you?"

"Five minutes of your time, Melvin. That's all I'm asking for."

Zachary looked down at the foot still wedged in the jamb, and after some thought, finally opened the door and showed him into a book-lined study off the hall. He did not offer Winter a drink, nor did he invite him to sit down, merely reminded him that he had just five minutes.

"I can understand how you feel about Tom McNulty," Winter said, choosing his words with care. "But in a way, we're both responsible for what happened tonight. The question is, are we going to let them get away with it?"

"I don't know what the hell you're talking about." Zachary jabbed a finger into his chest. "But I can tell you this, you're not going to come out of this business smelling like a rose if I can help it. Tom is dead because you filled his head with a load of shit about Korznikov, and the poor goddamned slob happened to be in the wrong place at the wrong time with the

223

wrong woman when some fucking pervert stole up on them."

Zachary was taking the easy way out. Somewhere along the line he had begun to suspect that Jessop was not all he seemed, but the younger man's star was in the ascendancy and he was on the way down, and frightened to admit that his protégé had pulled the wool over his eyes. So he'd used Tom McNulty as a sounding board and now, when everything had gone sour, he wanted to back off.

"That's the police version," Winter said coldly. "You and I know different. Tom was shot because he was close to upsetting the applecart."

"Now I've heard everything."

"We can prove it."

"Yeah? How?" Zachary demanded.

"Remember the intruder who broke into the Roosevelt Hospital? I think there's a chance the killer lying in the morgue on Georgia Avenue could be the same man."

"That's one hell of a long shot."

"It's still worth trying." Winter spread his hands. "What have you got to lose, Melvin? All it takes is a round trip to New York, and nobody's going to reproach you if the patrolmen who were on duty outside Korznikov's room that day don't recognize the killer's photograph. If anything, people will admire you for being thorough."

"I guess they might at that," Zachary said thoughtfully.

"You'll do it?"

"Well, like you said, what have I got to lose?"

"Good. When would you expect to know the answer?"

"Around noon tomorrow." Zachary ushered him out into the hall and opened the front door. "I'll call you at the Embassy soon as I hear from New York. Okay?"

"If I'm not there, they'll know where to find me."

"The Walter Reed?"

"Where else?" Winter said bitterly. Nodding a brief good-bye, he went on down the path toward the car, feeling cold and empty inside.

20.

Winter huddled inside his light topcoat. It was a dull afternoon, with a distinct chill in the air, and he had been sitting on a park bench near the zero milestone in the Ellipse for almost an hour. Apart from acquiring another layer of goose pimples, he thought it likely that if Zachary didn't show up in the next few minutes, the patrolman who'd been eyeing him suspiciously for some time now would eventually cross the road and ask him to move on. Determined not to be browbeaten, he met the patrolman's gaze unflinchingly, then slowly turned his head to the right, hoping to draw the officer's attention to the small group of demonstrators lining the railings outside the White House with their placards calling for "Peace Not War" and "Hands Off Cuba."

The ruse didn't work. When he looked back, the patrolman had already advanced to the curb, and was about to cross over when a large, black Ford sedan came between them, and an unseen hand unlatched the nearside rear door as it pulled up. The two men up front didn't look round. From the back, they appeared identical, broad-shouldered and muscular like athletes in the peak of condition.

"Goddamned peaceniks," Zachary said, glaring at the demonstrators. "They're a real pain in the ass. Ran into another bunch of them outside the State Department."

Winter assumed his remarks were another way of saying, "I'm sorry I'm late but I had to stop off on the way from Langley."

"You look bushed," Zachary observed. "Been up all night?"

"Yes, at the Walter Reed."

"So how are your people?" Zachary made it sound matter-of-fact, as though he were inquiring after the folks back home.

"Mrs. Franklin is as well as can be expected. At least she's off the danger list. Burman's lost the sight of his left eye."

"That's tough."

And Tom McNulty's dead, Winter thought; that's tougher still on Lois. He had gone to see Lois after leaving the Walter Reed, and he would remember her grief-stricken face for the rest of his life. "You killed him": those were the only words she'd uttered and she was right, though God knows he'd never dreamed for one moment that Tom would be in any kind of danger. But of course he couldn't tell Lois that because, even to his ears, it sounded like a pathetic whining excuse.

"Your intuition never lets you down, does it?" Zachary said.

"What?"

"The killer, he was the same guy who broke into the Roosevelt Hospital. We got a positive ID on him from one of the cops who was on duty that day."

"I guessed you had," Winter said, "as soon as I heard you'd phoned the Embassy and left instructions for me to meet you at the Ellipse."

"You know something?" Zachary said. "You could make a fortune on the racetrack. Every long shot you pick romps home a winner."

Winter shrugged. In his opinion, it hadn't been such a long shot. The whole business had started in New York and it was odds-on that whoever had organized Korznikov's defection at that end would be called in when things started to go wrong.

It didn't make sense to change horses in midstream, and at a time like this, the Soviet Embassy had every reason not to get involved. They would have roped in a few illegals though; keeping McNulty under surveillance was too big a task for one man to handle.

"That Lincoln convertible Tom owned," he said, "I assume you've looked it over?"

"We surely did," said Zachary.

"And found a homing device on the underside?"

"How the hell did you know that?"

"Pure guesswork." Winter glanced out of the window. They were heading east on New York Avenue and had just gone past the Travelodge Motel where Burman had been staying. "Where are we going, Melvin?" he asked.

"To see Korznikov. That's what you've wanted all along, isn't it?"

"Until I began to think he was a plant."

"You weren't the only one to smell a rat," Zachary said complacently. "The way the Soviets reacted when Korznikov came across struck me as kind of funny. Of course, they told us he was mentally ill and was about to be flown home, and naturally they demanded to see him, but they didn't get all hot under the collar about it like they usually do. Some of our people were inclined to think the Cuban situation had a lot to do with their low-key response."

But not you, Winter added silently, or so you would like me to believe.

"I still don't understand why or how he could do it."

"There's no mystery about it," said Winter. "Korznikov is a fanatic. For him, no sacrifice is too great for Mother Russia."

Nonetheless, there would have been certain compensations. Korznikov had acquired a taste for the good things in life when he was in London, and he could look forward to an even more agreeable lifestyle in the States. The CIA was very generous where Soviet defectors were concerned, and he would never be short of folding money. With a new identity, he could begin again and maybe set up house with another woman.

"I was referring to Jessop," Zachary said. "The white Anglo-Saxon Protestant who had everything going for him—a distinguished war record, good family background, and all the advantages money can buy. His father is the biggest real estate operator in the state of New York, and he married a girl out of the top drawer with all the right social connections. And yet he turns around and spits in our faces. Why?"

"Perhaps he thirsted after power?" Winter suggested.

"Power." Zachary scowled. "Yeah, that's what this whole thing's about, the reason why the KGB sent Korznikov across. For years now, they've been grooming Jessop for stardom and Vasili was going to provide him with the last few rungs on the ladder to the top. Can you imagine the dividends they'd have reaped with him in charge of the CIA?"

"It would be the greatest coup of all time," Winter said slowly. "I know I'd certainly pay any price to have the chairman of the KGB in my pocket."

"Right. The Kremlin saw Jessop as a long-term investment and they made a number of down payments: Steven Yarrow to get him into the agency and Fritz Briesemeier to help him get started on the ladder."

"Briesemeier?"

"A petty officer in the West German navy. Jessop unmasked him and put the Gehlen bureau on to the spy at Lossiemouth. You remember that case, don't you?"

Winter nodded. Horst Heinz Ludwig: Diana had mentioned that name over and over again. It was the only thing she'd said in her drowsy state after the operation which had made any sense to him.

"Now you know why they killed Deakin."

"I do?" Winter gazed at him, one eyebrow lifted quizzically.

"Aw, come on, you're not stupid. The KGB knew Korznikov would have to establish his credentials with us, so they told him to finger Deakin. In their eyes, good old George was simply a minnow to catch a whale, but sacrificing him did pose one very awkward problem. They believed that the moment he was blown, Deakin would tell the SIS exactly how he'd been recruited and the part Korznikov had played in the Suez crisis. And since that might be just enough to make us think twice about our prize defector, they decided Deakin would have to meet with an accident."

Q.E.D. The neat solution, except that Winter could think of one loose end. "Oleg Penkovsky," he said brusquely. "Where does he fit into your jigsaw, Melvin?"

"Well, that's where Jessop was real clever. He knew the KGB had had Penkovsky under surveillance for some time, but it would have looked a mite suspicious if they pulled him in for no apparent reason, when we'd told him to lie low for a while. On the other hand, the longer Penkovsky was left in circulation, the greater the risk he might get to hear rumors of what was in the wind. Therefore it was necessary to persuade the CIA to reactivate him, and the alleged power struggle going on in the Kremlin made a convincing argument for doing so."

The last *i* had been dotted, the last *t* crossed. Winter thought the KGB would have made things a lot easier for themselves had they chosen some other high-ranking officer to play out the charade instead of Korznikov, but that was only a minor cavil.

"Seems to me you've covered all the angles, Melvin."

"I like to think so," Zachary said modestly. "No two ways about it, killing Deakin was their one big mistake. Instead of protecting Korznikov, they turned a spotlight on him."

The skeptic had become a convert overnight because some police officer had recognized a photograph of a dead man. And like most converts Winter had met, Zachary had succeeded in convincing himself that he'd seen the light a long time ago.

"The joke is, neither Jessop nor the KGB knew that George was a double agent."

Winter didn't say anything. Washington was several miles

behind them now and they were heading east along a narrow country road. A signpost pointed to a Methodist church on the left, and up ahead on the opposite side of the road, he could see a small red-brick building fronting a used car lot. Then the driver slowed down and turned right onto a track leading to a copse a good half-mile back from the road.

"We're almost there," Zachary said, anticipating the obvious question.

They went on down the track, entered the copse, and pulled up outside a timber frame house. Both men up front got out and opened the rear doors, the driver staying with the Ford while his companion followed Winter and Zachary at a respectful distance as they walked over to the house. A burly man met them at the door carrying a pump-action shotgun in his right hand. Exchanging a brief nod, Zachary led Winter through the hall to a small room at the back.

"This is James Jessop," he said, introducing him in a flat voice. "Vasili you already know."

Winter shook hands with the American, his eyes on the Russian. Apart from a momentary twitch of the lips, he thought Korznikov didn't seem unduly perturbed to see him there.

"It's a real privilege to meet you, sir," Jessop said, mouth stretched in a brilliant smile. "Everybody knows you're one of the foremost experts on the Kremlin and I certainly welcome this opportunity to pick your brains."

"You're going to be disappointed then," Zachary told him bluntly. "This is strictly a fleeting visit. We're only here to collect Vasili."

"Oh?" Jessop released Winter's hand and stepped back a pace. The smile was still there, but it was beginning to look anxious. "Where are you taking him?"

"The State Department," said Zachary. "Some people there want to have a word with him. It appears Khrushchev is wavering and they'd like to hear from Vasili what their next move should be."

"Obviously, I'm not up to date." Jessop shrugged. "I suppose we should have listened to the newscasts on TV, but we've been kind of busy."

"I bet you have."

"Well, don't keep us in the dark, Zach. What's been happening in the great big world outside?"

"The *Gagarin* and the *Komiles* stopped just short of the quarantine line and the navy says that six other Soviet vessels have turned back."

"That's terrific." Jessop turned to Korznikov. "Take a bow, Vasili, you said Khrushchev would back off if we stood up to him."

"I don't think congratulations are in order, James," Korznikov said flatly. "The crisis isn't over yet."

"You're so right, it's only just beginning." Zachary snapped his fingers. "Better put your windbreaker on, Vasili, it's a mite chilly outside."

"Shouldn't I change into a suit?" Korznikov indicated the check shirt and denim jeans he was wearing. "I don't look very presentable dressed like this."

A malicious smile flickered across Zachary's face. "There's no time for that," he said. "They'll just have to take you as you are."

The innuendo was lost on Korznikov, but it registered with Jessop. Even though he tried not to show it, Winter could see he was rattled. The effort of holding the boyish smile together was beginning to tell on his facial muscles.

"Do you want me to come with you, Zach?"

Jessop tried to sound casual and relaxed, but his voice was brittle. What was left of his morale slumped even lower when the question went unanswered. The guard who'd met them at the door fetched a dark-blue windbreaker for Korznikov and helped him into it like a well-trained valet. Then they trooped out of the house, Zachary in the lead, Jessop a long way in the rear.

The driver threw away his cigarette when he saw them coming and quickly opened both nearside doors. Responding to a gentle tug on his coat sleeve, Winter followed the other CIA agent around to the far side of the Ford and got into the back, next to Korznikov, who sat in the middle with Zachary on his left. All four doors closed one after the other, then the driver cranked the motor, shifted into gear, and made a lazy U-turn in the clearing. Glancing back, Winter caught one final glimpse of a bewildered Jessop gazing after them, his mouth open, swallowing air. If Zachary had signaled the guard to keep an eye on him, Winter hadn't seen it, but he was standing to the rear and one side of Jessop, the pump-action shotgun cradled over one arm and pointing straight at him.

They drove back to Washington in silence, Korznikov sitting bolt upright between them, hands on knees, legs pressed together. His face was a death mask, the skin stretched tight across the prominent cheekbones, his eyes lackluster and unblinking. Only the shallow, undulating motion of his chest showed that he was still breathing.

The rain, which had been threatening all afternoon, started to fall as they neared the outskirts of town. Tires swishing on the wet surface of the road, they cruised on down New York Avenue to Mount Vernon Place, then turned into K Street.

"Where are we going?" Korznikov glanced left and right. "This isn't the way to the State Department."

"We're making a slight detour," Zachary told him. "I want to avoid the demonstrators outside the White House."

At the intersection of Sixteenth and K streets, the driver turned right and headed north.

"That's the Soviet Embassy ahead," Korznikov said in a low monotone.

"It certainly is," Zachary agreed cheerfully. "If you look real hard, you'll see there's a reception committee waiting for you."

"I don't understand. What's going on?"

"We're sending you back, Vasili. You came to us giftwrapped, but we didn't like what we saw when we undid the ribbons. It's as simple as that."

The car pulled into the curb and stopped. Grunting a little, as though the effort were too much for him, Zachary leaned forward, unlatched the door, and pushed it open. "Don't keep your friends waiting," he said.

Korznikov hesitated for a moment, then, bent almost double, he stepped over Zachary's outstretched legs and got out. Two men left the shelter of the Embassy building and met him on the sidewalk, their umbrellas raised aloft to protect him from the rain.

"They seem almost glad to have him back," Winter observed.

"They're just putting on a show for our benefit." Zachary closed the door and told the driver to move on. "I suppose you would have hung on to Korznikov in my place?" he said wryly.

"If I'd been allowed to."

"You've hit the nail on the head. State told me to throw him back into the pond. The missile crisis isn't over yet and it's their way of telling Khrushchev that he's no longer in a position to hoodwink us when we get down to the wheeling and dealing. I guess they have a point." Zachary sighed. "All the same, I'd have liked to have put Korznikov through the mangle and squeezed him dry. I would have taken a lot of time, and we would have had to check and double-check everything he told us, sifting the lies from the truth, but I think it would have been worth it in the long run."

"There's always Jessop," Winter said quietly.

"Yeah, that's right." Zachary brightened visibly. "We can persuade him it's in his interest to be cooperative."

Ten years instead of twenty, with the possibility of being paroled after five? Winter supposed Jessop would have little choice but to go along with that.

"Hoover would like the FBI to get in on the act," Zachary continued, "but we can keep it from them."

"You can?"

"Sure, no problem. The Police Department has McNulty's killer in the morgue. They don't know who he is, but a little thing like that isn't going to bother them. They've got enough

233

on their plates without looking for more, and it isn't as though they've got the media breathing down their necks. We can both thank Burman for that, even if it was unintentional. Any hospital other than the Walter Reed Medical Center and the press would have heard about it." He smiled lopsidedly. "One thing I like about the army, they're very security-conscious."

"You can't sit on the story forever," Winter pointed out.

"There's nothing so stale as yesterday's news," Zachary said. "Especially when Cuba is grabbing all the headlines. Three, maybe four lines on the back page, that's all it will rate. Naturally, we won't tell the newspapers that Tom was with the CIA, and I can guarantee Lois won't make any trouble for us."

Everything was to be swept under the carpet. Jessop would never be indicted, but there were other ways of bringing pressure to bear on him, and he would tell Zachary everything he wanted to know—who had recruited him, the name of his control, the cutout he used, and the location of every prearranged drop in Washington and New York.

"That leaves your people." Zachary turned to face him. "I understand Burman will be discharged from the hospital next Monday?"

"Yes."

"So when's he going home?"

"I'm not sure," said Winter. "It'll be another three weeks to a month yet before Mrs. Franklin is fit enough to travel. I think it likely he'll want to stay on until then."

Zachary mulled it over while they went on up Sixteenth Street and turned into Massachusetts Avenue. He was still thinking about it when the driver pulled up outside the British Embassy, shifted into neutral, and left the engine to idle.

"Can your man be trusted to keep his mouth shut?" he asked eventually.

"I can make it my business to see that he does," Winter said.

"Good. I guess that about wraps it up."

"Well, I certainly can't think of any loose ends." Winter

234

found himself shaking hands with Zachary, as though they had just made a very profitable deal on the stock market.

"You'll be returning to London then?"

"I think so."

"There's a Pan Am flight leaving tonight at twenty-one hundred hours," Zachary said. "I hear there are still plenty of seats for the asking."

"Thanks for the tip."

Winter got out of the car, closed the door behind him, and raised a hand in salute. The Ford pulled out from the curb and drove off down the avenue and he stood there in the rain until it was just a speck in the distance. Then he turned about and walked into the Embassy.

21.

The new PA was as different from Diana Franklin as a lemon from a peach. She was Winter's age, had rust-colored hair that was yellowish-gray at the roots, and wore severely tailored clothes which made her appear even more intimidating than she actually was. It wasn't her fault that she was decidedly plain, nor could she be blamed for having a name like Enid Potts, but the two seemed made for each other. An efficient if humorless woman, she had been determined from the outset to make herself indispensable and, within a week, every trace of her predecessor had vanished from the outer office. At first, Winter had consoled himself with the thought that she was only a temporary replacement, but then, toward the middle of November, Diana Franklin had followed Burman's example, tendering her resignation in a polite but formal letter, and he'd been forced to accept that Miss Potts was going to be around for a very long time to come.

It was a prospect which he knew Henry Ainsworth viewed with some considerable dismay. As a department head, Henry found it particularly galling that Enid Potts expected him to consult her whenever he wanted to see Winter. An obstinate man, Ainsworth had let it be known that he was damned if he would knuckle under to that old sourpuss, and had set out to prove it. Time after time he would try to sneak past her ever-open door; time after time Enid Potts heard his muffled footsteps and caught him in the act. A low mumble of voices in the corridor told Winter now that Henry had just lost another skirmish in his long-running battle and he waited for the intercom to buzz, then told his PA to show him in.

"Bloody woman," Ainsworth said, after she had closed the communicating door behind her. "Beats me how you can stand her."

"We get along all right," Winter said.

"Couldn't you persuade Mrs. Franklin to return? I know she's submitted her resignation, but I'm sure you could talk her out of it."

"I don't think so, Henry. Mrs. Franklin has a new interest in life, someone who means a great deal more to her than this dusty old building and its occupants ever could. His name is Burman."

"How very odd." Ainsworth frowned. "I would have thought she could have found someone much more suitable."

"Is that why you asked to see me?" Winter said coldly. "To discuss the love life of my former PA?"

"No, of course it isn't." Ainsworth sidled round the desk, removed a slim folder from his arm, and placed it in front of Winter. "This telex just came in from Moscow. I'm afraid it confirms what we suspected: Greville Wynne is being held in the Lubyanka along with Penkovsky."

First Korznikov, now Wynne. When one problem disappeared, another burgeoned to take its place. It was, Winter thought, the one constant factor in their twilight world.

"He should never have gone to Budapest," said Ainsworth. "The AVH knew he was coming and they had all the time in the world to plan just how they were going to kidnap him."

"He didn't have any option, Henry."

It sounded trite, but the truth often was. Greville Wynne had never been a professional intelligence officer; he was a patriotic businessman who had put a lot of time and effort into fostering East-West trade. The British Trade Exposition in Budapest had been arranged months beforehand and, although he was aware that Penkovsky was liable to be arrested at any moment, Wynne had been faced with what amounted to a Hobson's choice. Either he attended the trade show or else he sat back and allowed his business to collapse.

"What do you suppose they intend to do with him?" Ainsworth shook his head. "I mean, they can't keep Wynne in solitary confinement for the rest of his life, like they can one of their own citizens."

"I imagine the KGB will put the pair of them on trial when they're good and ready."

"And then what?"

"Penkovsky will be executed and Wynne will be sentenced to a long term of imprisonment. After a year or two, the opposition will put out a feeler and we'll make a trade; Gordon Lonsdale alias Konon Molody for Greville Wynne. We might have to throw the Krogers in for good measure, but that's the way it'll go." Winter uncapped his fountain pen, initialed the telex, and returned the folder to Ainsworth. "Anything else?" he asked.

"Well, there's Alik, the radar operator Deakin was worried about. Burman and I were trying to put a name to him before he left for New York."

"And now you have," Winter said.

"I think so." Ainsworth delved into his jacket pocket and produced a sheet of foolscap that had been folded in half and half again. "I'm afraid I'm not a very good typist," he said apologetically.

Winter unfolded the sheet and saw he wasn't being modest. Some words were joined together, others had letters in the wrong juxtaposition, and a considerable number had been blanked out with Xs. Deciphering the text took him all of five minutes and seemed hardly worth the effort.

"I don't see what all the fuss is about," Winter said, looking up. "What makes this particular American so special, apart from the fact that he discovered life in the Soviet Union was not all it was cracked up to be and decided to go home?"

"Look at the dates." Ainsworth leaned over his shoulder and stabbed a finger at the memo. "He left Minsk on the twenty-third of May with his wife and infant daughter and arrived in Moscow the following day. Then they spent a week in the Hotel Berlin while he arranged a repatriation loan and collected his passport from the American consul. They left Moscow by train on the first of June and spent two days sightseeing in Amsterdam before boarding the S.S. *Maasdam* for New York. They docked on the thirteenth of June. Five days later, George met Anatole Gorsky and was as chirpy as a cricket when I saw him the next morning."

"Because he'd solved the riddle and was convinced his pet theory was about to come true?"

"That's the conclusion I reached, for what it's worth." Ainsworth removed his glasses, breathed on them, and then polished the lenses with his tie. "Of course, that's not saying much. After all, it's hard to believe such an absolute nonentity is capable of doing anything that would rock the American people back on their heels."

The disclaimer said it all, Winter thought. They had gone down the wrong track because he had started with the preconceived notion that Deakin had been killed because he had stumbled upon something and had been conceited and foolish enough to try his theory out on Anatole Gorsky. From there on, all their efforts had been directed toward proving this was the case.

"You're right, Henry, it is hard to swallow." Winter drummed his fingers on the desk. "On the whole, I think I prefer Zachary's explanation; it has more credibility."

"Quite. That's why I didn't bother to pursue the matter when you returned from Washington." Ainsworth replaced his spectacles. "It's just that the notes were lying in my safe and I had a few spare moments in which to flesh them out." His voice trailed away and he shuffled toward the door. Opening it, he stepped out into the corridor, then turned about, a puckish grin on his face. "All the same, he's a very unusual nonentity, the only defector I know who was allowed to change his mind and go home. And with a Russian wife."

Winter looked at the typewritten memo again, the dates leaping at him from the page. The door closed with a faint click and reminded him of another time, another place, when Diana had phoned him at the British Embassy in Washington. There was probably an innocent explanation for those clicks he'd heard on the line, but he couldn't help wondering just whose idea it had been to send Korznikov back.

He got up, walked over to the window, and stood there gazing out at the darkening sky, uncertain what he ought to do. His head was full of preposterous ideas and he could imagine the belly laugh he'd get if Zachary knew what he was thinking. And yet, experience had taught him that nothing was impossible. Hesitating no longer, he returned to his desk, buzzed his PA, and told her to put through a priority call to Melvin Zachary at Langley.

There was no delay, no time in which to change his mind. Within a matter of seconds, the phone trilled and lifting the receiver, he heard a pleasant voice say, "I have Mr. Charles Winter on the line, sir."

Then Zachary said, "Well, this is a surprise. How are you keeping, Charles?"

"I'm fine, Melvin." Winter cleared his throat. "Do you mind if we switch to secure?"

"Not in the least," Zachary told him.

Winter depressed the button on the cradle, saw the bulb light up, and checked the black box on the floor under the desk. "I have two green lights," he said. "How about you?"

"Everything's jake this end."

"Good." Winter glanced at the memo a third time and began to feel more than a little ridiculous. "I'm not sure this is going to make a lot of sense," he said, "but we think there may be another reason why the KGB terminated Deakin."

"Yeah? Tell me more." Somehow Zachary managed to sound both interested and skeptical at the same time.

"It has to do with an ex-marine of yours, a radar operator who defected to the Soviet Union in September 1959. He liked to call himself Alik; at least, we believe that's how Korznikov and Gorsky used to refer to him in their conversations with George Deakin."

Winter paused, waited for Zachary to say something and got an unrevealing "Uh-huh." Less than confident now, he picked up from where he'd left off and ploughed doggedly on, trying to explain why Alik should be regarded as a major security risk.

"He's just a nut," Zachary said, when he'd heard him out.

Winter stared at the telephone. "You know all about him then?" he said in an empty voice.

"Sure we do. His ship docked at Hoboken, New Jersey, on the thirteenth of June. The guy you're referring to is Lee Harvey Oswald. Right?"

"I've been wasting your time, haven't I, Melvin?"

"Don't give it another thought. It was nice talking to you." Zachary produced a belly rumble which passed for a laugh, then said, "And don't give Oswald another thought either. The FBI down in Fort Worth is keeping tabs on him."

Winter heard him hang up, and slowly replaced the receiver. In the gathering dusk, he walked over to the door and switched on the lights. Retracing his steps, he then stooped under the desk, undid the black box on the floor, and removed the cassette. Zachary had found their conversation vastly amusing, but would it, he wondered, still appeal to his sense of humor should he hear it again a week, a month, a year from now?

CLIVE EGLETON *was a colonel in the British army until five years ago, when he retired to write full time. He is the author of nine novels besides* THE RUSSIAN ENIGMA, *including* THE EISENHOWER DECEPTION, BACK-FIRE, THE MILLS BOMB, SKIRMISH, THE BORMANN BRIEF, SEVEN DAYS TO A KILLING (*made into the movie* THE BLACK WINDMILL, *with Michael Caine*), THE JUDAS MANDATE, LAST POST FOR A PARTISAN, *and* A PIECE OF RESISTANCE. *He lives with his family in England.*